TO DO
NO HARM

TO DO
NO HARM

LESLIE GLASS

A Perfect Crime Book

DOUBLEDAY

New York   London   Toronto   Sydney   Auckland

A PERFECT CRIME BOOK
PUBLISHED BY DOUBLEDAY
a division of Bantam Doubleday Dell Publishing Group, Inc.
666 Fifth Avenue, New York, New York 10103

DOUBLEDAY is a trademark of Doubleday,
a division of Bantam Doubleday Dell
Publishing Group, Inc.

Book design by Tasha Hall

Library of Congress Cataloging-in-Publication Data

Glass, Leslie.
To do no harm / by Leslie Glass.
p.   cm.
I. Title.
PS3557.L34T6   1992
813′.54—dc20   92-14455
CIP

ISBN 0-385-42602-X

1   3   5   7   9   10   8   6   4   2

FIRST EDITION

To
Alex and Lindsey

For their unflappable good sense and persistence, I want to thank my editor, Amy Stout, and my agent, Sarah Jane Freymann.

For technical advice and their unflagging support, I want to thank Dr. Richard C. Friedman and Edmund Glass.

. . . I Will use treatment to help the sick according to my ability and judgement, but never with a view to injury or wrongdoing . . . I will keep pure and holy both my life and my art . . . In whatsoever house I enter I will enter to heal the sick, and I will abstain from all intentional wrongdoing and harm . . .

HIPPOCRATES, *The Physician's Oath*

TO DO
NO HARM

1

Ron Appleton, psychiatric resident at Chester Memorial Hospital in Chester, New Jersey, ran into Dr. Aaron Simon's waiting room and slammed the door.

"Is he with someone?" he demanded.

Lorna, Dr. Simon's matronly secretary, looked up, startled. She was there to protect Dr. Simon from people who got overwrought and hysterical like this.

"Is it an emergency?" she asked cautiously.

"Yes, dammit. Is he alone?"

She hesitated for a second and then nodded. "Do you want me to tell him you're here?"

He didn't wait for an answer. He plunged through the double doors into Dr. Simon's inner sanctum. Aaron was just finishing up with a phone call. He frowned and said good-bye to the colleague on the other end.

"What is it, Ron?"

"Jasper is HIV positive."

Ron dumped the file on Aaron's desk. "I'm sorry."

There was silence for a minute as Aaron thought about the repercussions for Alisa, who was already suicidal.

"What made you think he was?" Ron said finally.

"I interviewed him, Ron. Three times after that community meeting when the allegations started. First he denied having sex with anybody. Then he said he didn't know what the fuss was about. Then when Alisa became suicidal, he admitted having sex with her. Then he said he didn't feel good. He wanted to be tested. So I checked his arms. Needle marks all over the place. I take it he was admitted without anybody checking this out."

"He denied being an intravenous user," Ron said.

"He lies a lot. You should have checked."

Aaron felt like cursing and punching the young man in front of him. Ron was on the unit more than he was. He should know what was going on. But Aaron was the Head of the Department. He was responsible.

"What do we do?" Ron said.

"We have to make a report. Clinical Care will have a hearing. They'll investigate us. They'll make a report that will become part of the hospital record." It was a nightmare.

"We have to find out the whole chain, interview people, see if he slept with anyone else."

Ron grimaced. "What if he did? What will happen to me?"

Aaron frowned. "We'll have to talk about it later."

Ron got up reluctantly. He tried to make eye contact with his supervisor, but Aaron didn't look up to say good-bye.

Already he was thinking about how to handle it. It would all have to be made public. The patients would be upset. Alisa had to be told, and her parents. She had been a victim of incest, and unstable in the first place. The threat of getting AIDS was not likely to help the situation. They had to decide what to do about Amerigo.

Aaron sighed. Long before this he had gotten weary of his job as head of psychiatry at Chester. It wasn't just being responsible for the thirty psychiatric inpatients in his unit. Every month he found himself more and more drawn into general hospital business, into personnel difficulties, politics, ethical questions. All sorts of people in the hospital came to him and told him things about their private lives, about what was going on in different departments. Things that kept him awake at night wondering what, if anything, he should do. Now there was a lot he had to do.

His shoulders had gotten stooped with the weight of the world. He was tall, still slim and youthful. He appeared relaxed, even languid at rest, but tended to move quickly when he was out of his chair. His dark hair had not yet begun to recede, but was flecked with gray at the temples. He had a lean face, intense blue eyes that didn't miss anything, a broken nose from his basketball days, and a sensitive mouth that was now tight with fury over the lack of vigilance in his department.

In fact, his face was so expressive he had to constantly remind himself not to show everything he felt. Since he was not a passive person and had strong opinions about everything, this aspect of his profession had been hard for him to learn. But at the moment he was alone and didn't have to hide his fear and distress from anyone.

He was used to hearing unpleasant things, sad things, even dangerous things. Many of the secrets he was told had nothing to do with him or his department. Often he wished he didn't have to know, especially when there was nothing he could do to help. He didn't get paid extra for general listening or casual advice. But he never said no to anyone in trouble. He saw people on his own time.

At thirty-six he had been pleased to get this job, but now he felt embattled, like a fortress attacked on all sides by the unsuspected enemies. His precious time was hacked away by consultations, by meetings. He was forty-two, felt he was aging at a faster clip each day. He had no time to write his papers, to think, to do what he was trained for and liked best. He didn't have time to take on many long-term private patients. He didn't have time to heal.

Often he thought about having a different life. Psychiatrists in private practice could keep as much of the world away as they wanted. They could book ten patient-hours a day and keep the fees. To Aaron the dream of a lucrative private practice was as agonizingly appealing as Circe had been to Ulysses, a siren's song he didn't want to resist. But events at the hospital always prevented him from even thinking about taking the steps to get away. All of his personal wishes and concerns were insignificant in the face of what he had to think about. An HIV-positive patient who had seduced another patient and possibly others. He had to think of the chain and where it led. At least there was no problem with confidentiality. It had come out quickly. He thanked God for Adrienne, the depressed middle-aged paranoiac who complained about dirty things going on. As he often told himself, they might be sick, but they were rarely stupid. He was glad he had listened to her.

Well, he couldn't do anything now. He had a patient coming. He put the file of Jasper Amerigo into a drawer, as though to banish it, if only for forty-five minutes. He composed his face into the soothing mask of calm neutrality he was famous for in the hospital but rarely felt, and buzzed his secretary to send in his next appointment.

2

Bettina Dunne's first impression of Dr. Arthur Street's office was surprise. It was nothing like the plain, utilitarian, almost shabby offices of Drs. Cohen, O'Reilly, and Obermeyer across the street from New York Hospital that she was used to.

Drs. Street and Steadman shared an office in a modern brick structure three stories high called the Medical Arts Building. It was just off Main Street, four blocks down from the hospital in Chester, New Jersey. It had its own parking lot, surrounded by flowering shrubs. There were Japanese elms by the entrance and a weeping willow tree in each corner. Bettina was impressed by the parking lot, the weeping willow trees, and the pristine condition of the building, where there was also a "Group" of pediatricians, a "Group" of board-certified plastic surgeons, a "Group" of orthodontists, and several other specialties for which she would probably have a need eventually.

Everything about the suburbs was so nice it was almost spooky, she thought, not for the first time. Everything was so convenient, so pretty and quiet.

"Good afternoon; going up," the elevator said as she got in and pushed 2.

"How do you know it's afternoon?" she asked.

No answer. She found herself relieved the elevator could speak but not tell her anything really important. She walked down the tastefully decorated corridor, thinking the country might be making her crazy. She smiled at the thought, because anyone with a brain knew the New York City she and her husband Tom left a few weeks ago was truly dangerous.

She was threatened by a street person and almost run down by a van only the day before she left. Still, she couldn't help being nervous going to a new doctor in a place she didn't know very well. Everything was so nice—how did they know what to look out for?

She opened the door of "Suite B" and found an office so new, so perky and bright, so well appointed and light it looked as if it might have been created for a movie set. Modular sofas of pale green were lighted from below, showing how clean the ash-green, stain-resistant carpet was.

At the desk near the entrance sat a woman with bouncing black curls and an almost artificially white complexion. She had a very red mouth; and before she opened it, Bettina had the peculiar feeling that she might be meeting an aging Snow White come alive as a receptionist.

The red mouth widened into a welcoming smile. "Hi," the voice from inside bubbled, "I'm Isobel; you must be"—she looked down at the clipboard in front of her—"Bettina Dunne," she proclaimed triumphantly.

Bettina smiled, relieved that the voice, though perky in the extreme, was nothing like what Disney believed the sweetest girl in the world should sound like.

"Yes," she said. She was also momentarily reassured by the green tints on the walls and carpets. Everywhere was the color of money. Except in the pictures on the walls, which were of pink and coral shells and other marine objects that seemed to be floating in a very calm sea. Bettina understood these pink shells, with their succulent insides hidden from view, to be symbolic of the specialty practiced here. She was pregnant, and this was an OBGYN's office. Then she realized the place was empty and again began to worry.

"Nice to have you with us," Isobel said, taking up a pen. "Well, have a seat and we'll get the paperwork out of the way. He's almost ready to see you."

Bettina sat down, thinking wistfully of Rachel Obermeyer, the woman doctor she had left. She had recommended Dr. Street, but what if he was only Tom's age, just starting out, had decorated with a loan from his parents, and she was his only patient?

"Let's see, you're in your—?" Isobel looked at Bettina's stomach appraisingly, her pen held aloft.

"I'm almost in my eighth month," Bettina said, her eyes showing her excitement. Eight months sounded so much better than seven.

Isobel took a moment to suck on the end of her pen and consider the new patient. Sometimes they came in and talked a blue streak. It was hard to get them to move along. They told her the stories of their lives. They weren't very interesting stories, mostly filled with all the medical events they'd ever heard of, their fears of getting pregnant if they were young, their happiness and pride if they were older and married. Isobel was more than ready to be in the latter group, but that particular happiness had always eluded her.

She studied Bettina. On the other hand, sometimes getting the sketchiest history was as difficult as extracting impacted wisdom teeth. Some people didn't know themselves at all, couldn't describe their symptoms or their feelings. Isobel liked people who were open and friendly like herself, but not too friendly. She had her work to do and couldn't sit around gabbing about female subjects all day.

There was always a lot of work to do, but Isobel liked her job. She was an R.N., but didn't want to live with Emergency Room horrors anymore. Every time it rained, a dozen crashes on the highway, wounds of every description. And not neat ones like she had seen as an Operating Room nurse in her first medical life. She didn't want to see any more blood, and didn't want to spend her days in green pajamas, either.

In this job, where she liked to say that for the first time in her career the people she met were awake, she could use her head. Here she was the office manager, the psychologist, the dispenser of information.

"The doctor says not to worry. Blood clots are okay unless they're the size of a bread box and you have a fever. Did you take your temperature?'' The patients were more like hers here. She felt in control.

Now she smiled at Bettina. Bettina was beautiful, clearly a natural blond, but one of those cold WASPy types, Isobel decided, the kind who got everything just by looking good. She lowered her lashes, searching Bettina's hand for a diamond or a sapphire the size of a kidney bean. Bettina, however, had only a gold band on her ring finger, a Swatch watch on her wrist, and big silver dangling earrings on her ears. No jewelry to speak of. Isobel shrugged inwardly. She had long ago noticed it wasn't always the pretty ones who got the best stuff.

Isobel's theory was that sexual satisfaction had a lot to do with how much jewelry a girl got. Isobel was twenty-nine, had many gold chains and bracelets, amethyst earrings, tiny diamond studs, and a long history of not quite getting where she wanted to go. This failure to tie the knot was inexplicable to her, and the subject of marriage was never off her mind for long. If she had known herself as well as she thought she knew other people, she might have understood that sitting in this affluent OBGYN office surrounded by pregnant, pretty, well-kept, suburban housewives caused her far more pain than any fatality she ever saw in the Emergency Room. But she was no expert in anyone's motivation, least of all her own.

As she took Bettina's history, she felt superior in knowledge, and in practical experience. Bettina was new to the suburbs and didn't seem to know much about anything. Her husband an engineer. Humph. That was not as impressive as Isobel's new boyfriend Peter, who was a professional, a lawyer.

At the same time she felt the familiar gnawing ache that often came upon her before she knew a patient well, a strong sense of inferiority, even shame over her losses. She was filled with a confusing mixture of feelings. She felt superior because she could take care of herself and knew so much about life (did things in bed her little patients never heard of), had a boyfriend who was better looking than anybody she'd ever met, than anybody out of the movies, in fact. And she felt like a worm, somebody who was used, and stepped on and hurt over and over.

"A children's-book illustrator," she said, gushing at Bettina's occupation.

"What an exciting addition to our family. Would you tell us where we might get one of your books for our toy box?" she asked.

"Oh, I'll give you one," Bettina said graciously, pleased by Isobel's sensitivity in not asking for free copies. People so often forgot that authors had to pay for the books they gave away. Nothing in life was really free.

Bettina went into the bathroom and peed in the cup. Then, alone in the examining room, she weighed and measured herself. She was five foot six and seven months pregnant. She weighed a hundred and twenty-eight pounds.

A pregnant nurse came in and pricked her finger, drew out three or four drops of blood with a tiny glass tube.

Finally Dr. Street came in to see her. In New York Bettina had been known to wait for Dr. Obermeyer up to an hour and a half. In Chester, the waiting time seemed to be all of four minutes. She checked her watch, not knowing, of course, that the first appointment in the morning and the first appointment after lunch were always on time unless there was an emergency. It was one o'clock.

"Hello, Mrs. Dunne." Dr. Street bustled in. He, too, looked like something from Central Casting. Dr. Street was over six feet tall and weighed not a pound more than one seventy-five.

His freshly tanned face was unlined, amiable. He had no scars or defects that one could see, just a few wrinkles around the eyes, and silvering temples.

He was too close to fifty for his own comfort, but looked a lot better than Rachel Obermeyer, who was no more than thirty-eight. He had a thin mouth, sincere blue eyes, regular features, strong chin.

"How do you do," Bettina said.

Sitting on the examining table like a ripe melon still uncut in the field, Bettina held out her hand. She felt ridiculous in the pink gown she had been given, open in the back, and not really her color. She couldn't help being disappointed. She preferred doctors who were chubby and ate bagels. This person looked too much like her father, a man who seemed so pleasant and amiable, but was always off napping whenever he was needed.

She chided herself. Just because Dr. Street didn't show a lot of aggression and drive in the first thirty seconds of their acquaintance didn't mean he was lax and unreliable. It was possible, after all, for a man to be smooth on the outside and not entirely defective on the inside.

"Good to know you," he said, taking her hand and giving it a substantial, but not too familiar, squeeze. "I see you're referred by a student of mine. How is Dr. Obermeyer?"

"She was your student?" Bettina's mouth fell open.

"Yes, didn't she tell you?"

"No," Bettina murmured, "she didn't tell me," and wondered why.

"A very clever young lady," Dr. Street said. He held out his fine hands that had been much admired by his patients. "Good pair of hands," he said of Dr. Obermeyer's.

"I thought that was for football players," Bettina remarked, noting her new doctor's elegant fingers and manicured nails. He wore a white coat over a pink shirt with a blue and red striped tie and gray slacks. All very correct. Loafers on his feet.

He chuckled. "You'll see. A newborn is about the size of a basketball, a little bigger than a football. Can be slippery."

Bettina smiled, not entirely put off by the comparison. Tom would probably say the same sort of male thing.

"Well, any complaints, problems, before we get started?" He looked at her intently.

"The usual complaints, I guess," Bettina said. "Heartburn." *Anxiety,* she didn't say. *Miss my mommy, strangely enough. Wish I had a woman in my life.*

"Not much you can do about it. We're very conservative about medications these days. I guess you know that." Dr. Street smiled the benign doctor's smile.

I have strange feelings. I'm afraid. I don't know why. Is it because the vagina is so small, too small for a basketball to get out? Is it because pregnancy is so complicated? So many things have to go just right for the baby to be perfect. Do I feel guilty because I'm so happy, have a man I love, live in the American Dream House, perfectly clean, white with green shutters, when so many people are cold, are hungry, live in the street, without anything, not even the security of knowing they won't be stabbed, or strangled, or set afire in the night? What is it, this cold fear that follows me around the house and the garden when I'm supposed to be relaxed, thinking lovely thoughts? Can my fear infect my baby, make it nervous, deform it physically or mentally?

She sat there quietly, naked under the pink gown, with the appearance of perfect calm. She felt a bit betrayed somehow, because Dr. Obermeyer had not told her this man with whom she was sure to be "comfortable" had been her teacher. Surely this was information that would have made Bettina feel all right about the change. Now she thought she'd better not say anything. Dr. Street, who seemed so plausible and nice, would only toss off her worries with sports analogies, talk about massive hormonal changes. And how she didn't have that far to go to reach the goalposts.

She didn't want to hear it, but was relieved nonetheless when he said everything was still as okay as it had been when last she had been poked and probed in this undignified fashion. Dr. Street helped her up, shook her hand reassuringly, and said he'd see her in three weeks.

"Enjoy your pregnancy," he advised her. "You're a young, healthy woman."

Bettina made an appointment with Isobel, the perky receptionist with the red lips, and realized as she left that she had forgotten to ask the doctor what his fee for enjoying her pregnancy was.

"Going down," the elevator told her, and then, surprisingly, "enjoy the rest of your day," just before its doors slid open on the first floor.

3

The air conditioners were already on in Axam's sprawling suburban headquarters, even though it was only the end of May. In his office, Tom Dunne shivered as he looked over the final plans for an oil refinery he had designed. They were so immensely complicated that he couldn't really study them in less than several hours. He was looking at them because he needed a few minutes to compose himself. Suddenly, at the end of the day, he had been called into Highgate's office, and he didn't want to go. The unexpected summons from the boss of his boss made him feel like a kid in trouble.

For some inexplicable reason, he often felt like that these days. Since he had never worried about his job before, the worry itself made him anxious. He turned the large pages over one by one without looking at them. The plans were for a plant the size of a large house. Usually oil refineries were huge, but when the technology was new, they sometimes built a small model to see if it would work.

Some of the processes in the forty pages of future refinery in front of Tom had never been tried before. Even if the economy were in great shape, it would be normal for him to be a little apprehensive about it. But the economy was not in great shape. Oil companies were cutting back, even large ones like Axam. There had been layoffs. Management could cancel the project. They could fire him. They could do anything.

The phone rang. He picked it up. "Hello," he said cautiously.

"It's your girlfriend. Have a minute?"

It was Bettina. He relaxed a little. "Hi, Gorgeous." Did he have a minute? He looked at his watch. George was waiting. "I always have a minute for you. What's up?"

"I went to see my new doctor," Bettina said.

"I know. I was waiting to hear. How was it?" He had forgotten all about it.

"It was fine," Bettina said.

"You liked him?" Tom shoved the plans aside.

"How could I like a gynecologist?"

"You could *not* like him. What did he say?"

"He said I was fine. What's the matter?"

"Nothing. I'm just concerned about you and the baby."

"It sounds like something else. Did something happen?" she asked.

How did she know these things? He frowned, not wanting to worry her. "Absolutely nothing. I just have to go to a meeting."

"Why didn't you say so?" she said. "I'll talk to you later."

"I always have time for you, baby. Are you sure you're all right?" Tom didn't want to see George Highgate. He was scared of George Highgate. "Tell me exactly what he said."

"I'll tell you later. I love you." She hung up.

He put the phone down gently. How could they fire him? They'd just given him the mortgage on the house in Millville, so he and Bettina could get out of New York, live a clean and healthy life in the country. Have a nice place for their baby to grow up. They couldn't fire him; it was a crazy fear, irrational. But he knew they could.

He was an engineer who designed chemical plants and oil refineries. Bettina said it was kind of like being an architect for plumbing, except that he had to know chemistry. He had to know how to get millions of gallons of one chemical to move at a certain temperature and speed through a set of pipes. He had to know when and how to mix it with millions of gallons of another chemical at another temperature. He knew how to design machinery that could heat it up or cool it down, shove it along through miles of pipe, and have it turn out exactly right at the end.

He had been a troubleshooter at Axam's refineries for several years. He worked for brief stints in Texas, in Alaska, at Axam's mammoth refinery in Bayonne, New Jersey. Then they gave him an office at the headquarters in Morristown, where he worked on other engineers' projects. This little plant in front of him was his first project as supervisor of a team. Up to now his life had been going pretty well. He loved his wife. They had just moved to a farmhouse with eighteen acres of land far enough out of town to be a good buy. And now they were having this baby. He couldn't remember why.

Now he was worried all the time about Bettina's condition, even when she was fine. He had to worry about supporting the house and the two cars, the pregnant wife, and all too soon, the baby. What if his plans weren't any good? What if George Highgate were canceling the project?

The phone rang again. He could feel himself beginning to sweat. Never let them know you sweat, he told himself. "Hello."

"He's waiting."

"I'm on my way." Tom reached for his jacket.

4

"What are your fantasies about the baby?"

It was four o'clock in the afternoon a week after the AIDS incident began. Aaron Simon had forty-five precious minutes to do therapy, to help somebody without worrying about AIDS. For forty-five minutes he would only think about Laura Hunter and her problem. He looked at his watch. In forty-five minutes he would have to report to the Clinical Care Committee that the chain did not end with their seventeen-year-old patient Alisa.

Patricia Everet, the chief nurse, had cornered him in the hall a little while ago and told him that one of her nurses was feeling very depressed. It was a night nurse, an attractive girl, April Flanders. Patricia said April told her she had had unprotected sex with the same patient, and now that it was common knowledge he was HIV positive, she was terrified she was going to get the disease, too.

"Have her tested," Aaron said. "And have a preliminary interview with her. See if she'll tell you how many partners she's had and who they are." He paused, frowning. "She's the pretty one, right?"

"Yes, Doctor," Patricia said.

It was getting so that Aaron was afraid to leave his office. New things kept coming up. Amerigo was on room restriction. They couldn't have him wandering around, but they couldn't just throw him out on the street, either. Alisa couldn't be left alone. She had already tried to hang herself and was on suicide watch. And now a nurse had to be investigated and fired for sleeping with a patient and God only knew who else. It was a mess. He'd be dealing with AIDS for a long time.

Aaron forced himself to smile at Laura.

He was sitting in his swiveling desk chair that could tilt back so far he almost fell out at least once a day. Long ago he had found that keeping himself physically off balance helped him stay alert.

Until now he hadn't had that problem with Laura. She was a lovely woman, fair with high cheekbones and gray-blue eyes, a pert, upturned nose, and skin so fine the hollows under her eyes looked blue when she didn't get enough sleep. She was small and feminine, too, and didn't need the maternitylike dress she was wearing. Laura Hunter was only nine weeks pregnant. Her waist had thickened only a little and her stomach was just beginning to round out.

He gathered that Laura was not good at waiting for the

things she wanted, though. She was already wearing loose dresses and only a minute ago had told him she had run up the stairs because the elevator took too long. Except for the elevator, she said she liked his office. It didn't look like part of the hospital, and she felt safe there. He liked it when patients said they felt safe with him. That was what he was there for.

His office was on the second floor of the new four-story building that was attached to the hospital on that same level by a glass-enclosed bridge over the Emergency Room entrance. The way they were placed, the two buildings made a kind of courtyard that was at the same time very modern and almost medieval.

The view on one side of the new building was the glass bridge. Aaron thought of it as the Bridge of Sighs every time he went over it, because anyone who crossed it could see the continual flow of Emergency Room arrivals in every state of terror and distress. The view on the other side of the building was the parking lot. Neither vista was inspiring, but Aaron didn't let his patients look at either. He was a traditional psychiatrist in many ways and kept the blinds in his office drawn against distractions of any kind, even inspiring ones.

His suite consisted of a secretary's enclosure near the door on one side of the small waiting room, and his office behind it. The two shaded windows behind his desk faced the Emergency Room and the bridge, the entrance to which was just outside his door. He kind of liked the bridge, liked the office and the secretary a lot. When he considered leaving the hospital and going out on his own, he hated the thought of leaving them.

Laura blushed. "I don't have fantasies," she answered his question indignantly.

Aaron smiled gently. "Everybody has fantasies. They're the thoughts you have all the time."

He noticed that her arms tightly hugged her stomach and her hands were curled into fists. Immediately his sympathies were with her. He let his hospital anguish go.

"So what do you think it will be like after the baby is born? Tell me about that."

For a second her body tensed, as if with a sudden pain, and she grimaced. "Do you ever feel you don't have anybody to really love?"

"Do you feel like that?" Aaron asked.

She looked away guiltily. "No, of course not. I love my husband. But—I'm sure you've seen it. You know, when mothers talk to their babies and the babies watch them so intently. And then when they get to be about five months, they start to giggle."

Aaron watched Laura's hands relax.

She laughed. "Babies are so funny when they giggle." Then her hands closed around themselves again.

"Whatever love you give them, they give you back a thousandfold," she said wistfully. "I've seen it so many times."

"So you see yourself loving your baby and your baby loving you."

She nodded. "And talking to it, cuddling it," she added. "Bathing it, feeding it."

"And your husband. How do you see him?" Aaron asked.

Again she grimaced without realizing it. "Well, he's wonderful, of course. He loves me very much."

"What is it like?" Aaron prompted.

"What?"

"Your life together."

"Well, he's very—" She hesitated, chewing on her bottom lip. "I don't know. He likes things done right. It's hard to please him no matter how much I try." She laughed, as if at herself. "He's always disappointed, I don't know why."

She drew in her breath sharply. "But he's very sweet."

"What disappoints him?"

"Oh, I don't know. I never get it quite right. I can't get him what he wants fast enough. Or the dinner is cold. Or my closet is messy. I say the wrong thing." She looked down at her hands. "After making love he always says something, like I don't move enough, or I hurt his arm or leg."

Her lips trembled. "I don't think I'm very sexy. Maybe that sounds stupid."

Aaron shook his head. Not stupid. The man was subtly torturing her, criticizing everything about her. How could she feel sexy?

"He gives me everything I want," she said, shaking her head, as if puzzled by the knot of pain she felt.

"And what about the baby?"

"Oh, I think he'll be a wonderful father," she said doubtfully.

Aaron waited for her to describe him as a father, but she was silent on the subject.

"He'll be—very upset if I have another miscarriage," was what she said.

Finally the tears brimmed over. "Am I going to have another miscarriage? Dr. Steadman said you can help me. Can you really help me?"

Aaron didn't turn away from her anguish. He answered her as honestly as he could. "Maybe I can. I hope so. But it kind of depends on what's wrong, doesn't it?"

Laura sobbed into a tissue. "There's nothing wrong. They can't find a thing wrong."

Maybe not physically. But she was deeply unhappy and didn't dare admit it. That was something very wrong. She wanted the baby, but not its father. Maybe if she could deal with the father better it would work out.

He didn't say anything. He couldn't say anything remotely like that. All he could do was listen and ask questions and hope. Laura Hunter blew her nose and pulled herself back together.

"I don't understand how there could be nothing wrong with me, and I keep losing my babies," she said. "I *must* be doing something wrong."

"Who says it has to be your fault?" Aaron said.

She looked at him in surprise. "Who else's fault could it be?"

"I don't know. You tell me." He could see her close her mouth and start to think about it. The session was over.

His thoughts drifted back to Amerigo. Amerigo had said he wanted to be tested for AIDS because he had heard if he got early enough treatment he could have a normal life. One person like him in a hospital could ruin a lot of lives.

5

There was a topiary garden that could be seen from George Highgate's window. A number of large hedges had been carefully clipped into animal and fish shapes. In the middle was a fountain. The garden was supposed to demonstrate how hard Axam was working to protect the environment. Tom studied a green dolphin while he waited for Highgate to move some papers from one side of his desk to another.

Finally Highgate looked up. "We want you to go to Adam Adar, Tom," he said with no introduction.

Tom almost laughed out loud. "You're kidding."

"No, I'm dead serious. We've got that fifty-million-dollar thing out there and we've got to get it up. We need your help on this." George smiled.

Tom's mouth went dry. "But I didn't have anything to do with it. I hardly know a thing about it." Except that it was a desperately needed new refinery in nowhere Middle East that had taken two years to build and didn't work.

"We'll brief you. This is the kind of thing you've always done well with. We're putting our hopes on you, Tom. You know we think the world of you."

Tom hesitated for a long time. He wanted to ask George if George had seen the plans for *his* refinery. He wanted to know if his project was on course. Could one refinery have anything to do with the other refinery? Did he have any choice here? The Middle East was a long way away. The situation was still uncertain there. Fires still burning. He knew they needed the refinery, but did they really need him? He took a deep breath.

"My wife is having a baby in a month," he said slowly. Actually, it was more like six weeks, but a month sounded more immediate. "I'd hate to leave her right now, George. We just moved out here."

George Highgate was a wiry, leather-faced man in his fifties who was hard to beat at any sport, and very high up at Axam. His face turned the color of beet soup as he leaned forward and put his elbows on the desk.

"This thing is costing us a quarter of a million dollars a day, Tom. You know that," he said. He never argued. He just stood his ground like a bulldog, growling and pawing the ground until his opponent gave up.

"I know that," Tom agreed. Tom was a ginger-haired son of an Irishman with an unyielding chin and deep blue eyes that could get as steely as any they faced.

"I want you to go over there, find out what's wrong with it, and fix it." George sat back. He'd given Tom his assignment twice now and didn't want to hear any more about it.

"We just moved into a new place," Tom said. "Bettina's alone out here. I wouldn't feel right leaving her now."

Highgate frowned. "I know all about that place. I approved the mortgage on it," he reminded Tom. "I think you could say I paid for it."

Tom flushed. Highgate had never spoken to him that way before.

"Who else is on the team?" he asked.

"Eighteen prime acres and a house I hear you've done a lot with," Highgate went on. He looked at his watch.

"Yes, we did put a lot of work into it. It was a mess."

"I hear it's a showplace now," Highgate persisted.

"My wife is very talented," Tom said. "She knows how to do things. We appreciate the mortgage," he added, humbling himself for Bettina's sake. She wouldn't want him to stand up and punch out George's lights in a fit of Irish temper.

Highgate leaned back. "I'm glad you're happy there. Your wife happy, too?" George asked. He became expansive at the mention of Tom's wife.

Tom nodded. She was happy, in general. She wouldn't like this, though.

"Who else is on the team?" Tom asked again. "And when do you want them to go?"

Highgate shook his head. "It's just you, Tom. There's already a team out there. You tell them what you want them to do. And we've got your flight booked. The twenty-sixth, I think."

Tom paled. "That's the day after tomorrow."

"Yes, it is. Look, Tom, we're only asking for a few weeks. We'll have you back in time for the baby. We'll fly you back. I'll give you my word on that. And I'll give you another promise. We're a family here. We'll take care of Bettina. She'll have the support of all of us. Don't even think of her as being alone.''

Tom looked out at the dolphin, trying to control his impulse to kill George Highgate.

''By the way, Tom,'' he said, leaning forward as if to share an important secret, ''I was in Korea when one of my kids was born, and in Texas when the other one popped out. We didn't stand by with a videocam in those days.'' George gave a little shudder at the thought of a father participating in childbirth.

''And they did just fine without us. Do you read me?''

''Yes, George, but things have changed.'' Tom wanted to say more, but George's eyes glazed over. He got that ''Listen here, I can make it nasty for you'' expression in his eyes for a second. Then they refocused.

''Look, I think we might have even more incentives for you. You get that refinery on stream, Tom, and you can count on a lot of gratitude. Aren't you up for a promotion this year?'' George asked, scratching his gray hair, as if he really couldn't remember.

Tom nodded slowly, feeling boxed in on all sides.

Fifteen minutes later he drove slowly through Morristown, wondering if there was anything he could have done to change Highgate's position. He thought about the huge refinery that was shiny and new out there in some desert sheikhdom, where wars raged all around. The famous refinery they couldn't get ''on stream,'' which meant going. They just couldn't turn it on. It had some fault in it somewhere, like the space shuttle had for three years. And like the shuttle, if they didn't find out where the weak link was, and fix it, the thing would not just stand there useless when they turned up the power—it would blow to kingdom come.

Yes, Axam definitely had a problem, and now they made it

his problem. He drove slowly, looking at Morristown differently, thinking for the first time that they should have moved here instead of so far out in the country. All the reasons Bettina hadn't liked it were good reasons for her to be here now. It was built up, which meant that the neighbors were close enough to look in the windows and see if something was wrong.

Bettina didn't have any affection for the company wives who lived there, but she would have gotten to know them and warm up to them. They would have been there for her, like George said. So she didn't like the staid, well-appointed houses that seemed middle-aged to her. They had security systems that were wired into the police station. It was his fault for not thinking ahead. This would have happened eventually. Sooner or later, they were bound to send him somewhere. He drove out of Morristown to Chester, where Chester Memorial Hospital was. There was a hospital in Morristown, too, but Chester's was closer; and the doctors the company wives liked seemed all to be affiliated with Chester Memorial.

Tom thought of the Lamaze classes with regret. They had completed four of the series and had two to go. For the last month they were supposed to practice on their own. He felt guilty; would she go to the last two by herself?

Perhaps he should have said, "No way, George. Won't go for *three* promotions. Won't go even if the thing blows up." But there was the mortgage to think of. Axam owned his house.

He drove through Mill Valley out Route 5 into the country, where there were still horse farms and truck farms and orchards. Finally he turned onto Orchard and drove a mile to their farmhouse. The number 375 was painted in white on the mailbox by a huge magnolia tree, now spectacularly in bloom.

Tom parked the car by the house. The windows were open and he could see white curtains billowing upstairs in what would be the baby's room. He felt a pang, as if he had been struck by a dart. The room next door was Bettina's studio. He could hear music coming from there.

Tom's heart got heavier as he surveyed the house. It was white, the shutters green. A dozen newly planted azalea bushes under the first-floor windows were in bloom. It was a beautiful place. The front door opened onto a hall where there were stairs going up to the second floor. The dining room was on the left, with a huge, sunny kitchen behind it. The living room was on the right. Tom went upstairs, where there were four bedrooms and two bathrooms. Their bedroom faced the backyard, which had a trout stream running through it, a pond, and a number of fruit trees that were wildly and fragrantly in bloom.

"Hi," Bettina called. "Almost finished."

He walked into her studio, where she was finishing up a watercolor of the magnolia tree in the front yard for the spring chapter of the book on seasons she was illustrating.

He was hit with another dart of dismay. On the table was a pile of the tiny double-breasted T-shirts Bettina had embroidered with a spouting whale, a bunny, a squirrel, a fish, some flowers. A duck with the letter *D* on it. When had she done those? He felt like he was being tortured with these new images of domesticity.

As he approached her, he smelled the baby powder she now used daily, and was further sickened at the thought of leaving all this, of leaving her.

He kissed the back of her neck, then picked up one of the tiny T-shirts. "Wow, this is really cute."

Guiltily, he kissed her again. "Are you sure it's going to be this small?" He held up the T-shirt, a tiny jacketlike thing with short sleeves.

"Smaller," Bettina said. Finally she put down the brush and turned around to kiss him on the mouth.

"I love you," she murmured, shooting him with yet another dart. He had to pull away a little or die on the spot.

Then he became aware of something else. An odor wafted up from the kitchen that Tom had never smelled in anyone's house before. "What's that smell?"

"Bread," Bettina said, smiling widely. "Isn't it amazing?"

Tom's mother died when he was ten, but neither she nor the stepmother who came later ever served anything but packaged white bread that he could wad into a ball with a little squeeze and practically bounce on the floor. "Amazing" didn't begin to describe Bettina's idea of what home and motherhood were all about. He was horrified by all the work she was doing. He had no idea that pregnant women often have a nesting instinct and that Bettina was indulging hers to the fullest.

"I have bad news," he said suddenly, without knowing he was going to say it.

She got up, frowning. "What?"

"Highgate wants me to go to the Middle East."

"Oh." The color drained out of her face. For a second she became dizzy, and swayed. Tom grabbed her arm.

"Jesus."

"Are you all right?"

He helped her into their room, where she sank into a chair and covered her face with her hands.

"Baby?"

She didn't say anything. She told herself not to say anything. Tom could see her mind working. She was a WASP, not like his family, all of whom screamed and wailed and beat their breasts when they were upset. She was brought up to control herself. He could see her struggling now.

"Highgate was a real bastard. He kind of threatened me. But I can say no," Tom said quickly, "if you feel uncomfortable about it."

"I wouldn't say I feel 'uncomfortable,' " Bettina mur-mured. *Terrified, furious, outraged would come closer to the mark.*

"You promised me you wouldn't die," she said.

He laughed uneasily. "I'm not going to die. I'll go away for two weeks, that's all. But I can say no, if you want me to."

He sat down at her feet, put his hands on her stomach. The baby kicked. He laughed. His child always kicked for him. Good kid. Sitting on the floor in his own house with his arms around his beautiful wife, Tom thought it reasonable to tell Highgate to go to hell. It was right. He'd tell him in the morning.

"God," Bettina muttered. "All this time I've been wor-ried about the wrong thing. The baby's fine. It's *this* I have to be afraid of. The Middle East. No one comes back from there alive. They'll kill you."

Tom laughed again. "No they won't."

"Yes, they'll kidnap you and torture you. Oh, God, Tom. Can't you go to Alaska instead?"

Tom shook his head. "I love the way you think, but no, they don't need me in Alaska. What's that smell?"

"It's the bread burning," Bettina said listlessly.

"Oh, shit." He jumped up and raced down the stairs to save it.

She muttered, "Maybe you'll fall and break your leg. That would keep you home."

He called from downstairs. "It's okay. It looks fine. I got it in time." Tom came back into the room smiling.

"Wait till you take it out of the pan," Bettina said gloom-ily. "I'm sure the bottom's burned."

"Don't be a pessimist. What else is for dinner?"

She shrugged. "What difference does it make?"

"Oh, come on," Tom said. "I told you I wouldn't go."

"Thank you for the thought," she said. "I appreciate it. I really do. But you know you have to go."

"No, I don't."

"I suppose Highgate told you not to let the mortgage and the moving costs and your life insurance plan and the many fringe benefits influence your decision." Bettina laughed bitterly. This was the corporate game. She knew how it was played.

"I can still tell him no," Tom insisted.

"Did he tell you he was in Korea when his son was born?" Bettina asked.

"How did you know that?" Tom was surprised.

"Oh, he told me that at the company picnic years ago, pawed the ground as he said it," Bettina said. "He was glad to have missed it." She realized that her anger was bringing the color back to her cheeks.

"I bet he told you Alice and everybody else would be there by my side to comfort me in your absence."

Tom nodded gloomily.

"How long is this for, anyway?" *The rest of your life?*

Tom looked out the window at the magnolia tree, then at the watercolor on the artist's table. He loved Bettina more than anything else in the world. "A couple of weeks," he said. "Is that the end of the world?"

"A couple of years would be the end of the world," she admitted. "But they're probably lying. They'll get you there and keep you there."

"They can't do that." He laughed uneasily again. "I'm coming back. I always come back. You know that. Can I taste your bread?"

"Oh, sure, change the subject. Where are you going, anyway? I want to see where."

He went into his office for an atlas.

"Not between Iran, Iraq, and Kuwait," she said when he pointed to it.

"No," he said seriously. "You can see there's nothing between them. Anyway, that's over."

"Sure it is. Do the phones work?"

He nodded. "And they have flights out every day."

"Wonderful," she said. "If I get lonely I'll call my mother. Two weeks isn't such a long time."

He pulled her to her feet and they started down the stairs to the kitchen.

"It might be longer than two weeks," Tom said as casually as he could, "but I promise you I'll be back when you hit your ninth month."

Bettina kept going. There wasn't anything else she could do. In the kitchen two places were set at the table. Tom had taken the two loaves of bread and set them on the counter. Still cooling in their pans, they looked all right. Golden brown on top. The kitchen was all blue and white.

"My ninth month is in four weeks," she said.

"I don't think it will be that long. I hope it won't. I'm pretty sure it won't." He waffled. He had no idea what he was walking into. Better not say anything more. He tapped the sides of a bread pan while Bettina looked on, her hands on her hips, the irritated wife. The first bread popped out. It was burned on the bottom, as she had predicted.

6

It was only eight o'clock in the morning, but it felt like a hundred degrees in the offices of Drs. Street and Steadman. Isobel unlocked the doors and stepped into the thick, slightly medicinal, dead air. For a second the heat and the smell of the place made her so dizzy and nauseated she thought she would have to bolt for the bathroom and throw up in the blued water of the toilet.

Quickly she turned the lighting rheostat up all the way and hit the switch for the air-conditioning. Immediately the waiting room was cast in an unearthly greenish glow that managed to be both cool and warm at the same time. Almost as fast, the air took on a chill. Isobel held on to the edge of her desk, shivering as the beads of sweat on her upper lip, on her forehead, and between her breasts turned cold.

She was the first one there, as usual. She'd done this a thousand times—opened the offices, turned up the heat or the air-conditioning, depending on the demands of the season. Called in to the answering service for the messages and then walked around the place, turning on lights, running a finger over every surface she came to, making sure the place had been cleaned properly, the bathrooms washed down before her arrival.

There was a glass bowl filled with potpourri on her desk that charged the air with a new and different aroma every month or so. Neither Dr. Street nor Dr. Steadman liked the smell of potpourri very much, but Isobel didn't respond well to criticism. The doctors had talked about it and decided it wasn't worth the hassle to get rid of it. Now the pile of dried leaves and bits of bark gave off a spicy-sweet aroma that was called Autumn Rose.

It was this, Isobel decided, that was responsible for her nausea. The sickly odor, and maybe the fact that she had a hangover. She moved around to the other side of her desk and sank into her chair. She had fifteen or twenty minutes to pull herself together. She thought of making coffee, but could not bring herself to move. The lights on the board flashed, but the answering service was still picking up.

She watched the lights. Two, three, four calls. Now that she thought about it, this did not feel exactly like a hangover. The room was not spinning on a tilt. She exhaled, pushing the bowl of Autumn Rose as far away from her as she could. She had bought this particular fragrance over Tea Rose, Spring Bouquet, Summer Floral, Verbena, Lavender, and others because she was seriously in love. She was smitten beyond anything she had ever felt before, and although Peter never said anything specific about marriage, he did things no other man in her life had ever done. She felt they shared something very special. And she kind of thought that by autumn he'd be ready to marry her.

She would be happy right now to lie on the floor in the bathroom with her head hanging over the toilet. The tiles would be washed and cool. She groaned as the sick feeling did not pass, and teased herself with the thought that she might be pregnant. It was more than four weeks since her last period. She was sure of it. She had felt kind of crampy all day yesterday, but it had passed by the time she met Peter in the evening.

Peter wasn't always available, but the night before he had been in an expansive mood. He took her to Wilkies and only went off to talk on the phone twice. She accepted this popping up and down during dinner as a small disadvantage. Dr. Street had a beeper. Men who were on the VIP level, as she knew Peter was, were constantly in motion. The fact that other people needed them was what made them rich and important. But Peter was not like a doctor—not like the ones she knew, anyway, who were mechanics of the human body but didn't seem to know much about anything else. She was impressed by how he talked, how he did things, how his black hair, combed straight back, made him look like a movie star, someone almost dangerously attractive.

They had a bottle of wine, but she noticed he didn't eat his steak. They had most of another bottle of wine. That would have done it, she told herself, though she knew that she had actually drunk no more than three glasses at the most.

She put her head between her knees, kneading her stomach with her fingers as if she could tell from the outside what was happening in there. Last night he left his steak on the plate, complaining of lower back pain with that thrilling grin that turned her almost instantly into mush, a willing love slave. Whenever he said his back hurt, they had the best sex. Lower back pain could very well account for her being pregnant, if she was.

Her thoughts shifted to his great town house, everything leather and glass, big pillows made out of Oriental rugs. The wall of the second bedroom had been removed so that he had one huge bedroom upstairs with the Jacuzzi on a platform. Oh, God, she loved him so much. Wouldn't mind at all if she were pregnant. He'd marry her then. Even sick, she got turned on thinking of him. She took a gulp of air, almost lost it, then slowed down to deep breaths thinking about the Jacuzzi, the grass they smoked, the smell of chlorine and baby oil. The size of his penis, long, smooth, and thick in her hand, salty in her mouth.

There was a mirror on the wall, another one on the ceiling.

They could see themselves like they were a movie—drinking wine, smoking, doing things to each other not many other people did. Love with him was not like getting poked in the missionary position for a few minutes by an overtired doctor who thought he was the greatest and didn't give a shit about anybody else.

Isobel thought bitterly of Robert, the last man in her life. He had been a young resident who was in no way extraordinary. He took all he could get and gave only a few trinkets back. He sponged off her for two years—lived with her, allowed her to cook for him, wash his socks, pay for the food and rent. And then as soon as he started in private practice, he married the sort of cool blond Isobel despised. The kind of girl who had a good figure, a good accent, and some money of her own. One day he just cleared out his things. The next day the engagement announcement appeared in *The New York Times*. And he wasn't even good in bed, the shit. He left her three months ago. Now it was June, the traditional wedding month. Now she had a new life with Peter. By autumn she'd be married to him.

"What in God's name are you doing down there?" Jennifer parked her enormous belly proudly on Isobel's desk. The zipper on her uniform was ready to split any second.

Isobel jumped. She had been thinking that she wouldn't mind being pregnant, that Peter would marry her and she'd have a family at last. She knocked her head on the edge of her desk as she sat up. The first thing she saw was Jennifer's protruding stomach, resting on her territory. She had been feeling better, and now she felt worse again. Jennifer was having twins any minute, and the whole office had revolved around her needs, her discomfort, her excitement for months. She was a cute redhead, and it was all very hard to take.

"I didn't hear you come in," Isobel said, rubbing her head.

"Hard night?" Jennifer smiled.

"No," Isobel snapped. "I dropped something."

"I've heard that before." Jennifer laughed and walked off, swaying her spreading behind and switching on the lights as she went.

Isobel checked the calendar. June 5th. She *was* late. This cheered her up again, and she had to restrain the desire to call Peter and tell him right away.

Patients began coming in. She had no time, and knew she mustn't say anything until she was sure anyway. He had to be in the right mood. She had to be in the right mood. She didn't believe in abortion (for herself, anyway) and didn't want to make him angry. She got up to make the coffee.

7

"Peter, you're going to have to shape up and get a grip on yourself."

Aristotle Dennison came into the conference room, where Peter Balkan was dozing with his head on the table. He sat down opposite Peter. There were a number of open law books scattered around him, as if Peter had fallen asleep in the middle of working. But there were no notes on his legal pad. He hadn't been working.

Aristotle wrinkled his patrician forehead. He was considered the father of the firm. So he was the one who had to deal with the problems. Peter was getting to be a serious one. This was not the first time he had been found sleeping in the middle of the day. Usually he was discovered this way in his office. Whoever caught him just closed the door.

But now he was napping in public, and it gave the place a bad feeling. Aristotle was a very proper man who didn't like sloppiness in his firm. He didn't like the fact that Peter had used the conference room without looking to see if anyone had booked it for a meeting. Aristotle *had* booked it for a meeting, and felt Peter was now stepping into dangerous waters.

Peter sat up blinking, and shook his head. "What's going on?"

"You're sleeping in the conference room, Peter. This is getting out of hand. I'm trying to be understanding, but you're slacking off. I can't let it go any longer. You haven't done any work for—a long time, Peter. What's happening with you?"

"I was up all night. You know how I work. I'm a wee-hours man, always have been," Peter said with a wide, genial smile.

Aristotle shook his head. "I was here until eleven. I didn't see you last night."

"I was working at home," Peter said quickly. "What is this, the third degree? I make more for this firm than anyone. You're the managing partner. You should know that."

Aristotle shook his head. "Tell me the truth."

"Don't question me," Peter retorted. "I don't like it. I'm the best litigator here, the best in the state." He dragged a hand through his thick black hair and rolled down his sleeves as if to get down to work.

"Used to be. *Used* to be the best."

"Don't give me that shit. I'm still the best," Peter said angrily.

"What case were you working on last night?" Aristotle asked quietly.

"The, um, Gregory case. You know, the malpractice case where the—"

"I know the Gregory case. I'm handling it myself."

"What?" Peter said furiously.

"You let the ball drop on the Gregory case weeks ago. The family couldn't get you on the phone. You didn't return their messages, remember?"

"Yeah, well, it was a busy time for me. I had three major—"

Aristotle held up his hand. "I know."

"Shit, don't patronize me. You had no right to take that case. I'm just . . . it was unethical. How could you do that? I was going to talk to them. I'll talk to them today."

"Go ahead. I'd be glad if you got it together. I don't want to have to take cases off your hands. But you're costing us money now. You're falling apart."

"No I'm not."

"What is it? Are you sick? If you're sick, we'll do something about it. You're sleeping all the time. You've got a cold. Listen to your cough. We're worried about you."

"I'm fine," Peter said. "Just tired."

"Maybe you're sick," Aristotle said again. "Maybe you need some kind of treatment, medication, to get you back on track."

Peter flipped the books closed one after another.

"Look, if you're sick, tell me. We go back a long way. I hired you, remember?"

Peter nodded slowly.

"Whatever it is, you know I'll support you."

"Thanks," Peter said finally. "Thanks. I appreciate it. Maybe I will see a doctor." He looked at his watch and grabbed the books.

"You got the conference room now, right?"

Aristotle nodded. So Peter did know, the older man thought. He wasn't completely out of it.

"All yours. I'm out of here."

Peter trotted down the hall to his office and dropped the stack of books on his desk. He sniffed two or three times and then blew his nose.

I do feel like shit, he told himself. *I really do.* He smiled to himself. *Ari's right. I need some medication to fix me up.* He picked up the phone and dialed the doctor's office. It rang twice.

"Doctors' office."

"Is?" Peter said. "Isobel?"

"Yes. Peter?"

"Look, darling, I was thinking about last night," Peter said softly. "You were amazing, really amazing. I miss you already."

"Me too," Isobel whispered, "but I can't talk now."

"See you tonight?"

"What? Two nights in a row?"

"Yes. Can you handle it?" Peter teased.

"Prepare yourself."

He could hear her sigh as she punched the button to take another call. He got up and closed the door to his office, then buzzed the secretary he shared with another lawyer to hold his calls. It was true. He really felt like shit.

8

"I know I'm supposed to relax and have happy thoughts," Laura said as she came into Dr. Simon's office. There was no hesitation now. She was talking almost before she was in the room.

"Who said that?" Aaron asked as he closed the doors behind her. He had just gotten back from another difficult meeting and was beginning to think some people were subtly obstructing disclosure of the AIDS problem. He was concerned and puzzled by it. The danger wasn't going to go away and would only get worse if they didn't face it.

Laura sat down and leaned forward eagerly, as if it had been difficult waiting a week to continue the discussion.

"Everybody does. You're supposed to be only happy when you're pregnant. I have terrible thoughts." She frowned and hugged her stomach.

Aaron crossed the quiet room, grateful to be back where he belonged, if only for an hour or so before another staff meeting. Laura was starting exactly where they'd left off the week before. She was a hard worker; he liked that.

"Maybe you're human," he said.

"What?" She looked at him suspiciously, as if surprised not to have been scolded.

"Nobody has all happy thoughts."

Laura shook her head doubtfully. "But I have really terrible thoughts. Last night I had a dream."

"Tell me," he said, settling himself.

"Wendal was in a car accident. His head was all bashed in and there was blood everywhere. He died." She shook her head.

"Then I had the baby, and I had to bring it up all alone." She made a clicking noise with her tongue. "It was terrible. I was so upset."

Aaron was silent.

"What do you think of that?" Laura demanded.

"I don't know. What do you think of it?"

"Maybe I'm afraid I can have the baby or Wendal, but not both." She took a tissue out of the box beside her chair and started twisting it around her finger.

"Maybe," Aaron said neutrally.

"I was so upset. I had to be a single mother, do the whole thing myself. Tell me. What does it mean?"

Aaron's face didn't change.

"Come on. You're the doctor."

"It's your dream," he said gently. He didn't want to get into a conflict with her, but he couldn't tell her everything. It wouldn't help her.

"What's that supposed to mean? I know dreams are important. You're supposed to know what it means."

"It came from your head. You're the one who made it up. You should tell me what you think it means."

"Dr. Steadman said you could help me," she said accusingly, changing the subject.

Laura said this every time she didn't want to stick with a subject. Aaron smiled. Everybody thought he could solve their problems for them. It didn't work that way. He crossed his legs the other way.

"I can help you understand yourself, Laura. That's what the goal has to be here."

"No, the goal is to have the baby," she said forcefully. "Last time you told me it wasn't my fault. But this is the one thing that has to be my fault."

"Laura, you've told me your husband is very critical, and that frustrates you a lot. And makes you angry."

"I'm not angry," she said guiltily.

"Well, it must be rough to live under the burden of such high expectations all the time."

Laura chewed on her lips. "I don't see what this has to do with my dream."

"A dream tells a story, and the dreamer makes it up. Sometimes the meaning is all disguised."

"Why?" Laura asked.

"Why what?"

"Why am I doing this? Am I crazy? Why do I have to think about hidden meanings? I don't care about dreams."

"You're doing this," Aaron said, "because you want to help yourself. It's a good thing to do."

Laura looked away. "I'm in my tenth week," she said. "It always happens in my twelfth week."

"I know."

"What if I lose the baby?" she demanded. "It'll be the third time. I don't think I can take it."

"Well, don't be so pessimistic. What if you don't lose the baby?" Aaron asked.

"I'll be so happy. I really will." Laura started to cry.

She always cried at the very end of every session. It made Aaron sad to see her wait to let herself go, and then have to pull herself together a few seconds later.

She pulled herself together. "I don't get it," she said, laughing a little to cover her embarrassment. "Why are dreams so disguised?"

She wasn't going to let go of his refusal to tell her. Aaron got up. He had known Laura only a few weeks, maybe five or six, and he was impressed at how hard she worked. She avoided subjects she didn't like, but then she came back to them more quickly than most people. He worried that she didn't feel secure enough in her relationship with her husband to carry the baby to term. But there wasn't enough time to work on it.

"Well?" she demanded.

"Dreams are disguised," Aaron said, "to protect the dreamer against wishes that are too painful to cope with."

She stood there frowning. "But I love him. I really do. I don't want Wendal to die. Not really."

"See you next week," he said.

9

Tom jumped up from the clammy bed in his trailer to get a Coke. Then he took it to the door and stepped out into the hottest sun he had ever experienced. It was 110 in the afternoon, hotter than Texas, hotter than the California desert. Hotter than anything he could imagine. For a second he stood on the top step and stared out at his assignment. They called it Abdullah, and it was the first refinery in this oil-rich, rapidly developing, desert sheikhdom. Tom described it to Bettina on the phone as a sheikhdom because he couldn't bring himself to call it a country.

Downtown in its major city, once hardly more than an oasis, there were a few modern skyscrapers, scores of mosque-like mansions, hundreds of Rolls-Royces, and what seemed like millions of people in an endless bazaar. Somehow it managed to remain untouched in spite of the many hostilities and conflicts that continued around it.

On the outskirts of the city was machinery of every description with nothing yet to work on, and a massive airport. Surrounding this was nothing but desert and oil.

Tom sipped the Coke and smiled grimly over how excited he had secretly been about coming here. He liked the challenge. He didn't mind the trailer or the smell of three years' sweat on military-style furniture, covered with a petroleum by-product that did not split, scratch, tear, or give comfort in any way. He had a sofa—fifties modern—two matching "leather" chairs, and a dinette with four aluminum chairs. The air conditioner made dying sounds, groaned, wheezed, rattled. There was an endless supply of Cokes in the refrigerator. It could have been a remote Armed Services outpost. It could have been prison. He didn't mind. Roughing it went with the territory.

What he minded every day, after eating his tuna salad lunch in the company cafeteria where everyone but the Arabs ate, was the dead afternoon. The hours when it was too hot to work. It made him feel helpless. He couldn't bear the idle hours and sometimes worked very late at night to make up for them. Now, at the end of his second week in Adam Adar, he couldn't rest in the afternoon anymore.

The heat was like a wall in front of him, on top of him. The Coke only made him thirstier. He looked up at his nemesis— two square blocks of pipes of every size, gauges, tanks, and gridwork four stories high. He had been over it several times. There was something wrong with the pressure in one phase, and since every phase of the process was integrally linked with every other phase, they could not go on stream until everything was perfect.

A dozen experts had been over it and could not find the source of the problem. None of them could stay out here forever, either. Tom sighed, and decided he would go and check the errant gauge panels again. That was the first thing he had done when he arrived. He had had the gauges replaced, but the new ones showed no magical change in the situation. There was not the pressure there should be; the gunk (as Bettina called it) simply did not move through the pipes as it should.

He climbed up the stairs to the first level, marveling as he always did at this great silent Erector set. The stairs and the gridwork on the floors looked like an enlarged version of the toy. Actually it was not all silent; the refinery was very slowly going on stream, even with the defect. Millions of dollars were lost every week they were late and half the "people at home" wanted to go on stream no matter what was wrong.

Abdullah had been tested at higher temperatures, and greater pressure, and found to be "functioning inadequately," so the report said. Those who knew more about financial statements than refineries seemed to think that if Abdullah were put on stream gradually enough, the problem would straighten itself out—"God willing," or, as the Arabs put it, "Inshallah."

God, however, was not willing. Turning it on would be like putting a dirty pot in the sink, turning on the tap, and expecting the pot to scrub itself. Tom put that in *his* report. Except there were a few differences. The pot, unscrubbed, would simply not get clean. In a refinery, putting more and more pressure on a weak spot could result in an explosion. Tom did not want to be there to experience that.

Sometimes he had a nagging little suspicion that maybe a nasty end was what headquarters really wanted now. A way out of this place. He didn't want to die here, or live to find himself embroiled in an insurance investigation.

As he climbed around in the sun, checking machinery that had been already been checked and rechecked, Tom no longer looked at his feet. He knew the open gridwork and the stairs. What he concentrated on most now was holding on to the tools he carried. If he dropped something, it would go right through the holes and possibly land on someone's head. They were all required to wear their hats on site. But many of them didn't. "Candyass" was what they called people who thought about their safety.

Tom listened to the pipes as he moved around, looking at the needles on the gauges and twisting the handles a little this way or that. Somehow, even over all the noise, he felt he would *hear* the fault. Every day, every hour even, he felt there was a chance that the fault would make itself known to him. So he kept moving as much of the time as he could. He knew he would not find the answer in his trailer.

He hated to admit he was stumped. He hated the idea of giving up and going home. Slowly he climbed up to the fourth level and listened to the noise of the pipes. Every day he grew more frustrated and tired from his nightly vigils. The tension of all that money being wasted and worry about Bettina was getting to him. She always sounded cheerful when they talked on the phone every few days, but he could hear the depression behind her words.

Tom tried to shake himself out of his guilt. He had promised her he would be home by the time her ninth month began. He knew he had to leave immediately to keep his promise. And he also knew that if he couldn't get Abdullah on stream he was finished in the company.

Nothing. He couldn't find a thing.

He swayed on the ladder going down. He was not as brawny as most of the other refinery workers, or even the other engineers. He had never had the hard-hat look about him, and pushed himself hard to be as tough as the others. On the ground, he headed back to his trailer, disgusted at himself for having accomplished absolutely nothing once again.

10

Bettina had an eleven-thirty appointment. She was exactly on time.

Isobel looked up and smiled. "Hello, Mrs. Dunne. Husband back yet?"

Isobel knew that Bettina's husband was away, because she knew everything that was in every chart. The number to call in case of emergency on Bettina's chart was in some unpronounceable place in the Middle East. Isobel had put it there herself.

Bettina's blue-gray eyes clouded over. "No, but I spoke to him this morning. He said he'd be here by the end of the week." She sighed. "Is the doctor on time?"

"Yes," Isobel said, and turned to the ringing phone.

Bettina sat down and thumbed through a *Parents Magazine*. She didn't have to sit for long.

"Mrs. Dunne?" Jennifer came by and picked up Bettina's file, which was next in the pile on Isobel's desk.

"Yes." Bettina got up. "Still working?" she asked. "Aren't you due any minute?"

"Yes and yes," Jennifer said brightly. "I wouldn't want to sit at home and brood, would I?"

"Certainly not," said Bettina, who found herself at home and brooding quite a bit. She was lonely and hurt by her mother, who cried on the phone but said she couldn't, just *couldn't,* leave Bettina's father. She insisted he was sick and helpless, couldn't do anything for himself.

"It's the worst time of my life," her mother complained.

"You've never been there for me," Bettina wanted to say, but did not say. This wasn't new. Even before his heart trouble, her father had *never* done anything for himself.

But she tried not to be angry at Tom. "You've always been there for me," she told him. "I know you'll be back as soon as you can."

There was a commercial on TV in which an oil executive, who didn't look anything like Tom, went out to an oil rig in the middle of the ocean to fix something and kept calling his son, whose birthday he didn't want to miss. It was a commercial for an airline, and it wasn't clear at the end whether he got back in time for the birthday or not. But the sight of the oilman, out in the middle of the ocean, worrying about his kid every night during the evening news, made Bettina feel closer somehow to Tom.

"Pee in the cup for me, will you, and I'll be right back to get a blood sample and weigh you," Jennifer said.

In fifteen minutes it was all over. Picture-perfect Dr. Street straightened up, smiling. He threw the metal thing that looked and felt like an object of torture into a metal pan where there were many others. It made a nice clatter. He pulled off his gloves with a snap and tossed them into the wastebasket.

Clatter and snap. He did this fifty times a day, Bettina thought. She looked quickly into the garbage, and then away. This was medical waste. She thought of the sharp thing that pricked her finger, the dipstick that measured something or other in her urine, the glove with some kind of jelly on it. Where did all this stuff go?

Dr. Street held out his hand to haul Bettina to a sitting position. "Put on your clothes and come into my office. Let's talk for a minute."

"Is something wrong?" Bettina frowned.

"No, no. You're coming along fine. It won't be long now, that's all." He looked at his watch. "Can you hurry? I have to be at the hospital in twenty minutes."

He went out and closed the door before she said she could hurry. She pulled on the blue dress that matched her eyes and was Tom's favorite. She put on underpants that didn't begin to cover her stomach. She'd spoken to Tom only this morning, and he said he'd be home by the end of the week. She dragged a comb through her golden hair without looking at herself in the mirror.

Dr. Street saw her in the hall, and they both went into his office together. He had a big modern desk with two comfortable chairs in front of it, bookcases the length of one wall, and several photographs of himself and his two sons. In waders, loaded down with fishing equipment and going for trout; in a fancy boat off New England, going for swordfish. In Canada, fishing for salmon that, he told her, they smoked on the spot.

Bettina wondered if he knew how to dig for clams, as she did, wondered if he ate his catch or mounted it. Thought she'd like to tease him about the connection between his specialty and his favorite sport, but didn't. She didn't know him well enough, and was pretty sure he took himself too seriously to have any fun at anybody's expense, especially his own. She knew that she was thinking all these things and studying the picture of his wife—on a horse, no less—because she did not want to think about actually giving birth. She'd carried the baby, safe in her body, long enough. And now she wanted someone to hand it to her.

Dr. Street made church and steeple out of his lovely fingers, and smiled at the lovely woman sitting across from him. He had a very good nose and knew that her perfume was Fleur, perfect for the summer, and that she had changed it in the two and a half months since he met her.

"Well, Bettina," he began, calling her by her first name for the first time.

"You've begun to efface—just begun, though. I think you've got three weeks yet. Maybe four. It all depends on the whim of nature at this point. First babies, you know, like to stay put as long as they can." He fiddled with the reading glasses on his desk, looked down at her file.

Bettina sighed. *That* long? If thinning of the tissue that held the baby in had already begun, she didn't believe for a second it would be that long. "I feel ready to have it out now," she said with a rueful smile.

Dr. Street took this as a joke and laughed. "Don't you want to wait for your husband?"

"Well, sure I do, but it's getting so hard to move around."

"What do you hear from him?" He closed the file and put it down.

Bettina frowned at the mention of him. "I spoke to him this morning. He said he'd be home by the end of the week, no matter what." It was Monday.

She didn't like talking about this. She didn't know whether to believe him or not. And she was afraid all the time. Furious and afraid. It rained a lot and she was stuck inside, feeling pregnant and vulnerable. She thought constantly about how hard it would be to get away if someone came after her. She knew there wasn't a single window in the house that couldn't be opened by a ten-year-old. Anybody could cut the phone cord and cut her off from the outside world. And the outside world was very far away. There wasn't another house within view. Only those lovely fields and woods they had considered so charming when they first saw the house.

They had thought of themselves as pioneers, doing something different, relying on their own resources. But Bettina was a pioneer without a rifle, and now that didn't seem like such a good idea. Now she knew why the house had been on the market for over a year. Only a crazy person would want to be so far from civilization. It took half an hour to get the newspaper. It took so long, she didn't bother going for it anymore. So many things about their choice seemed wrong now that she was on her own. The house groaned when it rained. Animals scurried around in the eaves and the basement. The basement was almost unbearably scary.

She couldn't help it—even though she didn't mean to be, she was furious at Tom for leaving, and furious at her mother for not coming to be with her. She had the feeling she was being punished for getting what she wanted, like the people in the stories about the three wishes who never had enough judgment to get it right. She didn't know what to do, which way to go to keep herself safe, to protect her baby, and was so certain that her fear was her own fault, she simply could not let any of it show in her face.

Dr. Street opened his glasses and closed them. His face became serious.

"Bettina, have you thought of a backup in case he doesn't return in time?"

"Backup?" Bettina said, puzzled because she thought he meant Lamaze coach.

"Yes, someone to stay with you in the last week or so, be with you, take you home, that sort of thing."

"My husband told me he's coming back at the end of the week." Bettina just couldn't think about it, couldn't imagine him not being with her.

Dr. Street studied her face for a minute. "Well, make an appointment with Isobel for next week, then, and we won't worry," he said finally.

Bettina nodded and wondered if he meant him worry or her worry. In reception, Isobel was on the phone, swiveled around the other way, talking softly.

Bettina stood there for a few minutes and then sat down on the other side of the desk. Finally Isobel hung up and turned around, professionally cheerful again. "Well, Bettina, what can I do for you?"

"I'd like an appointment for next week," Bettina said.

"Oh, great, that means we're really getting close then. Did you buy that crib yet?" Isobel asked.

"You have quite a memory, don't you?" Bettina was impressed.

Isobel smiled. "I guess you could say I'm involved with all my patients. Did you get it?"

Bettina shook her head.

"Well, go right back there and choose. Right away. What if the baby is born early? You'll be caught without any equipment. You wouldn't want that, would you?"

Bettina frowned. "It's bad luck to have the crib before the baby."

Isobel laughed. "We don't let anything go wrong with our babies. You'll be fine."

"Well, maybe." Bettina couldn't help smiling back at her. Isobel seemed so sure of herself. She sat there twisting a curl around her finger and jiggling her foot. She had a lot of little gold rings on her fingers, and a gold anklet above the restless foot. Bettina also noticed she was wearing gold loafers, and that they didn't go with her uniform.

Nevertheless, she was right. Bettina got up awkwardly. She would have to get the crib herself, and the diapers and the bottles and the nipples. Whether it was bad luck or good luck made no difference. She had no choice; she had to do it.

11

"Dr. Simon, can I talk to you for a moment?"

Aaron was preoccupied, was hurrying back to his office from the psychiatric department's community meeting. Every week all the inpatients and some of the staff gathered together and talked about what was happening on the unit and their feelings about it. They had a lot to say about what was going on now. They didn't want dirty stuff going on in their community. Some of them wouldn't touch anything anyway, and now they knew for sure a touch could kill. Their neighbors could kill. Even the staff was infected.

He had passed the bridge and was just about to turn the corner into his office. At the sound of his name, he swung around to the stairs that came up from the entrance to the building below. A young woman was standing nervously at the top, as if afraid to come any closer. She looked familiar to him.

He crossed the hall. "Yes?"

She sank a few steps farther into the stairwell.

"I'm April Flanders."

"Oh," he said.

"I'm not supposed to be here anymore."

He nodded. "I know. Do you want to come into my office?" He looked at his watch. "I have five or six minutes."

"You won't tell anybody?" she said.

"Come on. My office is right here."

"I'm afraid I'll get in trouble." She looked around anxiously.

Aaron led the way and didn't say anything. She was already in trouble. She had sex with a psychiatric inpatient who was HIV positive, and been fired for it. She wouldn't have an easy time getting another job. What else could she get in trouble for?

Lorna was out to lunch. Her desk was empty. Aaron passed quickly through the waiting room and opened the doors to his office.

"Sit down."

April sat gingerly in the chair and looked down at her hands.

"You must be pretty upset," Aaron said. Now that he had a chance to look at her he remembered who she was. A dark-haired, lively girl. About twenty-five. Slim and attractive. She had an easy, relaxed way about her that made her popular with the patients and the staff.

She swallowed. "It's all a mess. I'm sorry about Ron. I didn't want this to happen to him."

Aaron closed his eyes for a second. Uh oh. "Did you have a relationship with him?"

She sniffed. "He didn't really do anything wrong. We were just . . . Well, it was the first time that first night." She stopped.

"You weren't on the floor. You were with Ron, is that right?" Aaron said.

She sniffed back her tears. "And he was mad."

Aaron shook his head, trying to be patient. "Who was mad?"

"Amerigo," she said impatiently. "I said I would—and I didn't."

Aaron shook his head again, confused. "You mean you didn't have sex with Amerigo?" Then why did she tell Patricia she had?

"I didn't do it with him *that night*. I did it with him before." She blew her nose. "I don't know. I had a blood test and it's negative, but I still could get it six months, a year from now. I feel so bad."

Aaron was frozen for a second as he tried to digest all this. "You mean you had a thing going with a patient."

"It didn't start in the hospital," she said defensively.

"The first time he had a weekend pass. We saw each other in the parking lot, and he asked me out then."

"He was still a patient, even in the parking lot," Aaron said. "Didn't you think of that?"

"I know. I'm sorry." She blew her nose.

"And then you began a relationship with Ron, is that right?" Aaron said slowly.

"He's not a patient," she said sharply.

"He was a staff member." There were rules about that, too. But it was hard to enforce them.

He frowned almost imperceptibly. Going off when they were on duty. That was inexcusable. If she had promised Amerigo she would come to his room, he would have felt angry and jilted. And entitled to a substitute. So he went down the hall and paid a visit to Alisa. Poor Alisa. This had happened to her before.

So now Aaron knew what happened. None of Ron's story had sounded right to him. But they couldn't shake him on it. He said he was off the floor when he should have been doing rounds because he had a stomach virus. He just didn't bother to report it. The Committee thought it was enough to terminate him.

And April, the night nurse, was off the floor, too. Patricia, the head nurse, was the one who found that out. She uncovered part of it. She was on the Committee. But April told her she hadn't had sex with anyone else. The Committee accepted that without further probing.

April sat opposite him, crying softly.

"Thank you for telling me," Aaron said.

"That isn't what I wanted to tell you." The underarms of April's pink blouse were stained with perspiration. "Oh, God," she muttered.

"There's something else?" Aaron said.

He watched her chew on her mouth for a few seconds. The chief administrator was waiting for him downstairs, but he didn't move. He waited, his distress mounting. "Go on."

"I don't want him to get in trouble," April said.

"Who?" Aaron asked.

"I just thought you should know," she said doubtfully.

Aaron nodded. "You're right, I should know. Is it another patient?" he asked cautiously.

"No, I would never have sex with a patient," she said indignantly.

He didn't bother to point out that she would and she had.

"Well, only with him. What are you going to do with him?"

"Amerigo? He's being transferred to a state hospital," Aaron said.

"Jesus, a snake pit." She looked at him sadly. "He was a nice guy."

Right. "I have to go in a minute."

"Look, what will happen if I tell you there's another doctor? It's a confidence, right? You can't do anything to him."

"You're telling me in confidence," Aaron said.

"He didn't do anything wrong. We didn't do it here or anything. It's just because of the, uh, the AIDS thing."

Aaron nodded. "Who is it?"

"Max." April said. "There, I told you."

Two seconds more and she was out the door. She told him, and she split.

Aaron sat back, stunned even though he knew he shouldn't be. Maxwell Starburn had been screwing the nurses for years. He was Chester's head of surgery. As a member of the Clinical Care Committee investigating this incident, he should be the most concerned of everyone, and yet at every meeting he downplayed the danger. Now Aaron could understand why. Max was part of the chain. He could even have the virus himself. Worse and worse. Now every patient he operated on could very well be at risk. Aaron would have to be careful how he dealt with this. It could get very nasty if Max was not open to inquiry.

12

Laura stood in the second bedroom squinting at the three samples of wallpaper taped to the wall. She had spent almost two weeks looking at them but didn't dare choose one. Now the twelfth week of her pregnancy had passed safely and she thought it would be good luck to go ahead and paper the room.

"Wen," she called, "come here for a minute, will you?"

"Honey, I'm late."

He was taking his last sip of coffee in the kitchen and reading the paper when she appeared in the doorway.

"Please come and look one last time. I promise you I won't ask you again," she said.

"Sweetheart, you know we don't need to paper that room. We had it painted only last year. We decided that yellow was best." He put down the paper and looked at her, frowning slightly.

"It's cheerful and sunny, and I like the curtains in there." He picked up the paper again.

"Oh, but Wen. You know I want to change it."

He put down the paper for the last time. "Can't even read the paper," he muttered.

"Look, Pumpkin, we don't need to do a thing around here. The place is perfect. I have to go. Where's my briefcase?" He started looking for it. It wasn't in the kitchen. He went out into the hall.

They had a two-bedroom condominium in The Oaks, a fancy building with a fountain in front, a swimming pool on the roof, and its own golf course. Wendal was an insurance agent, and Laura had been his secretary before they married six years ago. Since then she had taken college courses, gone to cooking school, and decorated their apartment.

The results of her decorating efforts were stunning. The apartment looked spare and expensive and modern. The parquet floors were bleached and pickled white wood. The dining area was mirrored to reflect the lights from the terrace and the fountain at night. They had two tweedy sofas in the living room, two leather chairs, a glass-topped table, and a marble table. The rug in the living room had a bold, modern design. The one under the dining room table was Persian and had a subtle design. From the many windows they had views of both the golf course and the sweeping entrance, with the fountain that spouted twenty-four hours a day from March to November.

Laura followed him. "Are you sure, Wen? They promised me they could paint the woodwork this week and put up the paper as soon as it's dry. You can't get better service than that."

"No, honey. If it could be done at the snap of a finger, I'd still prefer it just the way it is. Why can't you let well enough alone?"

"Because I think it will make a difference."

"Nothing like that will make a difference."

His back was to her. She couldn't see his face getting red.

"Don't you believe in changing things, Wendal? Like changing the room and changing ourselves?"

"Why?"

"Because we're human. We're not perfect. If we make some changes, our life will be better," Laura said.

"I don't know what you're talking about. Where the hell did you put my briefcase?"

"I could pay for it myself," she said softly.

"No new wallpaper," he said sharply. "No, and no. Can't you hear?" He searched the elegant living room for the briefcase.

"Yes, I can hear," she said, backing off. "I'll just get a crib and a carriage and a changing table and a layette. All right? Is that okay with you?"

"Why can't you wait, Laura," he said very deliberately so she would be sure to understand him. "Don't buy it until that baby is here, okay? Be realistic. You know your history."

"But this time it's all right," she said. "Last time I didn't buy the things, and I lost the baby. This time I'm going to be fine."

"You don't listen. You have a history and you don't listen. Where is that briefcase?"

He went back into the kitchen. Laura followed him. Dr. Simon said some men were insensitive. She looked at her husband, who was big, a former football player, and used to make her feel tiny, feminine, precious, smart.

"Wendal, are we happy?" she asked.

"What a stupid question. Of course we're happy." He turned to look at her. "Why do you ask me things like that when you know I have to go to the office and concentrate?"

"Well, you're so mad at me all the time. I can't bear it."

"What are you talking about? I'm not mad at you."

"Wendal, you're mad at me now."

"Well, you're making all this fuss. 'Baby, baby, baby.' I can't stand it. I don't know why you want a baby so much, anyway; you're so nervous you'd only have a breakdown trying to take care of it."

Laura's mouth fell open. "How could you say that to me? Do you think I'm crazy?"

"You have a shrink, don't you? Ah, here it is." He pulled his briefcase out from behind the bread box.

"Why did you put it there?" he said, touching his head with a finger to show his opinion of her mental state.

"I didn't touch it," she said numbly. "And I'm not crazy."

"Well, have a good day, then," he said. He leaned over and kissed her on the forehead.

"I don't think I will," she murmured as he went out the door. Her head and stomach hurt. She went back to bed and slept for many hours. When she got up to go to the bathroom, there was blood in her underpants. The sight of it was devastating. It was worse than before. Last time it was a shock, and that was bad enough. But this time she had gone for help. She was trying to understand herself. It wasn't supposed to happen. This time she didn't expect it.

As she stood there, too horrified to move, the flow increased. It seemed to pump out with every heartbeat. Suddenly Laura became dizzy. The blood made her think she was not just losing her baby, she was seeing her own death. She collapsed in a dead faint on the bathroom floor.

13

"If you want the valves checked on number four, why don't you climb up there and do it yourself?" Charlie turned on his heel and walked out.

Five of the team had been standing around in Abdullah's control room, where the computer equipment and control panels that monitored the whole refinery were. Everyone looked at Tom, but no one said anything.

Several days ago he had become convinced that Abdullah's trouble was in the number four distillation tower. There were half a dozen distillation towers all over the refinery, in several sizes, tall and taller, and tallest. Number four was the highest, about the height of a ten-story building. It was circled at intervals with gridwork platforms, and the stairs going up were ladders going around the tower in a circle. No one wanted to go up there.

Charlie argued that every one of the distillation columns had been carefully checked out as the refinery was being built. All the automatic gauges and monitoring devices indicated the machinery was in good working condition.

But when the pressure built up, Tom pointed out, a few key valves automatically closed. He was sure that the control valve on the top of number four was faulty. Or else the Freon gas in the refrigerating condenser was leaking out. It had to be checked. Tom was losing weight. He was taking more salt tablets, but water poured off him all day long. Every day he seemed to wither a little more. Charlie hinted that Tom had all the symptoms of sun sickness. Charlie's last post had been in South Africa. He liked talking about all the recruits from the states he'd seen fall apart in extreme climates.

Tom knew they were just stalling him. Theoretically he had the authority to order them to do anything he thought should be done, but he wanted them to agree with him. It took days of tight-lipped discussion to get to the bottom line.

He turned to Bob, who was still standing there, mouth open. Bob was a big, solid brute of a man, roughened inside and out from twenty years on one site or another, in cramped quarters away from what family he had, living on starchy food and beer.

"Is that what you think, too?" Tom asked.

Bob grunted, giving himself a moment to think it over. Then he nodded briefly.

"Okay, then. I'm not going to fight with you. I'll do it myself."

It wasn't Tom's job to go up there. And anyone could see that even if it had been his job, he wasn't in any shape to do it now.

Bob frowned at his scrawny supervisor, more than a dozen years younger than he. The company was nuts on safety. He shook his head. "I don't think you should. Remember Paul?"

"I do," Tom said. Who didn't remember the mechanic who went inside a half-filled tank to fix a pipe? He had gained a lot of weight since he last qualified for the task, but didn't want to risk losing his job by being examined and weighed again. He didn't care that his extra safety harness was now too small to fasten properly. As he was lowered into the tank, the straps slipped and the harness beneath them pulled off. He fell in, and they couldn't get him out in time. The three-hundred-pound man drowned in crude.

Tom set his jaw. "You, Tiny. You come with me. And get Indian Joe." It was two o'clock on a sizzling day in the middle of June.

Tiny, who was a six-foot-four Oklahoman, said, "Sure thing."

Indian Joe liked being high up, too, and the two men were buddies. Tom knew the three of them would be a fine team.

Tom set off for a knapsack of supplies, muttering to himself. Charlie pissed him off. Lazy prick. Tom didn't think he was sick. He was fine, and he didn't want to wait for morning. He wanted to go home and see his wife. He went into the prefab they used for a lounge and dining room, and got the cook to pack up some sandwiches.

He was going to do it right now, and Bob and Charlie be damned. Tom didn't once tell himself that Tiny and Indian Joe could do the job without him. He watched the cook make him bad sandwiches that would be all dried out before they were even in the bag and debated whether to take a six-pack of Pepsi or a six-pack of beer. Pepsi, he decided. Beer was too dangerous. He reached for a dozen bags of M&M's to keep them going. Chocolate in any other form out there melted before it got off the plane. Tom swallowed two salt tablets and then swung out of the building, the knapsack on his back.

Tiny and Indian Joe were waiting for him by the ladder at the bottom of column four. They looked at him doubtfully.

"I think we could handle this by our lonesomes," Tiny said after a long minute.

Indian Joe nodded his agreement.

"Hell, I'm coming," Tom said. He noticed that although there were a number of men around waiting to hoist things up to them, and generally hanging around to watch, Bob and Charlie were not among them.

"It's a long way," Tiny said slowly. "I wouldn't want to have to carry you down."

"Don't worry, you won't have to." Tom plopped his hard hat on his head without fastening the straps and started climbing.

It took more than a half hour in the broiling sun to climb to the top of number four. Surprising both himself and his companions, Tom got up there with very little difficulty. There was a slight tremor in the thigh muscles of his left leg when he reached the top, but he didn't pay any attention to it, and after a while the twitching stopped.

They set to work immediately, and for five hours the three of them hunkered over the various parts as they disassembled as much of the refrigerating condenser as they could. They stopped only once, to bolt down the sandwiches and half the bags of M&M's.

At eight o'clock, when they still hadn't found anything wrong, the sun started its rapid descent into the sand. Tom planned to turn on the spots all around them so they could continue to work after it got dark. They had all worked at night before, and Tiny and Indian Joe were just tough and crazy enough to work all night if Tom asked them to.

But they never had to discuss the matter. At eight-fifteen exactly, after five and a half hours on a sun-reflecting platform ten stories above the desert, they found a faulty joint in the main pipe leading to the control valve. The welding equipment needed to repair it was duly hoisted up, and in another hour the work was done.

When Tom reached out to congratulate Tiny and Indian Joe

for their good work, his foot made contact with a small piece of forgotten pipe. His ankle turned and he pitched forward. Tiny caught Tom by the arm before he hurtled right through the gap in the railing where the ladder was. Tom spun around, safe for a second, as his hard hat flew off and fell ten stories to the ground. Then there was a sickening thud as his head slammed against the side of the condenser they had gone up to repair.

14

Peter was leaving Isobel's apartment very late when he was jostled by two men leaning against the very unimpressive car he had gotten to replace his Ferrari.

"Hey, buddy, got a light?" one asked.

"Sorry, no," Peter said evenly. He felt a prickle of fear, but only a little one. It was past two in the morning. There was a little park between the building and the street, its bushes and trees fully in bloom. It was hot for the end of June, but any sounds not covered by air conditioners would not have traveled as far as the building anyway. He looked quickly at the building. All was quiet. Isobel's lights were off.

The two men lolled against his car.

"Excuse me," Peter said.

One of them stepped forward, as if to move out of the way, then shifted suddenly. His right arm lashed out and his fist connected with Peter's unprotected, unprepared stomach.

"Aggh," Peter choked.

He lurched forward, but the shorter of the two men caught him before he fell and propped him up while the other helped haul him back into the bushes.

Before, in the darkness of the quiet street, they had looked like kids, slouching against the car, vaguely threatening, but not seriously. Now they acted quickly. Suddenly their light summer suits fit snugly and their faces swam into focus as they straightened up. They were in their thirties, or more.

Peter tried to let go and fall down, but there were four strong hands on him, and he couldn't seem to get his breath through the pain in his heaving stomach. He gagged. Oh, shit, he was in trouble.

"Take my wallet," he gasped.

"Don't want your wallet."

Oh, shit. He had been prepared to lay down and let them roll him, play dead to get it over with. All he had was a twenty, a MasterCard, his driver's license, and a thirty-nine-dollar Swatch watch. They were welcome to it. But they didn't want that. One of them punched him again, and he gagged.

"He's going to heave, the mother."

"Go ahead, break the fancy nose, Smasher. What are you waiting for?"

Peter raised his head. His breath came back with a rasp. He knew who they were.

"Stop."

"When you get respect," the man called Smasher hissed at him.

"I got respect."

"Break his nose. For Christ's sake, teach him his lesson." Benny the Pipe, the little tank-shaped man, danced at Smasher's side.

Smasher paid no attention.

Benny kicked Peter fiercely in the shin. "Break his nose," he demanded again in the shrill voice that didn't match his body.

Peter buckled at the sharp kick in his leg, but could not fall. Smasher had him pinned against an oak tree with one hairy paw.

"I got the message," he gasped. "Tell him I got it." Oh, shit, make them stop.

"Break his *nose.*"

"Shut up. There are limits. You know the limits."

"Break a leg, then. Break a rib."

Peter made himself so heavy they could hardly hold him up. Oh, was he in trouble. He didn't cry out, just made "ouff" and "ahhh" sounds when they hit him. He knew how to plead only in court. He knew that here it wouldn't help his case. He saw the looks on their faces as they finally let him fall to the ground. They enjoyed it.

In the end they compromised, didn't break a leg, didn't hit him in the face. They cracked a few ribs with their kicks. And then, when he finally passed out in the dirt, they drove him home in his own car.

15

The day after their date, when Peter didn't show up at the office and didn't answer his phone at home, Isobel became uneasy. He had said he would call her in the morning, and he usually did what he promised. She drove over to his town house during her lunch hour and parked in his driveway. As always, she thought it was a beautiful place. She wouldn't mind living there. The houses were Tudor, Peter told her. The gardens were well kept and fragrant with blooming roses, the first of the year.

Everything looked normal. For a minute she thought she was crazy and should mind her own business. She sat in her car, thinking she ought to get out of there. Then something made her think she should just check. She got out of the car and went slowly up the walk, her face twisted with concern. It occurred to her that he might have had a heart attack and she could be the one to save his life. She liked that idea. She stood in the sun ringing his doorbell for a few minutes. When there was no answer, she tried the door. To her surprise and alarm, the brass knob turned and the door opened.

"Peter?" she called cautiously.

There were mud stains on the floor in the hall.

"Peter?" Her voice rose to a scream.

"Up here," came the croaky reply.

She ran up the stairs and found him lying on his bed in the suit he had been wearing when he left her the night before. It was muddy, bloody from a nosebleed, and torn in several places. He was sweating and shivering. His nose was running as if he had a bad cold. She was horrified.

"Oh, thank God you're here," he whimpered. "I need something for the pain."

"What happened?" she cried. "Oh, Jesus, what happened?"

"Just a little misunderstanding." He sniffed furiously and swiped at his nose.

"But you're hurt." She started pulling at his clothes. "You're hurt."

"Yeah. They hit on me."

"Who?" Isobel pulled off his jacket and started unbuttoning his shirt.

He twisted away from her.

"It hurts," he groaned. "Leave me alone."

"Shh, I have to see how bad it is." She probed at his bruises. He was filthy, covered with dirt. "God, what happened? It looks like you were beaten up."

"It's bad." He groaned every place she touched him.

"What *happened?*" she asked again. His sheets were filthy, too. "Tell me," she demanded. "I'll call the police."

"Ahhhh-ow. Shit, that hurts."

She got his shirt off. His body was a mass of bruises and lumps and scratches.

"I have to know what happened." She moved quickly, trying to make him more comfortable. She had to be back in the office in less than an hour. She had promised. But this was an emergency, she told herself. She ought to be there when the police came. He needed an ambulance, too.

"I'm going to call the police," she said.

"No," he said sharply. "Leave me alone."

"Somebody beat you up, Peter. We have to call the police. What did they take?"

"Nothing. Just leave it."

"You can't leave it," she said indignantly.

She looked around. The large-screen TV was gone from the bedroom. She was shocked. "You've been beaten and robbed."

She went to his closet. It was almost empty. Only one suit was in there. "Jesus. Your beautiful suits." She started to cry.

"Isobel," Peter croaked at her hoarsely, "it's none of your business. Stay out of it." He sniffed some more.

She turned to open the top drawer of his bureau, where he kept his watch and his expensive cuff links. All that was left were some collar stays and a tab. But why was he so dirty? She didn't get it. Did someone beat him up outside to get his keys? This was terrible.

"Peter, I'm calling the police," she cried. "You can't just let people break in and rob your house."

"It didn't happen here."

"What? Then where is everything?" Isobel looked around. Things were gone. A lot of things.

"If you love me, just stay out of it," he groaned. "I'll take care of it."

"What are you talking about? I can't stay out of it. You've been robbed. You're a mess. Someone beat you up. What am I supposed to do, forget it?"

"Just get me something for the pain."

"Peter, please, if you love *me,* tell me what's going on."

There was a long silence. His face was chalky. He sniffed two or three times. Finally he took a deep breath.

"It's a personal thing."

"What do you mean?" She stopped pawing through his drawers and came back to the bed, where he was lying in his briefs, groaning and hugging a pillow.

"I owe a little money, that's all."

"What?" She sat down.

"A bunch of punks, that's all. Jesus."

"For what?" She stood there with her mouth open. He was rich. He was very rich. He was successful. He made hundreds of thousands of dollars a year. What was he talking about?

"What do you think?"

She started to cry again. "Poor baby, look at you. I can't believe you're in debt. How much for?"

"Nothing, it's nothing. Eight thousand dollars. Big deal."

Isobel shook her head. It was a big deal to her. She didn't have anything like that kind of money. But he was rich. She frowned. Wasn't he rich? She knew he was rich.

"Maybe you should get an X ray for your ribs," she muttered.

"I need something for the pain," he said again.

She frowned, cocking her head, still puzzled. "What do you owe it for?"

"What do you think?" he demanded.

"What for, Peter?"

"Who do you think was paying for all that flake that went up your nose?"

"What?" She shook her head. How could that be? They did a little coke on the weekends. Nothing major. What was he talking about?

He turned his head away. "I got in a little too deep with my source."

"Eight thousand?" That was very deep. But he was rich. Eight thousand was nothing to him. He had a hundred-thousand-dollar car. She didn't get it. She frowned some more. Now that she thought of it, where was the car? She shook her head. No, no. They must have taken the car, too. They must have robbed him. He couldn't have gotten in that deep. Peter was not an addict. She just knew he wasn't. She didn't push him for any more details.

"I'll get you something," she promised.

She went back to the office, found some Demerol, some Valium, some Nembutal, some Tylenol with codeine, and whatever other samples were around, and came back two hours later. She gave him an injection of Demerol and cleaned up the house. There were a number of things she was sure were missing. She refused to accept the thought that he was in this kind of trouble. After a while she gave him some soup and another injection.

"You're an angel," he said.

"Why don't you pay it off?" she asked.

"Things are a little tight right now. I don't have it." He turned over and went to sleep.

She sat in his living room for a long time, wondering how a man as wealthy and successful as Peter didn't have eight thousand dollars, and thinking over and over that this couldn't be happening here. People didn't get beaten up for eight thousand dollars, not in Mill Valley. There must be some mistake.

But as she thought about it, and drank his vodka, she knew anything could happen anywhere. She had been raped by a young doctor at four o'clock in the morning when she first began working in the Chester Emergency Room. It made her sick every time she thought about how an innocent little flirtation could go so wrong.

He had seemed like a nice guy and he was new there. He started teasing and kissing her, and then got annoyed when she told him to stop. After a few minutes, he was all excited and wouldn't take no for an answer. He just got crazy. He unzipped his pants right where they were standing, in an examining area.

"Come on, cock tease—you started it, you finish it." He had his hands up her skirt and was pushing at her.

"Cut it out."

"Hell, no. You don't just turn me on and then walk away. Little bitch."

He wrestled her onto the bed, pulled the curtain around with one hand, and threatened to get her fired if she made a fuss.

"No." She didn't want to let him do that. It was mean and ugly. But when he had his thing out and was on top of her, pushing at her, all she could think of was how it looked and what he would say if someone caught them. He could get her fired. She was afraid to struggle anymore, didn't want to make a fuss and lose her job.

For a long, long time, she told herself it wasn't really rape. He wasn't a thug, a stranger. Rape was when someone held a knife to your throat. Rape was when you resisted and someone cut you. This nice young man, with all his degrees, stuck his penis in her and she didn't even scream. How could that be rape?

Later, all she wanted was not to get pregnant. She thought it was her fault, because she didn't think nice people with degrees did bad things like that. When she got her period, she was grateful.

Now, years later, she knew better. She knew every kind of people did every kind of thing. But not Peter. She was a week late with her period, and Peter could not be an addict. As soon as she told him, they were going to get married, have a child, and be like the rich and successful people who came to her office. She brooded for hours, wondering how this could happen now that she finally had a good man who loved her.

Not for a second did she think a little flake was bad. So he took a little something. So what? Everybody did something. Diet pills, pain pills, Valium. Uppers, downers. Isobel knew one woman who took too much of her thyroid medicine because it speeded up her metabolism and helped her to lose weight. She saw it all the time. The doctors did it, everybody. And nobody got beaten up for it. It wasn't fair. She couldn't even call the police. It was horrible.

She knew Peter wasn't a big user. She'd seen addiction. She had seen people change for the worse, teeter on the edge. She'd seen suicide attempts of varying degrees of violence and success. She'd been an Emergency Room nurse, after all. She was there when they came in. She'd seen slit wrists. She'd seen overdoses when people were gone and then were pitifully and painfully hauled back to life. She'd seen people die, more often than she wanted to remember.

What she didn't know about was what came before. She hadn't seen the deep, grinding depression day after day, the black hole of hopelessness so profound that living was a curse, that eating and breathing felt like hateful acts. She had never experienced the desperation that came before the violent act.

She put being a "user" in two categories. When it was not so bad, when it was explainable and manageable. Weekend partying, snorting, smoking grass, drinking wine all night. All that was all right as long as it was *nicely* done. It was not all right to drink until one toppled like a tree. It was not all right to snort coke *every day*. She had these standards. It was something she thought about.

All kinds of things were addictions. Eating to excess, starving, taking aspirin, diuretics. Isobel didn't consider herself a real user, because she did it only if it was there. She'd have a line of coke, and another when it was offered to her, but she wouldn't go out and find it for herself. Same with grass. She did buy wine and gin for herself, but never drank enough to make herself sick.

The other kind of people let their pleasures, their weaknesses, get out of hand. They were over the edge, sick to begin with. Isobel saw them when they came in on a stretcher, or when they were violent and uncontrollable in the middle of an acute psychotic break. They were like crazed beasts that had to be subdued by three or four orderlies and taken away screaming to some other hospital. She saw it only in a broken line and didn't connect the dots. Peter was like her. He was a user but not an abuser. And that was that.

As she waited for him to wake up, as she looked after him, shot him up with Demerol and whatever else she could find, all she thought about was how she could help him, how she could get the money he needed to pay off his debts. Eight thousand was not so very much money. He was a lawyer. She had worked with lawyers before. She could help him.

Peter did malpractice cases. He did injury cases. Maybe she could get him a case. What did she know about? She pondered the situation. She must know something about some case that could make him eight thousand dollars. In the morning she went back to work.

16

It was seven forty-five in the evening and finally quiet in Aaron's office. He swiveled his chair around to the computer behind his desk under the window and turned it on. He always took a few minutes at the end of the day if the phone was quiet to type up his notes and reorganize himself into a family man before going home.

There was a time when he used to stop at a local bar for a drink or two and let the pressure escape through gin, like steam released from a radiator. It was hard to be pulled in all directions at work and then go home without a break to his family, with its three powerful wills all wanting different things from him at the same time. No matter how much he loved his wife and children, he could feel himself vibrating with irritation at their demands. No quiet in his life anywhere.

It took some years negotiating the dangerous white-water rapids of marriage for Aaron to learn that rushing home just to be there as much as possible, regardless of his state of mind, was not always the best thing for his family. When he was preoccupied, they fought with each other more.

The days he came home a little high and boozy they didn't fight, but Sally was resentful at having to be the baby-sitter while he was out socializing with his colleagues. She didn't have a break from work and kids; why should he?

"Maybe I should go out drinking, too," she suggested in a way that kind of worried him. She was a good-looking woman, intelligent and humorous, with a toughness that matched his own. He didn't like being in conflict with her, but didn't like being bullied into compliance, either.

Ultimately it was his new computer and not Sally that changed his habits. First he had to learn how to use it. Then he started writing a paper from time to time. Finally he got into working on his notes every day. Before the Jasper Amerigo case, he had been thinking about writing a book. When he turned the thing on he was always thrilled by the sight of his own thoughts popping up on the screen like a big shaggy dog greeting him at the front gate. A half an hour with himself and he was human again.

For the last month, though, he had been deeply involved with both the practical and ethical questions of the Amerigo case. A lot of reports had been written and reviewed. A lot of meetings had been held. Ron and April were no longer on the staff. Jasper had been transferred to a state hospital and Alisa was scheduled to be transferred to a quality long-term facility within the week. But even though it all seemed settled, and he was never accused of any wrongdoing himself, Aaron felt the case was still far from resolved. There was still the issue of Max Starburn, who was operating on dozens of patients a week. If there was any question of his being HIV positive, they had to deal with it. But how? Aaron had been given the information in confidence. He could not reveal it. Max had to face it himself; and he had very good reasons for not wanting to.

Aaron had just turned on his computer and was considering what a rumor of that seriousness might do to the hospital and Max's reputation, when the phone rang.

"Hello," Aaron said.

"Aaron, it's Barney Steadman. I just wanted you to know that Laura Hunter aborted today."

"Oh, Jesus," Aaron said.

"Yeah, it was bad. Her husband brought her in in an ambulance about four o'clock. Apparently she'd been bleeding since noon."

There was silence for a moment while Aaron digested the information.

"What happened? Who met her in ER?" he asked finally.

"Why do you ask?"

The reply had a sharp edge Aaron didn't like.

"She's my patient. I'm concerned," he said. He was also worried about AIDS.

"She's my patient, too, Aaron. What's with you? Paranoia catching?"

Aaron took a deep breath. "Sorry. I'd hoped she'd make it to term."

"Me too. This was my third with her. . . . And I met her in ER," Barney said. "Any particular reason for asking?"

The Levolors on Aaron's windows were not completely closed. He could see the Bridge of Sighs and the ER entrance below. Now he had to worry about who touched his patients when they were admitted to the hospital, and if they were safe there. If he had been at his computer that afternoon he might have seen Laura come in. Shit. He hadn't wanted this to happen.

"No. Thanks for telling me. I'll go up and see her."

"Good. I'm going home. I'll talk to you in the morning."

Aaron shut off his computer with regret. Man's best friend sat there wagging his tail uncertainly as the screen went dead. Sorry, old boy. He reached for his jacket.

. . .

Upstairs they had put Laura on the maternity floor because she was an OB patient. Aaron stopped at the nurses' station to find out what room she was in. He was relieved it was a private room. He padded down the hall and knocked on the door.

"Come in." It was Laura's voice.

Aaron stepped through the curtain into the room. She was alone. Her husband must have gone home already. A hell of a guy. The air conditioner was on high, and he shivered involuntarily.

"Hi," he said.

She was very pale and looked tiny on the bed. His impulse was to take her hand, or to give her a hug and comfort her in some primitive and basic way. But touching was against the rules. The familiar wave of helplessness that returned like a bout of nausea whenever something really bad happened rolled in and crashed over him. He felt he had failed Laura and knew he was wrong to think that way. He didn't have control over people's actions, or their bodies. If he treated a drunk in AA who started drinking again, he couldn't blame himself. Dealing with almost anyone in his profession was a risk. He couldn't guarantee the outcome, like a bone man who sets a broken leg. Aaron worried all the time, though, almost as if he secretly felt he was God and accountable to his patients for everything.

Laura turned her head in surprise. "What are you doing here?" she asked. "Did Wendal call you?" Her eyes filled with tears.

"Dr. Steadman called me a few minutes ago. He said you had a bad time. How are you doing?"

"This is a maternity floor. How could they be so cruel?" Laura was fully awake and furious.

"I know it seems that way. I had the same thought as I came down the hall. You're an OB patient. I guess they had the room available here."

"Why didn't they just let me go home?"

"Dr. Steadman told me you lost a lot of blood. What happened?" Aaron stood there, stooped over a little, his blue eyes intensely focused on hers.

"I didn't want to lose it. It would have been better to die." The dam broke, and tears flooded her tiny white face.

"I've never seen so much blood. It was unbelievable. It was pumping out of me. It was all over the place, like a river. I wanted to die."

"Nobody else wanted you to die," Aaron said gently.

"It's easy for you to say."

"Yes, it is easy for me to say. I know it's true."

"They wouldn't tell me what sex it was. I asked them, but they wouldn't tell me."

"I don't think they knew."

"Oh, yes," Laura said. "They knew. They said it was just a mass of decayed cells, but that's a lie. The pro-lifers say it's a baby from the moment of conception. I lost my baby. You promised me it wouldn't happen."

Aaron sat down suddenly in the chair by her bed and clasped both of his hands between his knees. "No, Laura, I did not promise this wouldn't happen."

"Yes, you said not to think about it. You told me to imagine what having the baby would be like."

"That's true."

"You told me to look on the bright side, it might not happen this time."

"That's right."

"You never told me to imagine what it would feel like to lose a third baby."

"No, I didn't. That wouldn't have helped you."

"You didn't help me," she said, blowing her nose with fury.

"You can't always measure these things in absolute ways. Today you had a terrible loss. But you can recover. You're not alone."

"I am alone. I hate you." Laura turned her head away.

"Better me than you," he said with a tiny smile. "I can live with it."

"This is not funny. I'm not talking to you anymore."

Time to go. Aaron stood up. "No, it's not funny. It's very serious. I just meant that I could take it if you hate me for a while."

"I don't want any more therapy. Wendal *said* it wouldn't work. It didn't work for his aunt and it didn't work for me. So let's just forget it."

"I came to see you, Laura, not to terminate. This is not the moment for that. If you don't want to see me anymore, we can talk about it when you're feeling better."

Once again Aaron restrained the impulse to take her hand like a friend. She wasn't a friend. She was a patient. But her eyes were cold, cold, cold the way women's eyes get when a man they trust fails them.

"I won't call you," she said firmly. "I won't."

He had trained for this at the Institute—how to stand still when the whole of a person's fury hit him squarely in the heart, how to take it just right so the patient could come back to him and with his help head into the badlands they had to travel through to reach a happier place. None of it ever felt good.

"I hope you do, Laura. I think you need to."

"You hurt me," she said when he reached the door. "You made it worse."

He kept going, couldn't debate it then even though it worried him. The one thing he was not supposed to do was make it worse. It was his sacred duty. Did he make Laura worse, somehow upset her so she miscarried again? He didn't think so, but if she didn't continue therapy with him or someone else he would always worry. It was after visiting hours. The corridor was empty as he hurried to the elevator. At the end of the hall in the nursery, he heard a newborn's cry.

17

Tom lay unconscious in the local hospital for two days while frantic Axam Oil executives in Morristown and Houston tried to decide what to do with him. The doctor on site wanted him to stay put and not be shaken up any more than he already had been by the first helicopter trip sixty miles to the capital. Highgate was in favor of having him transported to Israel, where they were good with brains. The lawyers in the Houston office wanted to move him to the American Hospital in Paris, which was at least in the direction of home.

No one wanted him to stay comatose too long in Adam Adar, where there was no sophisticated equipment to test whether brain surgery was necessary, or to perform it if it was. There was also the sticky question of insurance should they start moving him around, and the possibility of damaging lawsuits if they didn't, or if they moved him too late.

The debate went on transcontinentally and transatlantically while Tom slept, the gash in his head neatly stitched up and glucose dripping into a vein in his forearm.

He opened his eyes on the third morning to find a nun sitting beside him, reading from a tiny black book and gently

fanning him with his chart. For a few minutes he thought he was
back in the summer of his thirteenth year, in the Holy Mother
Hospital recovering from appendicitis.

Then he tried to move his head and couldn't.

The nurse looked up. "Good morning," she said.

She had a heavy accent. "How do you feel?"

Tom tried to lift his hand to touch his head. The nurse told
him to lie still.

"I'm going to get Doctor," she said.

He closed his eyes, confused. When she stood up he saw
that she had no cross and no wimple. Not a nun, he told himself.

By the time the doctor came in he had drifted off again.

The next time he came around, Jim Albert, the company
doctor, was standing by his bed.

"Well, Tom, you sure had us worried," he said. "How do
you feel?"

Tom rolled his bloodshot eyes up to where the doctor stood
in a patch of sunlight. He had a feeling he might be dead, and
this was St. Peter, or maybe God Himself. He had no memory of
ever seeing this serious man with the white coat and gray crew
cut before. Nor could he identify the smells of the place, which
were different from the hospital smells in Rhode Island or Bos-
ton, or anywhere in America. A strong odor of sweat, of desert,
of some disinfectant with a vile odor. The place smelled the way
nausea felt.

Dr. Albert picked up his hand and turned it over. "You got
quite a blow up on column four. Do you remember?"

"Where am I?" Tom whispered.

"You're in Adam Adar. You were working up on the distillation column and you hit your head. You sure had us worried,"
he repeated. He checked his watch and started counting Tom's
pulse.

"Oh, God," Tom groaned. It hurt even to keep his eyes open.

"You have a concussion. We were very concerned. You're a lucky man."

"What day is it?" Tom asked.

The doctor put Tom's hand down. "You've been out for two days," he said casually.

"I've got to go home," Tom mumbled. "Send me home."

"What?" Albert leaned down close to Tom's face to hear him better. But Tom had gone back to sleep. The doctor waited for a few minutes to make certain that he was just dozing and had not lapsed into a coma again. When he was satisfied, he went to fax the home office that Tom was awake and lucid. Dr. Albert's judgment was that unless something very unexpected happened, Tom would probably be all right, though brain scans and other tests ought to be performed as soon as possible.

The next time Tom awoke, he was up long enough to ask about Bettina.

"It's all right; we've contacted her," Dr. Albert assured him.

"She's having a baby," Tom said. "I have to go home."

"You will," the doctor said vaguely.

Tom frowned and then winced because his scalp was sewn up. "I need to call her."

There was no phone in his room.

"You will."

This vague response filled Tom with fury. He could imagine only too vividly how distraught Bettina must be, thinking he was badly injured when she couldn't come to him. Every hour that passed was agony for him. His head throbbed when he thought of her, alone and worried. He didn't want the pain medication they offered him. It made him thick and foggy. It was hard to figure it out. It didn't seem possible that he could wake up after two days and not find some message from her. Some word of encouragement. Something.

They were very close. She had told him on more than one of their many calls that she couldn't sleep without him. He always held her. They touched even when sleeping. They breathed together; their thoughts and dreams were one. It was not right that he hadn't heard from her. The assurances that Bettina had not yet had her baby, that everything was all right at home, did not convince him. He wanted proof. He wanted to talk to her.

"Get me a phone now," he demanded, "or I'll sue this company for more than this place is worth."

"It's four in the morning there."

"That's fine. Then she's sure to be home," Tom said. "You found the problem, you know."

"Great. Call my wife and let's tell her."

"There's no jack for a phone in here," the doctor told him. "Look, we're doing the best we can for you."

"What does that mean, that you're keeping something from me?" Tom tried to sit up and couldn't.

"No," Albert said sharply.

"Then let me talk to my wife."

"As soon as you can get up."

"I can sit up. Put me in a wheelchair."

Albert nodded. "Sure, tomorrow."

"I don't understand this. In the movies people hurt worse than this go home the next day."

"That's because they're not really sick; you are."

"I want to go home."

The heavy bandage on Tom's head made him furious. He banged it into the pillow in frustration at Albert's bland face and then had to close his eyes from the dizziness.

Later, when Albert was gone, he swung his legs over the side of the bed and slowly inched off. As soon as he let go of the bed he fell down, knocking the water pitcher over with a crash.

A number of people came running in to see what happened. They hauled him back into bed.

"That wasn't wise," Albert said, coming in and grabbing his wrist because pulse was his specialty.

"The longer you keep me in bed," Tom said furiously, "the weaker I get. Look, I'm losing all my muscles. I need to get up; that's what I need."

"That isn't the way it works with concussions," Albert said calmly. "You're upset. Your pressure is way up there. This is not good for you, or your wife. You want to have a stroke and end up a vegetable?"

"I need some evidence that my wife is all right, understand? I've been here for days and I have only your word that you've spoken to her. I have no message, no calls from her."

"Look, I promise we'll call her tomorrow, okay?"

By the time the doctor had the promise out, Tom was tucked back in bed and his eyes were closed.

18

Peter's eyes unfocused.

"You didn't hear me, did you?" Isobel said. "You've got to go back to the office. It's been two days now. Won't they get mad at you if you don't show up?"

He shook his head. "I'm a partner, remember. I'm the best litigator in the state. They love me."

He needed to get more shit out of Angel. That was the only thing on his mind. It was all that counted. He was sitting up in bed holding the coffee mug Isobel had brought upstairs to wake him with. He was coming back into the world, slowly and sullenly. Sometimes he blanked out on what she said altogether. Sometimes he heard her. The one thing he wouldn't forget was that she had a name for him: Elton. He wouldn't forget it. He wouldn't forget where she left the phone number either. Beyond that, he was unglued, melting into a painful fog from which he had no interest in emerging.

He shook his head. "They love me."

It seemed that only a few weeks ago his symptoms came on slowly, like a decongestant wearing off. He didn't notice the changes until his nose was running all over the place and his body itched uncontrollably. Hours would pass when he was working furiously, or think he was working furiously. And then little by little, he'd slow down until nothing made any sense and he had to get a lift. He went on this way for a long time, with the highs slowly getting lower and lower. He needed more to get to a lesser place, and the times of comfort between became shorter and shorter.

Now it was like dropping off a cliff all the time. He could feel the downward pitch happen a lot sooner, the plunge as elation left him. It was like the long seconds when a paratrooper jumps out of a plane before the chute opens with a jerk. The moment before the suicide hits the pavement. Only when it happened to him, it was not seconds of agony, it was hours at a time when he was all nerves, his stomach left behind, as he pitched down, down, down with nothing to stop him. That's when they hit him. They hit him on the slide. Some scummy punk business.

He licked his cracked lips. His breath was foul. His mouth was dry from the pills he had left in his supply, which also was dwindling. There were only a handful or two left.

"Shit," he muttered.

"Honey?" Isobel stood over him with her lips moving.

He had no idea what she was saying. He focused. Oh, yeah, she was talking about his getting in the Jacuzzi when she left. For the bruises. He snorted, because the Jacuzzi was how he met Angel, the preppy sixty-year-old plumber who sold him the hot tub and became his source.

He nodded at her about the Jacuzzi, but the bruises on his body were nothing to the ache deep inside, the irritation in his nose, the itch so bad it felt as if he were covered with poison ivy and being eaten alive by mosquitoes at the same time.

He nodded yeah, he'd do it. But he was thinking about how to get some more crack from Angel. Isobel didn't know about the crack. She thought it was bad stuff. Just flake for her. Whatever.

Twice the day before Angel had asked for an apology from Peter for the difficulty he was causing. He threatened Peter with another "accident" if he didn't pay everything off to the penny by the Fourth of July. If only Angel would let him have a few hits to tide him over, Peter thought he'd be all right.

"Peter, my darling?" Isobel said. "I have to go to work. Are you getting up?"

"Get me some more Demerol, will you? The pain is still terrible." He felt his ribs. "Ow."

"All gone, precious," she said. "I can't just walk off with it. It all has to be accounted for." She paused sympathetically. "Anyway, by now the Tylenol 3 ought to take care of everything."

"It's not enough. I feel bad," Peter insisted.

"I know, but you have to make an effort."

She straightened the sheet briskly. "Do you want a list of fertility problems, too?"

He smiled. "You're a good girl. You got a good head."

"Thank you. I just want *you* to get well, and be healthy." She smiled fondly back. "You are the best."

"Best damn litigator in the state."

"Yes," she murmured.

"Then get me something," he demanded.

She smiled some more. "Fertility problems? I can get you a list by noon."

"That's not what I had in mind."

"There are many," she said brightly. "Lots of hopeless ones. I should have thought of this before. I used to help plaintiffs' lawyers in malpractice cases a lot when I worked in the hospital." She frowned. "I just can't do that kind of thing in this office. They're good doctors. They don't make mistakes."

"Yeah, yeah. Go to work." He needed a hit.

"But this is all right. This is helping everybody. You want the list or not?"

He shook his head. She'd been yakking at him enough.

"I can place a baby without your help."

He paused. "If the two I have in mind don't work out, I'll let you know."

"Okay, whatever you say," she said meekly, and blew him a kiss before running down the stairs.

He got out of bed and took two uppers. He dialed Angel's private number. Angel wouldn't talk to him. He called his office and said he still had the flu, then called the number Isobel had left on the table.

Two hours later he dialed Wendal Hunter, one of the people Isobel had been babbling about the day before. Wendal took the call.

"Well, well, Peter Balkan," he said. "Long time no see. What kind of trouble have you got for me now?"

Peter was still sitting on the side of his bed in his boxer shorts. He looked down at his shaking hands. He needed a hit pretty bad. "Hey, Wendal, old pal," he said, talking the way Isobel did when she was being a nurse.

"Just because we've been on different sides of a case or two in the past doesn't mean we always have to be on opposing teams."

"Oh," Wendal said. "I get it. We're on the same team, but you're about to tell me you're suing one of my clients for six million dollars."

"Oh, come on, you know that's the way the game is played. You were lucky to get away with fifty grand in the Patterson case and you know it. Hey. You've got the wrong idea about me. I'm in this business to help people with their troubles. Who knows—I could even help you."

"I don't think so, Peter. I haven't got any troubles."

"Sure you do. I heard about poor Laura. That's a tragedy, man. Terrible. Really great little person like her." He paused.

"Who told you?" Wendal asked sharply. "Oh, yeah, I forgot. You probably had the ambulance tagged, paid off the driver for the name of the injured party. Well, forget it. This isn't that kind of case."

"This is a real tragedy, Wendal. I know how bad she felt after the last one."

"Look, there's nobody to sue here. This is nature. You can't sue fucking nature. So thanks for your interest, but forget it."

"Not so fast. What would you say if I told you I could solve your problem?"

"I just told you—"

"A first-class white baby. Mother a cheerleader, looks just like Laura, father a football player. A couple just like you, Wen. Except they're teenagers who got stupid. They planned to get married, but the boy's going to college instead and won't do it now. She's fifteen, a beauty."

There was silence for a long time.

"Are you shitting me?" Wendal said.

"No way. I talked to the girl and her parents this morning. She's been hurt and needs some support right now. You pay her college education, and the baby is yours."

"Jesus," Wendal said. "I don't know. We never talked about it. I mean adoption, that's—"

"No muss, no fuss. But they're not a wealthy family. They need a little impetus to make up their minds. They've been approached before, but they weren't ready. They're ready now."

"Jesus, this is very sudden." Wendal's voice was doubtful.

"Yes, you could almost say it's a miracle. God takes away and God gives." Peter's hands were steady now. He was still the best.

"Laura hasn't even recovered yet. I mean she's—I don't even know if she'd go for this."

"Trust me on this one. You want a happy wife? Let God give."

"Jesus," Wendal said for the third time. "I just don't know. What kind of money are we talking about? I mean, I have to talk to Laura. We have to think about this for a while. This is too fast."

"Well, sometimes you got to move fast to save your life. The girl is due now. She's not going to keep the baby on hold while you make up your minds. I can't promise, but I think thirty-five should do it."

"Thirty-five thousand dollars?" Wendal said. "You're kidding."

"How much is happiness worth? A happy home? A happy wife? Huh? You got the money. You know that's what it takes for a quality baby, and you know you got it. Talk it over. I got to know right away. I have other interested parties."

He could hear Wendal saying "I don't know about this, I just don't know" as he put the receiver down. Peter's hands were shaking again. He called Angel. He still wouldn't take the call.

19

"What are you doing here?" Laura looked up at Wendal in amazement.

She was sitting at the kitchen table with an empty coffee cup in front of her. It was noon, only three days after her miscarriage. Except they didn't call them miscarriages anymore. They called them spontaneous abortions. She had been sitting there for a long time with her elbows on the table, unable to move in any direction, when suddenly Wendal was standing there with his face all pink as if he were having a heart attack.

"How are you feeling?" he asked.

"What are you doing here, Wendal?" she asked again. He never came home in the middle of the day.

"I came to see how you're feeling," he said.

She regarded him suspiciously. "Well, I'm fine. What about you?"

"I'm all right."

"Good." She turned away. "Now that you've seen I'm all right and I've seen you're all right, you can go back to work."

He frowned. "Hey, you don't have to be that way."

"I'm fine. I'm not any way." Laura turned her head even more so she didn't have to see him.

Wendal sat down heavily. After a few moments of silence he picked up her hand that was resting on the table. It was limp and listless.

"Laura."

She didn't answer.

"I guess it's been pretty bad for you, huh," he said finally.

"I told you I'm fine. I don't know what else you want."

"I don't *want* anything."

"Then what are you here for? I said I was sorry."

"I don't want you to say you're sorry. Look, I feel bad about this. Maybe I feel worse than you do." He stroked her hand.

"I don't know what you're talking about."

He leaned forward to try to make her look at him. "You could have died, Laura. The doctor told me that. I'd be pretty stupid if I didn't wonder why my wife would rather bleed to death on the bathroom floor than call me for help."

He paused. "I don't even know what made me think I better go home. How do you think that makes me feel?"

Her eyes filled with tears. "You did think of me."

He nodded. "I'm always thinking about you. How do you think I felt when I saw you like that? I never saw so much blood."

He shook his head. "I almost lost you. They had to give you a transfusion. Nothing in the world is worth that."

Her fingers curled around his just a little.

"What made you do it? Did you hate me? Did you want a baby so much?" he asked.

There was a long silence. She looked at their fingers, linked on the table.

"I guess I just didn't want it to happen again. I feel so . . . I don't know. Like my own body is my enemy. I don't know why the poorest refugees, the homeless, anybody can do it —but me." She looked at him, her forehead furrowed with confusion. "Why?"

He swallowed. "It means that much to you."

She nodded. "I know some people seem to do okay without children," she murmured. "They get over it." She shook her head. "I'm not one of those."

"Do you want me to do something about it?"

She sniffed. "You? What can you do about it? You can't have the baby." She smiled suddenly, as if the thought of Wendal's having a baby amused her.

"Maybe I *could* do something. I'm in a position to hear about things. I have friends." He cocked his head to the side and raised a shoulder.

The smile disappeared. "What are you talking about?" she asked.

"I'm talking about another baby. Adopting a baby."

"You said you never wanted to do that. It wouldn't look like us." She choked back a laugh. "What about the Murphys with their Asian baby?" She shook her head.

"I don't see us running around the world trying to find some third-world baby. That's not for us."

He looked hurt. "No. That would take a lot of time, and maybe set us up for more disappointment."

"Thank you anyway." She smiled faintly.

"There's another alternative, though."

"Oh? Macy's, Bloomingdale's?"

He shook his head. "You know that lawyer, Peter Balkan? The one who came to one of your theater things? You thought he was so good-looking? He called me a little while ago."

Her eyes widened with surprise. "You mean you're serious."

"I'm dead serious."

She screwed up her face in doubt. "You're really serious?"

"Yeah." He nodded. "What would you say if I told you there is a baby? Right here in Mill Valley. A teenage mother due in a few weeks. Doesn't want to keep it." He raised his eyebrows. "Peter says she's got your coloring."

Laura put both hands to her mouth. "You mean it?"

"Oh, yes, I mean it."

She shook her head in wonder. "I was ready to wait nine months three times for my own baby," she murmured. "This is very sudden. It's weird to think of getting one in just a few weeks."

"Well, you don't have to do it. It's up to you. It's just an opportunity. Something to think about."

She got up and threw her arms around his neck. "You'd do this for me? I don't believe it."

He put his face against her stomach and breathed in her scent, tickled her a little.

"I don't know what that shrink said about me, but I'm a good guy. I want you to be happy."

"I'll be happy," she promised. "I am already." She thought of Dr. Simon asking what kind of father Wendal would be and how she couldn't answer because she thought she'd never know. So much for him.

20

A week went by. It was the end of June. Bettina had not spoken to Tom for several days and could not get through to him. Every time she called she got a different answer. The last two times she was told he wasn't there. Since this was his own deadline for his return, her fantasy was that he was on his way home. He was going to surprise her, just show up.

Her next appointment with Dr. Street was a repeat of the last one. The week before he had said it would be three weeks, probably four. Now he said it would be two weeks, maybe three. His tone was flat and matter-of-fact. He pulled off his right rubber glove with the snap he liked to make and tossed it into the wastebasket. Bettina tried to resist looking at it, but her head turned in spite of herself. The glove was lying palm down on a soggy pile of used paper towels and soiled disposable equipment. There was blood on the index finger.

Another two weeks, she told herself. Tom would probably be home tomorrow. Maybe today. It was going to be all right.

Dr. Street was in a hurry. He didn't have time to stop and talk. As he washed his hands at the sink with his back to her, he reminded Bettina to make another appointment before she left. But Bettina didn't stop to do it. There was an uncomfortable, almost frightening ache inside where he had probed with his gloved fingers. Suddenly she didn't think she'd need an appointment the next week. As she stood in the talking elevator, she told herself that millions of women in remote and backward parts of the world have babies every day with no help at all and survive. She'd have lots of help and the best in modern equipment. Tom would probably be home tonight. Tomorrow at the latest.

"Enjoy the rest of the day," the elevator said as the doors slid open.

Bettina didn't think she would. She looked down to watch her step. Recently her stomach had sunk. Dr. Street told her the baby's head had engaged. If that was so, there was no way the baby would be in there another two weeks. She wondered why he said it would.

She walked across the parking lot to the car, reminding herself over and over that hundreds of millions—billions, in fact —of babies found the way out, proving that such a thing as birth was possible. How would *hers* happen, though? Would she scream? Would she make a fuss and disgrace herself? If it happened today, could she make it to the hospital by herself?

She reached the car. The handle was hot from the sun. She swung the door open and climbed in. It was ridiculously awkward now and when she was settled, her stomach touched the wheel. She had put the seat so far back her foot almost didn't reach the pedal, but still her stomach touched the wheel.

No one else seemed to worry about how babies got out. Why did she?

Bettina didn't like to go out anymore. She was enormous. She looked overdue, she thought, like a beach ball that had been blown up past its limit. When she got home she called her mother.

"Bettina?" Her mother picked up on the first ring.

"How did you know it was me?" Bettina asked.

"A mother knows," her mother said.

"Oh, Mother, I think it's going to be soon. Please come up here for a few days."

"Tina, I wish I could. I hate your being alone. I can hardly sleep at night thinking of you in that big house by yourself. But I know you'll be fine."

"I don't want to be alone."

"Your father"—Bettina's mother lowered her voice—"is being very difficult. He's afraid he'll die if I leave him with a nurse."

"I know he says that, Mother, but he won't die. I haven't asked you before. I'm asking you now."

"Well, you're not going to die, either, Tina. Childbirth is a perfectly natural thing. You're going to be fine."

Bettina could hear her mother crying on the phone.

"What can I do? My daughter is having a baby, and my husband of thirty-two years has *become* a baby."

Bettina blew her nose. "All right, Mother. Don't get upset. I'm fine. I really am."

But how did one measure "fine"? How do you know when you aren't? She knew she could function. She could get up (by rolling out of bed). She could make herself a cup of herbal tea. She could eat some cereal. Wash the cup, spoon, and bowl, and put them away. Was that fine? Was moving through a day, with all the doors locked, fine? If so, she was fine. More than anything else, Bettina wanted her mother. It was odd how much she wanted the woman who had never actually mothered her, never combed her hair or held her tight that she could remember. *Why am I so scared?* Bettina asked herself. The little girl in the white party dress standing by the coffin of her baby brother was always in her mind.

"Say good-bye to him," someone said. "You won't have another chance."

"Why?" she asked. "He didn't say good-bye to me."

"Don't say naughty things," her father said.

Her mother slapped her hand when she reached out to

touch him. He looked like a doll in the box lined with white satin. She had been astounded by the slap and the sharp sting that accompanied it. Her mother looked surprised and turned away.

I'm just having a baby. I'm going to be fine, she told herself. She sat there looking at the phone. After a few minutes she decided to call headquarters to find out when Tom had left. She dialed the number and listened to it ring. Five, six, seven times. Then came the message that the offices of Axam Oil were open from eight to five-thirty. It was late now, way after six.

21

At eleven o'clock that night, Bettina felt she might like to vomit. For twenty minutes or so, she hung on to the sink as far over the toilet as she could get. As she stood there, her whole body in a cramp, scenes from her life, particularly her life with Tom, flashed through her head. She felt loose now, adrift. Other pictures from her childhood made her wonder if this was what it was like to die. It occurred to her that by the time you really are dying you don't care anymore. Then the nausea passed. She must not be dying.

She went back to bed. All around her she could feel the house, dark and quiet. She put her hand on her stomach. In the past few hours, since her visit to the doctor's office, the baby had become strangely still. There seemed to be no struggle now, only a profound quiet. For the second time she thought she might not live through the night, and knew she would. She put the telephone on the pillow beside her, closed her eyes, and tried to think of someone to call to be with her, but couldn't think of anybody. She dozed off.

At two o'clock her eyes jerked open. Her body was covered with a fine mist and her thin cotton nightgown was drenched. A pain as sharp as anything she had ever felt shot through her, causing her to grunt with surprise and hold the pillow in front of her like a shield. It didn't help, though. Once, twice, three times she was struck through with the blade. Then it was gone and her body relaxed.

She waited for a few seconds, then moved as quickly as she could to the bathroom. As she retched again and again over the toilet, amniotic fluid poured out of her onto the floor.

"Call me as soon as your waters break," Dr. Street had said.

Bettina dressed herself and then got back into bed. She didn't feel well enough to leave the house. It was quiet, almost mystical, there in the dark. She wanted to stay there forever, isolated in the pain. It yawned at her, trying to envelop and swallow her up. It was not at all what she had expected. It brought tears to her eyes and took her breath away. She started to cry.

And then it went away, making her think that she might have made a mistake and nothing was really happening. She turned her head to the wall and decided to wait a little longer. She didn't want to go to the hospital alone. She wanted to wait for Tom. Then it got worse.

At three-thirty she called a taxi in Chester and somehow dragged herself out of bed. She was sitting on the front step with her suitcase by her side at four when the twenty-year-old taxi driver pulled up the drive.

"Why didn't you call an ambulance?" he said, getting out nervously.

"I didn't think of it," Bettina said softly.

Twenty-three minutes later, they drove honking up to the lying-in section of the hospital. Bettina held out the crumpled wad of five five-dollar bills she had been clutching for an hour.

A guard came out. "You have to go to Emergency," he said.

The driver shook his head. He helped Bettina to a bench by the door and put her down.

"Hey, you can't do that." The guard stepped forward.

"Call a doctor. Can't you see she's having a baby? Do you want her to have it here?" the driver said, his voice rising in volume.

"It's against the rules," the guard said uncertainly. "You got to take her to Emergency."

"Are you crazy? Get a doctor. There must be one somewhere."

A nurse having a cigarette popped her head around the corner of the building, attracted by the noise. "Hold on," she said when she saw Bettina huddled miserably on the bench.

She disappeared inside the doors. A moment later she was back with a wheelchair and an attendant.

"Come on, honey, it's okay now." She and the attendant lifted her gently into the chair.

"Go into Emergency and fill out the forms," the nurse said to the driver.

"I'm the cabbie. I don't even know her name."

"Never mind then. We'll do it later," the nurse said.

In a second, they were in the hospital, and then in the elevator. Soon they were upstairs in a cold prep room where there were four beds, all empty.

"I'm Bettina Dunne," Bettina whispered as a nurse efficiently stripped off her clothes and put on a hospital gown. "Dr. Street is my doctor."

"He's in the hospital," the nurse said. "Don't worry."

She covered Bettina with a white sheet and called for the resident.

He showed up while she was writing up the chart.

He pulled on a rubber glove with a snap. "You sure took your time getting here," he said when he lifted the sheet and had a look.

The nurse had the blood pressure equipment out and was wrapping Bettina's arm. The doctor reached under the sheet with his gloved hand. Bettina closed her eyes.

"Do you want her prepped?" the nurse asked.

The hand went in.

Bettina started to retch, making a lot of noise.

"Too late for that. Take her down the hall," the doctor said sharply. He pulled off the glove and walked out of the room.

The nurse followed him and left Bettina alone. They had forgotten to cover her up again and half of her body was exposed. She lay there chilled from the air-conditioning, holding a kidney-shaped plastic container under her chin. The pain was now unrelieved. It was a pain without a shape, in her stomach, in her back, in the bones in her pelvis. She kept her eyes tightly closed. She was afraid to sit up and rearrange the sheet. She was alone. No one was with her.

In a minute the nurse was back with a stretcher on wheels. The nurse and orderly moved Bettina to the stretcher. The nurse picked up the clipboard as they headed down the hall.

Bettina started panting the way the book said to. Her mouth was dry, and she was trying not to panic.

"Age?" the nurse asked.

"Twenty-nine."

"Any miscarriages or previous births?"

Bettina shook her head, still panting.

"Then this is your first pregnancy. Mother and father living?"

"Yes."

Tears leaked out of Bettina's eyes and ran unchecked down her neck. "I think I need a shot," she cried.

"When was your last meal? Is your husband here?"

Bettina shook her head.

"All right, honey, we're almost there now. Here's Dr. Street."

Dr. Street was covered in green. Even his shoes were bagged. He took Bettina's hand briefly, then let it go.

"Dr. Milligan tells me you took your time getting here."

"It didn't seem bad enough," Bettina mumbled.

"Okay, let's get the show on the road," he said.

A nurse wrapped her arm to take her blood pressure. Another nurse was trying to shove an IV into a vein in her hand. It seemed to take ages. Bettina thought her back was breaking. They moved into the Delivery Room.

"I'm Dr. Simpson, your anesthetist." A woman's voice came out of the mask but nothing showed of her except the eyes, which were neuter.

Bettina groaned. Now four people were arranged around her. Dr. Street sat on a stool between her legs. She couldn't see him over the tent that covered her from the waist down. It felt like her bones were splitting. They put some kind of thing over her mouth.

"We want you to sit up on your next contraction."

"You're kidding."

"Ready? Breathe."

Four arms raised her up and shoved a pillow under her back. She screamed into the plastic tube. They lowered her down, but not all the way.

"Okay," Dr. Street said. "You're almost there. On the next one we're going to get the baby out."

"I just got here."

In barely a second she was supported from behind again and commanded to push and breathe at the same time. Oxygen from the tank at her head filled her lungs. Suddenly she felt no pain. Bettina pushed and felt something emerge.

"Stop. Don't push anymore."

The head was out, then a shoulder. There was a communal sigh as the baby slid out.

"It's a girl."

It made a tiny cough and was silent. Bettina was shaking all over as Dr. Street held the baby up in his rubber gloves for a moment and showed it to her. She couldn't seem to stop shaking. The baby was kind of gray and pasty all over and still attached by the umbilical cord, but even in that condition it was clear she had red hair and was perfect in every way. She wasn't even mad enough at the shock of birth to cry.

"I did it," Bettina murmured in awe.

22

At the office the next morning Dr. Street told Isobel that Baby Girl Elton was born at eleven o'clock the night before with a few problems they hadn't expected. She had a faulty valve in her heart, and the right ventricle was much too small for her to grow and be healthy. Isobel didn't know what to do with the information. The adoption she had found for Peter needed a heart transplant to survive her childhood. It was a disaster.

Isobel almost broke down and cried when Dr. Street told her. She knew there was a couple that had agreed to take the baby, but she didn't know who they were and didn't think they'd had time to give Peter any money yet.

"How can that be?" she asked Dr. Street incredulously.

He shrugged. "It happens. One in ten thousand maybe, but it happens."

When he disappeared into his office, she collapsed like a leaking balloon and put her head in her hands. Later, when he caught her ignoring flashing telephone lights, he was furious. He hadn't had any sleep all night and was in no mood for shirking from others.

"Shape up, Isobel; we can't have you sleeping on the job," he scolded. "The files are mixed up, too."

"Sorry, Doctor," she said in her mechanical nurse's voice. "It won't happen again."

As soon as he was gone, she was lost in thought again. What would happen to that poor girl's baby? Peter couldn't offer a sick baby for adoption. No one would take it. Not only that: If he couldn't place it, he wouldn't get his money. She couldn't help thinking about what would happen to him if he couldn't come up with the money. For some reason he wasn't getting better, wasn't pulling himself together and getting up. She'd already given him most of what she had saved, but she couldn't go on nursing him and working. He had to go back to work.

She bit her nails and reviewed how much money she had. Five hundred dollars in a savings account. It had been added to at the rate of fifty dollars a month and earmarked for a vacation in the Virgin Islands before she met Peter. He could have it. She'd already given him all but a few dollars in her checking account. She'd always spent most of her money on her clothes. She liked nice things, wanted to be pretty, wanted her men to be proud of her. She had expensive accessories, too. Shoes, handbags, belts. She owned nothing else.

Her car was leased; she couldn't even sell it. A lot of help she was. Her apartment was rented. She was afraid to tell him. She felt guilty, as if she, her office, the doctor she worked for, were all responsible for Peter's trouble. She was afraid if she didn't find a way to help him now, she might lose him. He'd be mad, or desperate. Or murdered.

She slunk into his house at noon full of dread, and climbed the stairs to his room on the second floor, where he was still hanging out after almost a week in bed. All that was left in the room was a round bed and a Jacuzzi upon a platform that wasn't real marble.

"Where have you been? I thought you were going to come by and give me a shot," he grumbled. He was lying in bed staring at the ceiling. "I need a shot."

"I went to work," Isobel said softly.

"Where's my shot?" Peter said. "It hurts something awful."

"You should be feeling a lot better by now. Did you take the Tylenol?" she asked, straightening the sheets on his bed mechanically.

He turned to her suspiciously. "Why do you ask?"

She shrugged. "Just asking. I told you over and over, you should try the Tylenol first. That should do it for this kind of thing," she said.

"I prefer the shot. I've been beaten up," Peter said pathetically. "I'm in pain."

"You were beaten up a week ago. You'd be over heart surgery by now. I can't give you any more," Isobel said. "This time I really mean it. We have to talk."

"Why do we have to talk? I don't want to talk about it

now. Don't you see what's happened to me? I have to get well first. I can't go to the office broken in a hundred pieces. It would ruin my image."

"Chrissie had her baby last night," Isobel said. She sat on the bed and took his hand.

"Wow, that's early, isn't it?" he said, waking up suddenly. "Thank you, thank you, God."

Then he jerked his hand away, galvanized into action. "I'm getting up. You'll have to give me something so I can go to work. I have to get the papers ready; there's a lot to do." He pulled the sheet aside, groaning.

"Don't just sit there, get me something. What shall I take?"

"Wait a minute. It's not good news," Isobel said.

"Why not? Is something wrong?" He shouted at her harshly when she hesitated, "Come on, what is it?"

"The baby has a bad heart," Isobel said. "I'm sorry."

"So?"

"A really bad heart. Anybody would pick it up. It may not even live."

"Oh my God." He punched the pillow. "Oh my God." He punched it again. "Shit." Punched the headboard. "No, no, no!"

Then he stopped and turned to Isobel with a wild look she hadn't seen before. "Listen, were there any other babies born last night?"

"Well, sure," Isobel said.

"What was it?" Peter demanded.

"What was what?" She looked at him blankly.

"Chrissie's fucking baby. What was it?"

"A girl," Isobel said mechanically. "So what?"

"Did anybody else have a girl last night? A *healthy* girl?" he said.

"Yes, Bettina Dunne," she said, finally understanding.

"Switch them," he said. "Go over there and poke around. You know everybody. Make it a reunion. Take a box of doughnuts. Visit your patients. Find the right moment. Is, you know just how to do it. They only have one nurse in the nursery. She can't be there every second."

Isobel listened to him very carefully.

"When she goes to the ladies' room. When she gets their little bottles, whatever. Switch the bracelets on their wrists."

For a long minute, Isobel looked at him as if he were crazy, really wacko. Then she said, "I can't do that."

"Why not? Why the fuck not?"

"Because it would be—" She was at a loss for words at how terrible, how wrong it would be. Yet, in the corner of her mind she knew she could do it. It was a small hospital. There was not a lot in the way of security. She always wore a nurse's uniform because the Drs. Street and Steadman insisted on it. She still had her ID tags. She knew the fat girl in the nursery, Janine —not very bright, but loved children. Yes, indeed, doughnuts would distract her.

"It would be an act of charity. You'd be giving that poor baby its only chance for survival. With real parents, it may get a new heart, and the care it needs. Otherwise it will become a ward of the state. It will never leave that hospital alive."

Isobel's jaw dropped. "But still, it's like—like changing the news. Reporters are not supposed to do it."

"But they *do*. They do it every day," Peter said. "Be a good girl, Is. Give me a shot and get out of here. You're the only one who can save my life. Otherwise, I'm history."

Isobel chewed the inside of her cheek and tears sprang up in her eyes. "Oh, God, switch the bracelets?" she said.

"You'll have to switch the babies, too. Don't forget that.

Their names are on the card on their—um—containers.'' Peter sat back.

"What if I get caught?" The tears fell down her face.

"Don't get caught," Peter said. "And you have to do it today. For God's sake, do it today."

"I don't know," she said doubtfully. "If they think the baby is sick, they won't release it for adoption."

"Just do what I tell you, okay? I'll get the baby released. Trust me. Promise me, and I'll promise you."

"What?" she asked tearfully.

"I get out of this, and I'll take you to Paris."

"Oh, God. I don't know." Isobel blew her nose into a tissue. How could he manage it? It didn't make sense.

"And I'll marry you when we get there. How about that?"

"Marry me?" She couldn't believe it. He was going to marry her.

"Yes ma'am, if you'll have me," he said solemnly.

"Oh, I'll have you." She smiled through her tears. "You're the best."

"Today," he whispered into her neck as he took her in his arms. "Do it today, Is, before the Dunne woman has time to recognize the baby."

23

Soon after Isobel left, the phone rang. Peter picked it up warily.

"Hello?"

"Good morning," Angel said. "It's June Twenty-ninth."

Peter took a deep breath to control his panic. "I've had an accident."

"Another one? I hope it's not serious. You owe me thirteen thousand dollars," Angel said smoothly.

"Thirteen?" Peter sputtered. "I thought it was ten."

"I guess you can't add. I'm beginning to worry about your future."

"Don't do that, Angel. Don't threaten me. You know I'm good for the money. I told you I'd have it by the Fourth. I've had a setback, but I'll straighten it out today. How can I get anything done if you're hanging over me?"

Silence on the other end.

"Come on, give me a break, Angel. Help me. Let me have a couple of hits and I'll help you. I'll give you something you want."

There was a click as the phone went dead.

"Angel, Angel." Peter slammed down the receiver in a rage. He hurt. He hurt all over. He needed a hit badly. He wanted it more than he'd ever wanted anything. It was more persistent than hunger. It was deeper than anger, deeper than any love that ever existed.

He got up and found his leather toiletry bag, where he kept his stuff. There was almost nothing left in it that was of any use to him. He threw it against the wall. A few minutes later he called Sam, a broken-down old quack who would do anything, testify to anything, and get him anything as long as the price was right. The Doc was out.

24

Bettina was put in a private room because she came in so late. She fell asleep right away, in spite of her excitement and desire to tell everybody she knew that she had a little girl, seven pounds, three ounces. But there was nothing in her room yet. No telephone, no television. The hospital administration offices didn't open until nine, and she was told no one could arrange for these things until then.

In the morning when the nurse came in, Bettina asked to see her baby again right away. She wanted to memorize her face and breathe in her baby smells, examine her tiny hands and feet. She wanted to determine whom she most resembled, Tom or her. She hadn't seen her for more than a few seconds and was pretty sure she had red hair and blue eyes. But all babies have blue eyes when they're born, she seemed to remember someone telling her.

The nurse ignored the request and hauled up the sheet to have a look at Bettina's incision.

"Looks okay," she said. "Now you gotta urinate."

"Can I wait a little while? I don't really have to yet."

"Nooo, you can't. Up, up—now, or I'll give you a bedpan."

"I'll get up," Bettina said. "Is there a pay phone around here?"

"Yes, but it doesn't look like you're ready for that." She hauled Bettina to a sitting position and helped her get out of bed.

Bettina felt very shaky. Three steps to the bathroom were suddenly a long way. Then, a moment of privacy in which she was too trembly in her knees to do more than accomplish the assigned task and wash her hands. Three shaky steps back.

"You'll have to wait for the office to open to get your phone." The nurse deposited Bettina back in bed as if she were a rag doll and slapped an ice pack on the wound.

"Half an hour on, half an hour off," she admonished before leaving.

Bettina didn't get a phone in her room until four in the afternoon. She called George Highgate's office at Axam.

"It's Bettina Dunne," she said when his secretary asked who was calling.

"Where are you?" the secretary cried. "Where have you been? We've been trying to reach you for days."

"Why? Has something happened?" Bettina suddenly felt cold all over, as if the ice pack between her legs had traveled up and chilled her heart.

"Well, yes. But I'm just supposed to find you. I'm not supposed to tell."

"Tell," Bettina demanded.

"Well, your husband had an accident. But he's all right," she added quickly.

"When?" Bettina fired back. "What happened?"

"Uh, let's see. The twenty-third, I think. Do you want Mr.

Highgate to tell you the details? He's in a meeting now. I could have him call you back."

"The *twenty-third?*" It was the twenty-ninth now. "Why didn't someone tell me?"

"We tried to reach you."

"I don't think you did. I was home all the time. Dammit, I want to know what *happened.* Now."

"He hit his head. They put him in the hospital."

"Where is he? I want to talk to him." Bettina's voice was rising with shock and fury.

"I think he's in Zurich." There was a pause. "Or maybe Geneva, I'm not sure."

"What? Don't you even know where he is?"

"I'm not sure. I can ask Mr. Highgate. He knows. They didn't want him to be up in the air too long without his having an MRI scan first."

"What?" Bettina said wildly.

"It's a kind of brain scan," came the cautious response. "But really, he's fine. They just want to make sure there's no blood leaking in his brain."

"What?" Bettina began to cry.

"Where are you, Mrs. Dunne? In case he calls again."

"You've spoken to him?"

"Well, *I* haven't. But I know he's called here several times trying to find you."

"I'm in Chester Memorial Hospital. I had a baby," Bettina said. "Tell him I had a baby."

"Congratulations. What is it?"

"A girl," Bettina said, pride bubbling up for a minute. "Tell him to call me. I had a girl."

"I'll tell Mr. Highgate. He knows what hospital. They'll get in touch with him."

"You promise?"

"Oh, yes, don't worry. We'll take care of it," the girl said. "I'm making a note right now."

A few hours later, an elaborate arrangement of flowers and a porcelain music box in the shape of a cradle that played Brahms's "Lullaby" were delivered to Bettina's room. But she had no call from Tom. Switzerland was six hours later. She figured it was the middle of the night.

At eleven Bettina was still waiting. From down the hall she suddenly heard the cries of the seven babies in the nursery that had been born in the last four days. They all seemed to be screaming in concert. The sound pierced her as nothing ever had before. Her breasts, which were heavy and hard, ached terribly. As she listened for a moment, milk began to leak out and wet her nightgown. She didn't know a baby's cry could do that.

The whole corridor was quiet now except for the nursery. The visitors had all gone home. In this section of the hospital no one woke the patients every few hours to make sure they were still alive. Bettina shuffled carefully down the empty hall toward the nursery. There were no nurses and the lights had been dimmed for the graveyard shift.

When she got to the nursery window she peered in, looking for her baby. The one nurse there was dressed in green. She was taking the babies out one by one, and changing them swiftly and mechanically, tucking each one under her arm when it was done, like a football.

She was absorbed in her task and didn't see Bettina's face peering through the glass, fascinated by the two rows of snaillike creatures. Except for the color of hair and some variation in size, they all looked the same. Finally, Bettina saw the Dunne card on a bassinet. It said, "Baby Girl Dunne." The baby was all the way in a corner wrapped in a pink receiving blanket. She was propped on her side with another blanket behind her so that she couldn't flop over. And she alone was sound asleep.

Bettina was overcome with excitement and pride. Her breasts felt pierced through by a thousand needles. She went around to the nursery door that said "No Admittance" and pushed it open.

"What are you doing up?" the nurse said sharply.

"I wanted to see my baby," Bettina said meekly.

"Well, you can't come in here." The nurse was tall and very thin, and did not stop the wrapping and unwrapping job she had begun. She was as grim as a morgue matron, Bettina thought, if there is such a thing.

"Why not?" she asked.

"There are babies in here."

"I'm not coming from the outside," Bettina pointed out. She clutched her breasts.

"Outside of here is outside," the nurse grumbled. She shrugged her bony shoulders, bounced the shrieking infant in her arms, then looked Bettina up and down. "Which one is yours?"

"The Dunne baby," Bettina said proudly. "Is she all right? I mean, how come she's sleeping when all the rest are making such a racket?"

The nurse smiled a little. "Who do you think woke them all up?"

Bettina sighed. "I heard the crying and knew it was mine," she said softly.

"Well, scoot; I have work to do," she commanded, but not unkindly now.

"My breasts hurt," Bettina said. The front of her nightgown was soaked by now.

"Take a hot shower."

"Now?"

"It's too late for her. I don't think she'll wake up for anything until two."

"Please let me try," Bettina asked.

The mistress of the babies looked at Bettina uncertainly. "Well, you're not supposed to take her at this hour, but if you can get her to your room by yourself . . ."

"I can do it," Bettina said confidently. "Thank you." She realized she was thanking this prickly nurse for letting her have her own child.

A few minutes later, she was shuffling slowly down the hall pushing the cart with the tiny plastic bassinet on top. Below was a shelf with a box of Pampers, a comb, some undershirts, receiving blankets, and some small bottles filled with sterilized sugar water. When Bettina got back to her room, she hopped in bed, wincing, and then pulled the cart close to her.

The baby was sound asleep. Bettina lifted her out carefully and held her for a minute, just looking at her. She unwrapped her just enough so that she could examine her hands and feet. It was amazing. The baby had reddish hair, delicate eyebrows, plump cheeks, and a compact little body. Her mouth was like a rosebud and her hands and feet, though tiny, were long and slender, exact miniatures of Tom's.

"I love you," Bettina whispered. She lifted the baby closer to her so she could feel its soft breath on her cheek. The baby stirred for a second. When Bettina stroked her hand with one finger, the baby opened her fist, took Bettina's finger, and squeezed it.

Bettina was thrilled. "Yes, I'm your mommy," she whispered. "And your daddy will be home soon."

She held the baby close to her heart and decided not to take her back to the nursery. She would keep her in the room all night.

25

Isobel typed the two names on four pink strips of paper. Pink for girls. Baby Girl Dunne and Baby Girl Elton. They used to put the tags just around the wrist, but now each baby got two, one for the wrist and one for the ankle. She used her office typewriter at the end of the day after everyone had gone.

All afternoon Isobel considered what time would be best for her to go. It couldn't be too early. It had to be sometime after eight, when visitors were required to leave. Even though these two babies wouldn't have fathers and grandparents sitting around playing with them, it was more than likely they would be out of the nursery during that time anyway. And it couldn't be too late. It would look suspicious if she came in at two in the morning.

Isobel didn't want anybody to know. Peter suggested she offer Janine a thousand dollars to keep her quiet, but Isobel didn't want anybody to know. It wasn't so very bad a thing, not as bad as other things she'd seen people do. She had no doubt she could change the babies and go on with her life, get married, and not think about it again. She might leave Dr. Street's office, but the episode wouldn't really count, any more than the other terrible things she'd seen in her life that had come before. It would be like water under the bridge. Married ladies had better things to do than worry about events that had happened in the past.

No, she could not let anyone know why she was there that night or allow anyone to help her do what she had to do.

She came in through the Emergency Room.

"Hi, uh, Geoff." She looked at the name tag pinned on the male nurse at the desk. Recently, it had been glassed in for security reasons. She couldn't get to the desk, where she knew exactly which drawer had the tags she needed.

Isobel had the box of doughnuts in one hand, was wearing her nurse's uniform and white, soft-soled shoes. She didn't know him.

"Can I help you?" he said without looking at her.

"Is Alice around?" Isobel asked.

"In the cafeteria," he said laconically, and turned the page of the magazine he was reading.

Isobel couldn't think up a reason to go behind the glass and reach her hand into the drawer where the bracelets were kept.

"Oh," she said. "I guess I'll look for her there."

It was nine o'clock. What was Alice doing up there? They wouldn't be serving food at this hour. Isobel felt stupid. She should have said she could leave a note, and gone inside the glass enclosure to write one. But he had his feet up on the desk. She couldn't have gotten into the drawer without his moving them. She should have thought of some excuse, but it wasn't so easy to think of things on the spur of the moment.

Upstairs, she sat in the cafeteria with Alice and some other girls for what seemed like a year. She had to open the box of doughnuts and offer them around. They were smoking there, because they were not allowed to smoke downstairs. And they were in no hurry to get back to their stations. Isobel watched six of the doughnuts disappear and thought it was a good thing she had bought two dozen.

It was an hour before they casually gathered their things

and wandered off. Alice went downstairs and Isobel went with her. It was another half hour before Alice had to go to the bathroom. She relinquished her spot at the desk to Isobel with relief, because she didn't want to ask Geoff, "that prick," to sit in for her again.

"He has it in for me," she said.

As soon as she was gone, Isobel reached into the drawer and took out four identification bracelets. She inserted the pink pieces of paper with the babies' names typed on them into the slots on the bracelets, and put them in her bag.

Ten minutes later she got off the elevator on the sixth floor and strolled down the hall to the nursery.

It was eleven o'clock. Isobel looked in the window and immediately saw that plump Janine was not on duty. Skinny Marilyn went off duty at twelve and liked to leave everything perfect when she left. There was a word for people like that.

Isobel waved.

Marilyn nodded, and deftly tucked a very dark-looking infant with long black hair into its plastic home.

Isobel quickly scanned the names on the bassinets and didn't see Dunne. The back of her neck prickled with anxiety. She couldn't have gone home yet, could she? She just had the baby this morning. No, she always knew when the patients went home. She tried to relax. Three of the bassinets were turned sideways so she couldn't see the names.

She pushed open the swinging door that said "No Admittance."

"Hi, Marilyn, what's new?"

Marilyn shrugged. "Oh, same old shit," she said, and smiled grimly at the joke no one else ever seemed to enjoy.

"Very funny," Isobel said. She started looking at the names on the three bassinets she hadn't been able to see from outside.

"You tired of your desk job or something?"

"No, just stopped by to say hello to my babies. Hi, sweetie." She stroked the nearest chin with her finger.

"Kind of late for stopping by, isn't it?"

"I was in the hospital," Isobel said coolly. "I thought I'd come by before I left. Several of our patients had babies last night. Want a doughnut?"

"Thanks, I'll keep it for later." Marilyn reached in the box and took one.

"Dunne," Isobel said as if she had just thought of it. "I don't see it. Girl, isn't it?"

"Oh," Marilyn laughed. "Yeah. She's down the hall with her mother."

"What?" Isobel's mouth went dry. "Why?"

"She wanted her. There's no harm in it."

Isobel's mouth fell open. She didn't want any more difficulties. She was covered with sweat. Her heart had been beating triple-time ever since the Emergency Room doors automatically slid open for her. She had had enough trouble getting the damn identification bracelets, and now the baby was with its mother. It was too much.

"It's too late. Isn't that against the rules?" Isobel spat out in as angry a tone as she felt.

"It's only for a few minutes," Marilyn said uneasily, because Isobel was frowning at her as if she hadn't washed her hands, or something even worse than that.

"Well, you're not supposed to be in here, either," she said. "So maybe you better go."

"I'm sorry," Isobel said hastily. "I just wanted to see her, that's all. I like the mother."

Marilyn sniffed. "I'll get her in a minute."

"Thank you." Isobel looked at her watch. "I can't stay more than a minute."

In fact, she had only forty-five minutes before the shift

changed. After eleven, when the night nurse came on, it would be hard to explain her presence there. It had to be done, and she had to be gone, by then.

It's all right, she tried to assure herself. Both Bettina and Chrissie were blond. Bettina wouldn't know the difference. By tomorrow she won't remember. They all looked pretty much alike at this stage, anyway.

After a few minutes Isobel's tapping and sighing and yawning made Marilyn nervous enough to go fetch Baby Dunne.

It was then, while Isobel was alone in the nursery, that she realized Baby Elton wasn't there, either. She noted three boys and two girls. One girl was enormous and had black hair. The other one was clearly an Indian or an Arab.

There was another section in the nursery. Isobel nervously pushed aside the curtain that separated the two areas and went inside. There, one baby was isolated. It was in an incubator, had a tiny breathing tube down its nose, and was attached to a heart monitor.

Isobel put her hand to her mouth and gasped. It was a tiny thing, a peanut with bowed legs and no flesh. Seeing it was like walking into a land mine or a shotgun blast. This couldn't be mistaken for a healthy baby with a deadly, hidden flaw. This child of a football player and a cheerleader probably wouldn't last a week. Its head was bald. Its eyes were squeezed shut, and it was attached to tubes and monitors and life-support systems in so many places. The name "Elton" was everywhere—on the chart, on the incubator, on the baby's wrist and ankle.

Isobel was soaked through, and now she could feel her bowels turning to water. It had seemed a lot easier when they'd talked about it. She sniffed back her tears. No one told her it was in intensive care. She didn't know. She hadn't used her head.

She realized she was groaning aloud. How could she have made such a mistake? And there was no way to fix it. They weren't alike. Not alike at all. Each one was different and distinct. Blindly, she went back to the nursery, desperate to get out of there before Marilyn came back. She grabbed the box of doughnuts because it was hers. She didn't want to leave anything behind.

Hurry, hurry, she told herself. She ran out of the swinging doors and down the hall to the elevator without looking back. The elevator was in the basement. She took the stairs, skipping down them without watching her feet. A baby wasn't just a baby. They weren't all the same. They were not the same, she tried to explain to Peter in her mind. It didn't occur to her until she was on the street that she was safe: She hadn't done it.

26

There was a moment of crackling on the line between Zurich and Morristown, and then Tom spoke.

"Is that you, George?"

"Ah, Tom, Tom. Yes, it's me. Good to hear from you. You did a good job over there. We're all proud of you. And we did a good job here," George said.

"Did you find my wife?"

Tom had been sitting impatiently in the chair by the bed in his hospital room in Zurich for the four hours since he awoke before dawn. Now he knew he hadn't heard from Bettina because she'd never been told about his accident. They seemed to have misplaced his wife after promising to take care of her.

Untouched and still in front of him on the table were the coffee and newspapers in several languages that had been brought to him earlier.

He was furious. He was also a peculiar sight. A big patch of hair had been shaved off where the stitches were, and his head was still bandaged. He had not shaved for over a week, and did not have the strength to do so now. But he was dressed and had his shoes on, was ready for his escape the minute he could bring it about.

"We did, indeed," George said heartily. "It took some doing, though, because she's an independent lady—"

"Well, where is she? Is she all right?"

"She went off," George said. "She went off, just like I told you they do, and she had herself a little girl."

"What?" Tom jumped to his feet and was overcome with dizziness. "You mean she had the baby?" He eased himself down into the chair, his heart racing.

"Yes, Tom. She had the baby. Congratulations, you're a father, and I hear the baby's just gorgeous. A red-head."

"A redhead." Tom's eyes filled with tears. "Oh my God, she had the baby. This is tremendous. How is she?"

"Mother and child are doing fine."

"Oh my God," Tom said again. "I just can't believe this. I'm so excited. A girl. She had a girl. I'm glad she had a girl. I think she wanted a girl." He realized he was babbling and stopped.

"You there, Tom?" George asked after a few seconds of crackling.

"I've got to get out of here, George," Tom said. "I want out of here today. I've got to get home."

"Now calm down, calm down. We can't rush these things," George murmured.

"What do you mean we can't rush these things?" Tom said furiously.

"Look, the crisis is over. Your wife had the baby. She's fine. Relax; we'll get you home in good time."

"I don't want to get home 'in good time.' I want to get home now."

"Well, we can't do that."

"Why the hell not? If a refinery were down and you needed a part, you'd charter a goddamned jet."

"This is not the same thing, Tom, and you know that. Your best interests are our only concern here. We want to get you home healthy, and we're not moving you until we're sure it won't do you any harm."

Tom's head throbbed. "Jesus," he said. "They haven't done a thing. Not a goddamned thing. George," he shouted, "they gave me an enema. That's it."

"Well, the equipment is down," George said slowly.

"What do you mean it's down?"

"Well, they expect to have it fixed by tomorrow. You get your scan," he said soothingly, "and then if everything looks good, we'll have you out on the first flight day after tomorrow."

"Shit."

"What, Tom?"

"I want to talk to my wife," Tom said.

"Tom, I think you'll be glad to know that we're sending someone with you, and you'll be flying first class," George added.

"Fine. Can you patch me through?" Tom didn't care about the concession of being sent first class when nobody, not even the president, went first class at Axam.

"And we'll have a car out at Kennedy to pick you up."

"That's nice, George. Thanks. Now, do you think you can put me through to my wife?"

"Uh, hold on. I'm not sure how this new electronic phone system works. Listen, if we get cut off, I'll call you right back."

Tom waited on hold for ten minutes. Finally, when he was about to hang up in disgust, Highgate's secretary came on.

"Mr. Dunne?" she said.

"Yes," Tom said.

"Hold on, I have Mrs. Dunne on the line."

"Thank you," Tom said.

"Mrs. Dunne, go ahead," the secretary said.

"Tom, are you all right?"

He had to either take the phone away from his ear or have his eardrum shattered. "I'm fine. You don't have to yell. It's a good connection."

"What happened? I was so worried." She seemed frantic, almost hysterical.

"I love you. You had a girl." The sound of her voice tore him apart. More than anything, he wanted to be with her that moment.

"She's beautiful," Bettina whispered. "So beautiful you won't believe it. Tom, tell me what happened?"

He swallowed, trying to find some words. His head throbbed from his rage before and his yearning now. He didn't like to tell them, but sometimes his vision was a little foggy. It was foggy now.

"I did a stupid thing. I went up column four in the middle of the day."

"Why?"

"I wanted to come home. I didn't want to wait."

"Did you fall?"

"No, no, nothing like that. I got up all right. We were up there about seven hours." He gave a short laugh. "We found the big leak. That's where it was."

"Oh, Tom."

"I look pretty awful. They had to shave off some of my hair. I have twelve stitches." He touched the bandage.

"They didn't tell me," Bettina said. "I didn't know."

"I thought so. I was out for three days. There was no message from you when I woke up. So I knew there was something wrong."

"Oh, my love, I'm sorry," Bettina said.

"I'm the one who should be sorry. I missed it. I wanted to be there so much, and I missed it."

"Well, maybe we can arrange for you to be there at the next one," Bettina said with a laugh.

"Can you say that already?"

"You don't think about the pain the minute that you see it, Tom," Bettina said.

"She's that good, huh? Do you love her more than me?"

"Is that a real question? You know I love you a hundred percent. The whole way, Tom. Do you have any doubt?"

"Just checking," he said, a little sheepishly. "I miss you, and you have something to hold."

"When are you coming back?"

"Day after tomorrow. They want to give me a brain scan before I go up in the air again, but the machine that does it is being fixed. I can't have it done today."

"Oh."

He noted the drop in her voice. "It's all right," he assured her. "I know there's nothing wrong in there. It was a nasty bump. I have a concussion. It just takes a few days to heal."

"I'm sure it's all right," Bettina said, without the least idea of whether it was or wasn't.

"I'll come and get you. Stay where you are," Tom said.

"Why? I want to go home as soon as I can."

"Just stay in the hospital where you're safe, and there are people to take care of you," he said fiercely. "I know how

independent you are, but do as I tell you just until I get back.''
He laughed. ''Then we'll go back to normal and I'll do as you
tell me.''

''All right. Take care of yourself.''

''You too.''

A few moments later Tom hung up. He went to the window and looked out, wondering if Bettina still liked the name
Katherine.

27

Isobel went straight home from the hospital and took several
pills to calm down. Then she fell asleep holding the teddy bear
her father had given her when she was six. It wasn't much of a
teddy bear. It didn't have any plush left on its body, but its eyes
and smile were intact.

The next morning she dressed carefully and took what was
left of the box of doughnuts to Peter's house. She opened the
door with the key he had given her and found him downstairs,
sitting in the kitchen.

''Hi. Looks like you're feeling better,'' she said brightly.

''Where have you been?'' He was dressed for work for the
first time and had a glass of vodka in front of him on the table.
''Didn't you know I was waiting to hear?''

''Sorry,'' Isobel said meekly. ''I was exhausted.''

''Well, did you do it?''

"It was in intensive care." She said it flatly because it was a fact.

"What?"

"Chrissie's baby was all hooked up. She was the size of a chicken. I couldn't do it."

"Jesus Christ." Peter threw the glass at the wall, where it shattered noisily. A couple of ice cubes bounced across the floor.

"God damn it!" He slammed his fist on the table. He turned to look at Isobel, who had begun to pick up the pieces of glass and collect them in her hand.

"Why didn't you think of something else?" he demanded.

"Like what? I couldn't exchange two others."

"Why not?"

"Three were boys," she said as calmly as she could. "I couldn't very well use a boy. And the other two were too dark. One was an Indian. The other weighed twelve pounds and had black hair. Besides, Chrissie's baby was the one we needed for an exchange to work."

"Jesus," Peter said. "Jesus, I don't believe this."

"I'm sorry," Isobel muttered. "I tried." She dumped the pieces of glass in the wastebasket.

"I already told them the baby is coming. They're getting the money for me."

"I'm sorry," Isobel said again.

"We'll have to do something else," he said.

"Like what?" Isobel regarded him blankly as he poured himself another drink.

"Take the baby."

"What baby?" Isobel put the top back on the vodka bottle, as if drinking at seven-thirty in the morning were the most normal thing in the world. "There isn't any baby."

"Oh, yes there is. There's still the Dunne baby. We'll take that one."

"Oh, sure. Go to the hospital and walk out with it."
Isobel's hand twitched.

Peter shook his head.

A weak little laugh escaped from her throat like a hiccup.
"For a minute I thought you were losing your grip."

"Shut up. Go to work. I don't need you. I can do it
myself." He turned his back on her.

"I'm sorry," she said weakly. "I can't do anything else."

"Beat it," Peter said harshly. "No one's asking you to."

She walked across the kitchen very slowly, as if the glass
were still there and she was barefoot. As if it were a mine field
and she might be blown away at any second. Why was this
happening to her? Why? Just when everything was going so well.

"And don't come back," he shouted after her.

He called her in the office a few hours later.

She punched the lighted button with the end of her pen.
"Doctors' office," she said mechanically.

"Look, I'm sorry I lost it this morning," Peter said. "I'm
under a lot of pressure. Chrissie Elton wants her money. She
thinks she did her part, and the outcome is not her fault."

Isobel's heart jumped at the sound of his voice, but the
hurt was not relieved by his apology. She continued filling out
the bill she was working on, switched her mind to another tack.

"Is?" Peter whispered.

"You told me to get lost," Isobel said, swiveling her chair
toward the wall so no one could see her face.

"Hey, you know I didn't mean that. Where would I be
without you?"

"Maybe better off," she murmured. None of this would
have happened if she hadn't gone through the files and thought of
Chrissie Elton. The whole mess was her fault, in a way. At times
like this she was afraid there was something bad in her that made

these awful things happen. Something opposite to the Gardol Shield in the commercials for toothpaste in her childhood. She couldn't remember what toothpaste it was, but there was an invisible shield that protected a huge tooth from decay. She wanted a shield like that for herself, something that could stop all terrible things from touching her. She'd become a nurse to help people and to be wrapped in goodness. But wearing the white dress and a name tag on her chest had not turned out to be a protection against anything. She was rarely appreciated, and people often got hurt in spite of her efforts on their behalf.

Over the years, she watched the girls she went to school with get married. They had the shield. They met nice men who fell in love with them. Isobel watched them disappear into domestic tranquillity, have babies, be in car pools, go to PTA meetings, never work again.

Sometimes, watching the pregnant women come to the office in their expensive cars, saying "my husband" this and "my husband" that, gave Isobel so much pain in her stomach she thought she had ulcers. She wanted to be a wife, yet she, alone among all the girls, couldn't get what she wanted.

"Better off without you?" Peter said. "What gives you that idea? I'm nowhere without you. Flat, empty."

"You told me to split," Isobel said. Her stomach was still knotted up with anguish over it. Men had disappeared on her before. Some just dropped off the deep end as if they had never been. Some acted like they were still friends when it was over, slapped her on the back as if it was all okay. Their eyes were clear. The last one packed up and left while she was at work. She never even knew he had been engaged to someone else for months. But no one had ever told her to get out before.

"I didn't mean it forever. I'm sorry if you misunderstood. You're a sensitive flower, Is. I'm rough. Forgive me."

"You hurt me," she said. "You gave me a stomachache; I'm still in knots."

"I wouldn't hurt you for the world," Peter said. "You know that. I'm just"—he sniffed—"I'm in trouble, Is. I need you more than I ever did."

There was silence as Isobel looked at the polish on her nails. It was perfect. One thing that could be said for her was she always took care of herself. She sniffed. And she took care of him, too. Where else was he going to get someone who wouldn't squeak with indignation at some of the things he liked to do?

"I know you do. But there's nothing I can do to help."

"Yes, you can help me through this. I just need to get to the other side. It's like climbing a mountain. One foot in front of the other until we get to the other side."

"What do you want me to do?"

"Just make me dinner tonight and let me borrow the five hundred. I'll pay you back triple at the end of the week."

"Well, that I can do."

At six-thirty she drove over to his place with the five hundred dollars he had asked for and her car loaded with groceries. He was still at the office. Isobel let her breath out. She wished she could pour herself a glass of wine, but she couldn't find anything. She looked around in the living room, saw that there were even more things missing than before. She took the money out of her purse, put it on the table, and went into the kitchen to start cooking dinner.

Peter came in more than an hour later. His face was sallow and waxy. He had deep black circles under his eyes and his mouth was so narrow and drawn he seemed to be missing his lips altogether. Isobel stared at him.

"What are you looking at?" he demanded.

"Nothing. You look tired," she said quickly. "Have you eaten anything today?"

"What are you, my mother?" he snapped.

She stepped back, hurt. "I just asked," she said. She put her hand to her breast. Things were not starting well, and she wanted a drink badly.

"I brought the five hundred," she said. "I got it from the cash machine. Did you see it?"

"Yeah, I got it." He softened a little, reached in his pocket and pulled out a joint. "Here, calm down." He held it out across the counter, where she was standing awkwardly in tights cut off at the knees and a halter top, black and pink, with the apron over it and a terry-cloth headband around her forehead to hold back her curls.

She took the joint gratefully. "Thanks," she said when he lit it. She inhaled deeply and held it in her lungs as long as she could, then passed it over to him with a shaking hand.

He passed it back. "I have a way to solve the problem of the baby," he said after his second drag.

"I thought you gave that idea up."

He put the joint down, and smiled. Then he reached into his pocket and pulled out a vial of clear, yellowish liquid that had a distinctive packaging Isobel had seen before. G.E.F. Series II, it was called. Peter handed her the vial.

"Jesus, where did you get this?"

"A friend gave it to me." He smiled. "That should do it. Don't you think?"

She looked at him blankly. "Do what?"

"Do you know what it is?" He reached for it.

She nodded and didn't hand it back. "Nasty stuff. Hallucinogen."

"Hey, it's perfectly harmless in small doses."

"I wouldn't take it for the whole world." Isobel handed it back.

"It's not for you. It's a way to get the baby," he said.

"Are you nuts?"

"Listen, it's a perfect plan. We get the mom after she comes home, Is. We give her a little shot. When she wakes up, the baby is gone, and she doesn't know what happened. Isn't it beautiful?" He lit up another joint.

Isobel frowned. "If you give her that, she won't be able to remember her name. It's a drug that makes people go crazy. They only use it on rats. It didn't work so well on people. They tried it and a few people died."

"So?"

"Be reasonable, Peter. You can't do that." Her fingers felt funny. She dropped the roach in the sink, where it fizzled out. A giggle escaped her. "Oops, sorry."

"Have you got a better idea?" He reached into his pocket for another joint.

Another giggle erupted from her mouth as she exhaled a drag so deep there was no smoke left when she let it out.

"Sodium pentothal," she murmured. "If I were doing it, I'd use that."

"Nah, that would knock her out," Peter said.

"I thought that was the idea."

She passed the third joint back to him and sat on the kitchen stool seductively. He took two drags before replying.

"No, if she's just sleepy and compliant, she'll be angry when she comes to. She'll be rational and blame someone else."

"So?" Isobel said.

He shook his head. "She can't know what she did with that baby of hers."

"Oh."

"See, if she's had a bad trip, if she's thoroughly confused and out of it, she won't know what happened."

Peter uncorked a bottle of wine he had pulled from the back of a cupboard and poured Isobel a glass.

She did not wait to smell it or swirl it around in her mouth as she had been told was the right thing to do with wine. She drank it down in gulps and wiped her mouth with the back of her hand. She felt better. He always made her feel good.

"Peter, she may be out of it *forever* if you give her that." She pointed to the vial. "She may even die. We don't want that nice woman to die."

He shrugged.

"It would be murder. People go to jail for that." She laughed. Jail was suddenly funny.

Peter shrugged. "A woman offs her baby, goes berserk, and jumps out of a window, hangs herself. Better her than me." He poured out some more wine.

Isobel cocked her head. "It's a jungle out there."

Better her than Peter. Suddenly it occurred to her that Bettina's husband might not be around. She was alone. It could work. She ran the movie camera in her head, considering it. She speeded up the picture the way she did when she and Peter had sex and she watched in the mirror. Pain came from far away, or in real close, depending on her frame of mind, how tired she was, how high. But it wasn't ever really her being slapped or bitten. It was some other naked girl with her hands tied, getting roughed up a little before being pronged from behind—hmm, *sodomized,* hard enough to break the skin in a dozen places.

She giggled. The words "Hurt me" bubbled up, and her stomach turned over. Peter looked kind of wild. She wondered if he had any coke, if he was up to it.

She sneezed, running the reel again on the other girl, probably younger than she was. Yes, she remembered. Bettina was younger than she was. Hell, a prick in her thigh. That wasn't real pain. Now Isobel knew real pain. She knew real hurt. This wouldn't be hurt. This would be a bad moment, an episode. Only one episode in her whole life.

Worse things than this happened in hospitals all the time. Isobel had been present at enough of them to keep her awake whenever she felt bad about the way her life was going. One doctor sewed up a young boy from Rahway with a tiny perforation in his colon because he was late for a party. The boy died. And residents prescribed fatal drugs to patients without checking their charts first. The reports that came in days later said the patients had failed to respond to emergency treatment. At four o'clock in the morning, or even at noon sometimes, the most terrifying things happened.

A twenty-year-old girl bled to death during a routine tonsillectomy while the doctor stood there panicked and raging because no one had checked to see if she was a bleeder. Isobel was holding the girl's hand as the blood filled her lungs and she drowned.

This was nothing to that. Isobel could smell the chicken in the oven. The skin must be very crisp by now, the way she liked it. She was starved. After they ate, maybe she'd ask Peter if he had any coke. She looked over at him. He was dozing on the sofa.

28

On Thursday, Aaron shut down his computer for the night earlier than usual. He'd promised Sally he'd stop at the liquor store for supplies. The barbecue they always had on the Saturday of the Fourth of July weekend was in two days, and he hadn't started thinking about it yet. She had nagged him about it all week.

"What's the matter? You said you were going to take care of it. I told you I have to take Delia to rehearsals after work this week." She threw the dishes in the sink for later and dashed out before he did.

He seemed to recall her saying something about a play. He scratched his head for a second, trying to remember what it was, gave up.

He did remember promising to help with the food, though. He had to get the liquor now, so he could spend all day with Sally on Saturday. He liked choosing the steaks himself and starting the grill. Usually he did. This year he was lacking in enthusiasm. In fact, the whole thing was making him uneasy. He didn't feel like having a party for his colleagues from the hospital.

There were a lot of unpleasant things going on under the surface. He could feel it. He sighed as he put his jacket on and closed the door of his office. The hall was empty. Everybody who could get a head start on the weekend had already taken off.

It was seven-thirty, still fully light. The quaint liquor store with the sawdust on the floor down the street from the hospital was open until eight. Aaron ambled across the street, trying to work up some excitement for margaritas and planter's punch. He had gotten to like the mixed drinks, especially in summer. But most people preferred beer or wine. Beer was easy. Maybe he'd just do beer and wine this year. From the corner of his eye he saw Max Starburn heading into the Recovery Room.

The sight brought him down. He'd had a bad feeling in the pit of his stomach about Max ever since they sat across from each other at a certain Committee meeting. There had been a heated discussion going around the table about further investigation of April Flanders and Jasper Amerigo. Max had argued quite eloquently that it was a waste of time. Ultimately his view had carried the day.

Then a huge smile of satisfaction had spread across Max's face as he clapped his hands together and said, "Well, that's that."

Without meaning to, Aaron changed course and headed for the Recovery Room. He hadn't been there for many months. It was a small place, wood-paneled. It was always open, always busy, and always dark, no matter what time of day. It happened to be the only decent restaurant and bar in the neighborhood, and was right across the street from the hospital.

He took a seat next to Max at the bar and nodded affably. "Hi. How's it going?"

Max swallowed down half the beer in front of him before turning his head. "Haven't seen you in here for a long time. What's the occasion?"

Aaron shook his head. "Nothing special. Just taking a break." He ordered a beer and looked around. "What's going on?"

"Not much. It's been pretty quiet."

Aaron's beer came. He drank some.

"You don't come around anymore," Max said after a brief silence. "What have you been up to?"

"Oh, you know me. I get into these pychiatric and psycho-analytic association things." Aaron sighed. "Always overcommitted."

"It's a drag."

"Well, now I'm a member of the Medical Ethics Committee of the APA."

"No kidding," Max said with a smile. "Leave it to the shrinks to find things to worry about. What area of medical ethics?"

"Physicians and AIDS."

Max made a face. "Jesus."

"We've appointed a task force to explore the moral and ethical issues of doctors with AIDS continuing to perform high-risk procedures."

Max snorted. "And you're on it."

"It's getting to be a serious problem. I wouldn't mind getting your input on it."

Max shook his big leonine head. He was a rebel. He had hair growing way down over his collar. The beer stein looked small in his hands. "I don't know. I'm on the front line. Thinking about risks is not my thing."

"Lot of people have it, pass it around," Aaron said, working his way into the subject carefully.

Max shrugged, turning away.

"Look at our own situation. A few people sleeping together in the hospital, and the whole community has a problem."

"Maybe you're making too much of it."

It was Aaron's turn to shrug. "It's a question of who should be protected. The patients have to be protected, all of them."

"It was your psycho," Max pointed out.

"Yeah, and he's out of here because there's no problem about violation of confidentiality," Aaron said. "If he were a physician, we couldn't demand the test. He'd still be hitting on the nurses and practicing."

Max shook his head furiously. "This whole thing is a tempest in a teapot."

"The people involved don't think so. The Flanders girl had a breakdown. She's had a number of partners since then. *They* must be concerned." He looked at Max questioningly. "Don't you think so?"

"Maybe not," Max said evasively. "It doesn't transfer woman to man."

"Oh? Is that true? I don't have the numbers on it." Aaron swallowed some beer. He didn't think that was the case anymore.

"Maybe one in a thousand. It's not a big deal."

"Must be a big deal," Aaron argued. "There are hundreds of doctors who are HIV positive in this country doing thousands of procedures a day. How do you think they're getting it? Intravenous drugs? Homosexuality?"

Max laughed bitterly, as if Aaron were an idiot for not knowing.

"What do you think about testing?" Aaron persisted.

"I think testing is fine. I've done it myself. It has to be an individual thing, though. Let people take care of it their own ways." Max's fingers drummed restlessly on the bar.

"I'm not sure about that," Aaron pressed on, ignoring his discomfort.

"Look, you can't ruin a man's career, destroy his family, his whole life," Max said explosively. "You ethics people. What do you know?"

"I know the problem," Aaron said calmly. "I don't know the answers."

Max finally faced him squarely, his face bright red. "I know what you're asking. But you can't touch me. Don't even think about challenging me."

"You're the head of surgery here. You've operated on some of my patients. I'm sure you'll operate on others. I'm not asking you anything. You want to talk about it; I'll talk about it. That's all."

"They don't get it from nurses," Max said suddenly.

Aaron looked down at his beer. It was almost gone. In a minute he'd have to order another one. He didn't want to do that.

"So what do they get it from?" he countered quickly.

Max looked around. It was after eight. The place was crowded. There wasn't an empty table anywhere. Finally he turned back to Aaron and looked at him contemptuously.

"I guess it's been a long time since you were covered with blood in an operating room." His beer stein was empty. He raised his hand for a refill. "It doesn't matter how careful we are. The patients are more dangerous than the doctors. Think about that."

Aaron took his breath in and let it out slowly. Sometimes it was hard to say where the danger was. He'd been shot at a couple of times. A patient had come at him with a knife once when he was a resident. He looked at Max, working on another beer and probably lying about a lot of things. It was going to take many months of careful groundwork to get him to reveal the results of his blood tests. Aaron brooded dejectedly. One thing

Max said was true, though: Aaron had never been covered with anybody's blood.

He sat there for a while and then paid up. It wasn't until he got home that he realized he had forgotten the liquor again.

29

On Friday morning Bettina decided to check out of the hospital and go home. It was July 1st, three days since she had given birth. When Dr. Street didn't come by in the morning, she called his office and asked the nurse if she could leave. Isobel was on duty.

"Dr. Street is gone for the weekend, but there's no note here that you can't. It's up to you. What time do you want to go?" she asked.

"This afternoon, as soon as you can arrange it."

There was a slight pause. "Uh, will your husband be with you?"

"He's coming in tomorrow afternoon," Bettina said. "Is that a problem?"

"Not on our end. I just hope you have someone to help you. Is there anyone at the house, your mother?"

"I have a car coming to get me." Bettina paused. "But I can manage one night alone."

"Fine."

That was it. The release form appeared within the hour, while Bettina was collecting her things. Then one of the nurses brought her the baby and a shopping bag full of manufacturers' giveaways. She went downstairs and checked out. No one asked her anything.

She went out the hospital door with her handbag, one suitcase, one shopping bag, and one baby fully wrapped in a cotton receiving blanket to guard against dust, germs, and other foreign agents. As she waited for the taxi, Bettina thought about how surprised and pleased Tom would be to get home and find her already there. Save him a trip.

The taxi came in a minute. She gave him her address and sat back. Then she raised the corner of the blanket. The baby was asleep. For a second her tiny lips puckered, as if preparing for a cry, and then they relaxed. Bettina smiled with delight. See, she could do things for herself—give birth, get home . . .

She settled the baby more comfortably on her lap, and looked out at suburban New Jersey as if for the first time. It was mid-afternoon on Friday of the Fourth of July weekend. The trees and sky had that special clarity of early summer. It was brilliant and still, as if everything were suspended on the quietest, laziest moments of summer. Very little traffic, no school buses on the road.

They turned into the long drive. The gracious white house with the dark green shutters came into view. Bettina inched forward on her seat. She put her handbag into the shopping bag, hoisted the baby high on her shoulder as the taxi pulled to a stop.

It was awkward getting out with the baby and the shopping bag and the suitcase, but there were only two steps up to the front door. Bettina struggled up the steps, put down the shopping bag and suitcase, opened the door, and went inside. Then, still holding the baby, she went back outside for the baggage and brought it in. Thinking of Tom, she closed the door and locked it.

She went in the kitchen first, made herself a cup of decaffeinated tea, and held the baby on her lap at the kitchen table as she drank it. She realized she needed a place to put the baby downstairs. She stood up and washed the teacup and saucer with one hand, left them on the counter to dry.

The wall phone in the kitchen rang. She reached for it.

"Mrs. Dunne?"

"Yes," Bettina said.

"This is Andy Rappaport."

"Who?" Bettina searched her memory for the name.

"Of Rappaport's Baby World."

"Oh, yes," Bettina said. "I didn't recognize your voice. That's funny, I was just this minute thinking about all the things I didn't get." No place to put the baby. She laughed at this unexpected connection to the outside world.

"Just checking to see if everything was all right with your order."

"Yes. Thank you for assembling the crib for me. I couldn't have done it myself."

"No problem. By the way, congratulations—you had a girl."

"How did you know?" Bettina was surprised.

"Oh, we have a service, Mrs. Dunne. I'm sure I told you about it. We do baby announcements. We'll come out to your house, photograph the baby, and attach the picture to whatever announcement you choose. We get the lists of births from the hospitals, and, of course, many of the mothers are our customers already."

"Oh." Bettina didn't remember anybody at Rappaport's telling her that, and she had been there several times.

"I'll be by this afternoon, if that's convenient for you."

"Oh, no. That's very nice of you but my husband won't be here today," Bettina protested, "and I couldn't make any decisions without him.'' Bettina didn't want formal announcements anyway. She was an artist, after all. She wanted to do her own cards.

''No problem, I could just drop off the sample books for a day or two, and you could decide at your leisure.''

''Well, that's very nice of you, but I don't know if we'll even use them.''

''No obligation at all. Look, we're here to make you happy. If you look through the books and don't find what you want, we can do whatever you like. You can even design your own. We'll print them for you.''

Bettina hesitated. She didn't want to be short with him, but his pushing made her nervous. This sudden niceness was the opposite of what she had experienced in the store. The man she remembered had been quite impatient with her. He was the least likely person in the world to have any sort of service that would require him to go out of his way for anybody.

''How's five-forty-five?''

''I really think it's kind of premature. I'd feel better just coming in when I'm more settled. I have to come in for a lot of things anyway.'' She jiggled the baby against her shoulder.

''That's great. Then you can bring the books back for me. It'll just give you a head start. You don't want to let your announcements go too long. It's a sign of a disorganized household.''

Bettina frowned. ''All right,'' she said finally, ''if you want to. But I'm not making any promises I'll buy anything.''

After she hung up she was annoyed at herself for giving in. She wouldn't even have time to bathe or change her clothes. She went upstairs, taking the shopping bag with her. When she changed the baby, she saw the identification tags still on her wrist and ankle. There was a pair of scissors among the items in a container on the changing table. Bettina cut the tags off to save them forever. She tossed them into the shopping bag with the freebies. Then she fed the baby and rocked her to sleep in the old-fashioned rocking chair she and Tom had bought with such excitement. Finally she put her down in the crib. The baby was sleeping peacefully when she went downstairs to answer the doorbell.

The door was solid wood. There was no peephole. She opened the door and someone shoved a rag into her face. She didn't have time to scream. Her cry reached no farther than her chest. It was like being thrown into water so cold the heart all but stops.

Bettina went down without a sound.

30

The Nuclear Magnetic Resonance machine that scanned Tom's brain was huge. It was designed to enclose a whole body about as tightly as a coffin. Tom was rolled into the round metal cylinder and parked there. There was no circulation of air in it. He broke into a cold sweat. A few minutes later a pounding noise started reverberating through the machine and into his head. It sounded like a dozen three-year-olds banging on metal pots. The technicians spoke German and wouldn't let him out. He was in there an hour without a break. Two hours after that, back in his room, he was still shaken by the experience. His head hurt so much he couldn't see. He was afraid they'd gotten mixed up and given him a lobotomy.

No one would tell him anything until the results were faxed to Highgate in Morristown. It wasn't until the next morning that Tom got a call.

"Vell, hello, Thomas Dunne. This is Herr Doctor Otto Gutenhoffer."

"Ah, Otto, help," Tom said. Otto was a Swiss economist with whom Tom had once worked to develop a presentation for a refinery in Brazil.

"How can I apologize?" Otto said. "I vas not here ven you arrived. I am sorry for your misfortune. How are you feeling?"

"I feel fine," Tom lied.

"Gut, because I have the results of your tests here, and they look like you are feeling lousy."

"Oh," Tom said.

"But not an endangered species, after all," Otto said, and laughed loudly.

"Oh." This was an example of Otto's humor. "You mean I'm lousy, but I'm all right."

"Exactly."

"That's great," Tom said. "Help me get out of here."

"I'll take you home as soon as you feel up to it," Otto added.

"I had a baby," Tom said. "I'm ready now."

"I thought you had a concussion, but congratulations." Otto laughed some more.

He was a great laugher. He was still laughing when Tom interrupted him.

"My wife had the baby, Otto."

"That's gut. I have a present for the baby," he said. "A cuckoo clock, what else?"

Tom smiled. "Thank you, Otto, that's nice of you. Would you do one more thing for me before we go?"

"Of course. This minute you are my job. I'll do whatever you want. What do you want?"

"They won't let me out of here to go shopping. And I have to bring something for my wife. I haven't seen her in a month, and she just had a baby. Something nice—"

"You don't have to make explanations to me. I'll take care of it. Feel better; we go tomorrow."

"We go tonight," Tom said firmly.

There was a pause.

"No flights tonight, Tom. We go tomorrow. Don't worry. I'll take care of it."

Tom knew he was lying. "I'm not going to sleep at all tonight. I'm not getting any rest."

"Yes, you will," Otto said. "You'll sleep. Good mountain air."

"What mountains? I don't see any mountains."

"Well, tomorrow you'll see mountains. Bye, Tom." Otto hung up.

31

Peter took Bettina to a house set far back from the road in a tangle of weeds five feet high. There was a hedge in front and on the sides that hadn't been touched in years. Huge, leafy spears shot up all along it. Behind the house the woods had encroached practically to the back door. A sign in front of the crumbling Georgian mansion read, "This lovely acreage is the site of the soon-to-be-completed Fabulous Leisure Village." There was an architect's drawing of the "village," but no indication that any steps had been taken toward beginning the project.

"How much time do we have before she wakes up?" Peter asked.

He drove the rented car into the driveway and switched off the motor. In the backseat, Isobel was cooing to the baby.

"About seven and a half minutes. If you want to be exact," she said.

"Well, let's get her inside then." He got out of the car and went around to the passenger-side front door, where Bettina was slumped against the window.

Isobel looked at him blankly. "What should I do with the baby?" Isobel asked.

"Leave it there. It won't walk away."

Isobel propped the baby on her side so that her back rested against the back of the seat. She opened the receiving blanket just a bit so that the baby's cheek was resting on her own blanket. Then she opened the car window so the infant wouldn't suffocate in the summer heat.

"Come on," Peter said impatiently.

"I'm afraid it's too hot in there," she murmured.

"Then move faster."

Reluctantly she got out of the car and moved around to where Peter was standing.

"Hurry up."

"All *right.*"

They pulled Bettina out and half-walked, half-dragged her up to the front door. It was chained and locked with a Yale lock. In a minute Peter had the door open and they went inside.

"Take her in there," Peter said, indicating a paneled room at the back.

Bettina stirred.

"Dammit, you forgot the masks," Peter said irritably.

"She saw the masks once, isn't that enough?" Isobel asked.

They tried to prop Bettina up in a sitting position against the wall, but she slid down until her face was resting on the filthy floor. Isobel's mouth twitched. She reached out to lift Bettina's head.

"Isobel, forget about that. Get the masks." He gave her a push in the direction of the front door. "Come on, are you crazy? Do you want her to see your face?"

He followed her out, restlessly wandered into the ruined living room while Isobel headed out to the car. Some of the windows were broken, and there was glass on the floor. A desiccated bird lay in the fireplace.

Isobel went out to the car grumbling. "She wouldn't remember. I'm sure she wouldn't." She paused to check the baby.

A minute later she came back with the two rubber Frankenstein masks Peter insisted she buy in a five-and-ten-cent-store the day before.

"Put it on," he demanded, pulling on his own mask.

Isobel hesitated.

"It's just a mask," he muttered.

"I never liked them. If I were her and I woke up to one of these, I know my heart would stop."

Peter headed toward the library.

"Where are you going?"

"Come on, we're wasting time." Peter stopped to urge her on.

"I don't know why you brought her here." Isobel shivered.

The house smelled like a crypt. There were mouse droppings all over the floor. Everything was covered with dust. In the summer heat the odor of decaying wood and mold, and some kind of dead animal, was suffocating. Huge spiderwebs filled in all the corners. An accumulation of dead flies lay in heaps under each one.

"It was your idea to lock her up so she wouldn't hurt herself," Peter said.

"I don't see why we couldn't have left her in her house. I never said we should move her."

"We couldn't leave her there. What if somebody came over and found her locked in the closet? It would be clear she hadn't locked herself in the closet. We've been over all this."

"I know, but it's creepy." Isobel shivered again. "I hate it here."

"So does everyone else; that's why it's a good place. Let's do it before she wakes up." Peter turned toward the paneled room.

"It takes a long time for them to be aware, about forty-five minutes. And about twenty-four hours to get it out of the system. Maybe we don't need anything else," Isobel mused.

"Put your mask on, Isobel," Peter said very slowly. "You know we have to use the stuff. Don't go soft on me now, or I'll use the rest on you."

"Don't threaten me. I'll do it." She put on the mask.

In the other room Bettina lay the way they had left her, her cheek against the floor. "See, I told you there was plenty of time." Isobel studied her.

"Well, take care of it, and let's get out of here," Peter said.

At the sound of their voices, Bettina stirred again.

"Shh," Isobel said. She moved over to where Bettina was lying and squatted down next to her. She brushed Bettina's hair away from her forehead and started gently stroking her face. She had forgotten how she looked with the mask on.

This time Bettina came up sobbing.

"It's all right," Isobel said softly. "It's all right." She dug a handkerchief out of her pocket and wiped the wet face.

"Christ!" Peter said in alarm. "She knows."

"No, she doesn't," Isobel said sharply. "A lot of them come out of it like this." She leaned over and crooned in Bettina's ear.

"What happened?" Bettina moaned.

"Shh," Isobel murmured to her.

"Hurry up," Peter said angrily.

"For God's sake, wait a minute. She's reliving something. Look at how she's moving. She thinks she's in labor."

"What are you doing?" Peter cried.

"Bettina, wake up," Isobel said softly. "Wake up. Open your eyes now, it's all right."

Bettina's eyelids fluttered.

"Open your eyes, Bettina. Come on."

"Are you crazy? Why are you waking her up?"

"Because if I give it to her when she's unconscious, she may not come out of it again. Do you want her crazy, or dead? Come on, Bettina. It's all right."

Tears poured out of Bettina's closed eyes, but she stopped writhing. It took her a few more minutes to open one eye.

She screamed.

Isobel touched her mask and swore. She had brought many patients back from unconsciousness, but this was the first time anyone had screamed at the sight of her. It was a stupid move getting those masks. Bettina would never have remembered them, never.

"Christ," Peter muttered. "I thought you knew what you were doing."

"What did you think would happen when she saw this face?" Isobel demanded.

"I didn't expect you to wake her up," Peter barked.

She tried to pull the mask off, but Peter moved across the room quickly and held her arm backward in a painful grip.

"Are you crazy?"

"Ow," Isobel whimpered.

"Don't try that again. Give her the shot, and let's go."

"All right. Go check the baby," Isobel said, rubbing her wrist.

"Shit," she muttered when he was gone. What a mess.

Isobel drew the vial of distilled water out of her bag. She had the syringe half-filled when she heard Peter's step behind her.

"All set," Isobel said in her nurse voice. "Just wait in the other room for a second, will you?"

"Cut the crap, Isobel," Peter said. "That's just water."

"No." Isobel looked shocked.

"It's clear. There's only water in there. Damn you."

"Calm down," Isobel said sharply. "I know what I'm doing. I had to put some water in it. If I gave it to her undiluted, there'd be a black-and-blue mark so big they'd see it in California."

"Where is it? I don't believe you." He lunged forward and grabbed her bag. The unopened vial fell out.

"Damn you. I knew it. Squirt it out," he said, indicating the water in the syringe.

Isobel flinched but didn't do as he asked. "I don't want it to be any worse," she said. "I did it for you."

"The fuck you did. Squirt it out."

Isobel shook her head with disgust, but pushed the plunger. Some of the water squirted out onto the floor. Peter handed her the vial. All this time Bettina sat there with her blond hair tangled, her face dirty and tear-stained, and her eyes half-closed.

"That's not enough," he barked when Isobel drew half of the yellowish liquid into the syringe.

"She only weighs a hundred and ten pounds," she said calmly.

"He told me all of it."

"All of it for an army. If you want to kill her, you give her the rest." She held out the syringe.

"All right, all right, do it your own way." He retreated to a safe distance.

Isobel considered the situation. She wanted to give Bettina the shot in her hip, at the top of her buttocks; but she couldn't really do it without help. She didn't want to do it in her arm in case it "told a story," bruised, or was painful. She decided the thigh was the best choice and reached for Bettina's skirt.

Bettina's eyes flickered as Isobel looked her thighs over for a good spot, squeezed a chunk of flesh above her right knee, and aimed the syringe. Bettina did not flinch as the needle plunged into her. She put her head down and was unaware a few minutes later when she was half-carried upstairs.

32

On the ride going back, Isobel sat silently with the baby on her lap. She tried not to think of Bettina Dunne locked in the walk-in closet on the second floor of that disgusting house. She looked out the window so she wouldn't have to look at Peter. She felt filthy and miserable. Her white pants were badly soiled and her matching shirt was wet. In her handbag were the remains of the disposable syringe and its wrappings, the drug vial marked G.E.F. Series II, the masks, and the distilled water. The signs of the crime were all over her, but Peter was as spotless as he had been when the afternoon began. It didn't seem fair.

"When I drop you off," Peter said as they neared Mill Valley, "I want you to burn your clothes."

"Burn my clothes?" she said sharply.

"Yes, burn them. That's what I said."

"How do you suggest I do that?" It was summer, and she had no fireplace in her apartment.

"Well, get rid of them. And the stuff in your handbag. Take each thing and put it in a different garbage can."

Isobel thought about that for a minute. "What do you mean, drop me off?"

"I'm taking you home," he said.

"Peter, I can't go home now."

"Of course you're going home. Where do you think you're going?"

"I thought I'd be going with you," she said softly. She looked at her dirty hands. She couldn't believe she had gotten her hands so dirty. It was a crime to touch a newborn with such dirty hands.

Peter shook his head. "Not tonight."

"Tonight especially. I don't want to be alone," she said.

He didn't answer. They stopped at a red light and both of them stared straight ahead, waiting for it to change. She didn't want to think he would make her stay alone now. He couldn't be so cruel as that. After everything she'd done for him.

"What about the baby?" she said finally.

"What about the baby?" he said irritably.

"What are you going to do with her?"

"Deliver her, what do you think?"

Isobel looked down at the sleeping face again. All this trouble for her. She wondered what her adoptive parents would think if they knew how this beautiful baby had come to them.

"If you take me home, who will hold the baby?" she said after a minute.

"It will be all right there on the seat for a few minutes."

"What if she cries or vomits, or falls off?" They had no car seat. It was against the law.

"Isobel, I want you to go home and get some sleep," Peter said. "You deserve it."

"I think I better come with you," she said stubbornly.

"No way."

"Why? I've come this far."

Peter's mouth thinned out into a line of solid, furious opposition. "Because I said so."

"Come on, Peter, don't turn me off now."

"You're a mess," he said, taking a quick look at her. "Look at you. You have to go home. Now forget it."

"It would make me feel better later. I want to see where they live," she argued.

"We've been all over this before," Peter said, more gently now. "It's for your own protection. If you don't know, then you can't hurt yourself or anybody else."

Isobel chewed on her lips. "Who am I going to hurt, Peter?"

He didn't answer.

"I've done a lot for you," she said slowly.

"Come on now. Cheer up. It'll all be over tomorrow. We'll celebrate."

They were nearing her building.

"All right, I'll wait in the car, then. You can leave me down the block if you want. Then I won't know which house it is." Isobel wouldn't let it go.

Peter was silent for a minute.

"I'll hold the baby. That's all. And then you can take her in. I just want to make sure she gets there all right." Isobel crossed her heart. "That's all, I promise."

"You're conscientious, I'll say that for you."

"And I won't ask any more questions, okay?"

"All right." He went through Mill Valley without slowing down and headed toward Oakwood, where there was a complex of luxury apartment buildings made of glass and concrete with little gardens dotted here and there. It took only five minutes to get there.

He stopped two streets away and parked the car.

"Should I change her?" Isobel said.

Peter shook his head. He climbed out of the car and came around to the other side, reaching for the baby.

Isobel handed her over without looking at her again. She noticed that Peter was not put off by the wet patch on the blanket, and that the curve he made with his arm was exactly the right one for a newborn. It was clear he had held babies before. Unconsciously she patted her stomach.

"Be sure to hold her head," she said, and jumped out to get the shopping bag she had taken from the baby's room and stowed in the backseat. "Can you manage both?"

"I don't need that," he said.

"You better take it. They might not have any formula."

He took the shopping bag and looked inside. "What's in here?" he asked suspiciously.

"Just hospital giveaways. I took out the personal stuff," she said.

He poked into it, saw nothing objectionable, and took it. "Now get in the car and stay there. You're a mess. I'll be back in a few minutes."

Isobel nodded. She got back in the front seat and closed the door. She had resolved not to watch him walk away, but turned her head at the last minute in spite of herself. For a second she forgot everything horrible that had happened. She was touched by the sight of Peter carrying the baby and the shopping bag full of baby things. He looked the way she imagined he would when he was a father himself.

She watched him walk away in the opposite direction from the two buildings they faced. He went through a garden and out the other side, past the entrance of the building on the opposite street. He moved quickly, without looking around.

As he strode through the garden, Isobel lost sight of him. She turned around and looked out the front window. In a few seconds an unmarked van pulled up and parked on the other side of the street. When no one got out, Isobel became uneasy. Peter had been beaten up in the park in front of her building.

She tapped her fingers on the window for a second thinking about that, then got out of the car and ran in the direction Peter had gone. She caught sight of him a block away. He was hurrying faster now, taking big strides and looking around from time to time as though afraid of being followed. He looked suddenly peculiar to her. She wondered if he had seen the van.

The next time he turned around she ducked behind the corner of a building.

When he reached the apartment house he was looking for, he stopped and waited for a minute or two, looked at his watch, and resettled the baby in his arms. Finally he went through the glass door into the building.

It was a very nice building with a fountain in front. Isobel moved closer to it. She could see Peter raise his hand and run his finger over a list of names, looking for the right button. His finger stopped on one, and he pushed it. She couldn't tell which one it was. All she knew was that it was one of the buttons on the end row.

He turned around twice, then walked into the building and disappeared into the elevator. Isobel hesitated for a second, then followed him into the building and examined the name panel. She was sure he had pushed a button in the A line. But which one? She turned and looked dejectedly into the building. The elevator was going up. The numbers of the floors flashed on the panel above: 7, 8, 9. It stopped on 9. Isobel turned back to the names.

The name beside 9A was "Hunter." She almost laughed out loud. It was a name she knew almost as well as her own, a name she'd given him herself.

33

It was seven o'clock when Laura ran across the wood floor in her bare feet and flung open the door. Peter Balkan, whom she had met exactly twice in her life, stood in the hall, disheveled and wild-looking. He was holding a small, sodden bundle. With an absence of ceremony, he handed the baby over. "Here, take it," he said.

This was not exactly how Laura had dreamed of becoming a mother. "Uh, thank you," she said.

She reached for the baby awkwardly. "Oh, she's wet." She laughed nervously.

"Come in here while I change her." She led the way.

"Where's Wendal?" Peter asked.

Laura moved through the living room into the bedroom she

had fixed up for the baby she couldn't have. The walls were pale yellow. White, frilly curtains covered the windows. The light fixture in the center of the ceiling was a merry-go-round. The white wicker changing table was covered with white terry cloth. Underneath, its shelves were piled with colorful, new, freshly washed baby clothes and newborn-size Pampers. It had all been expensive. This was a baby she had shopped for and was confident would arrive.

Peter followed her in and tried to talk over the baby's wail. "Where's Wendal?" he asked again.

"He went to the store for some formula. I bet she's hungry, poor thing." Laura started to unwrap her with trembling fingers, then stopped.

"Turn off the air conditioner, will you? It's too cold in here for such a tiny little thing."

Peter looked around for an air conditioner but didn't see one.

"On the windowsill. It's central," Laura said.

Peter found the dial and switched it off.

She waited for the room to warm up before opening the blanket. When she did and saw the baby's silken, strawberry blond hair, she sighed with relief. She had been afraid that the baby would be dark and look nothing like them. That would have been a constant reminder to Wendal. She couldn't see the color of the baby's eyes because they were squeezed tight with every wail. But she was fair enough. That was the main thing. Often they were born with darker hair that fell out at six months and grew in lighter. She hoped that would happen with—Anna. They would call her Anna.

"See what a nice place she'll live in," she said with pride.

"Would you like a drink? I'll get you one in a second." Laura peeled off the receiving blanket, finally satisfied that the room was warm enough. Under it was the tiny T-shirt Bettina had put on to replace the jumpsuit the baby had worn home from the hospital. There were two ducks embroidered on it, and some flowers, plus the letter *D*.

Laura drew her breath in sharply when she saw it. She felt cold and clammy.

Peter also paled at the sight of it. *"D for duck,"* he said quickly.

"Did you bring her from the hospital?" Laura asked.

"Yes," Peter said.

Laura accepted his answer. She stripped the shirt off and dumped it in the little hamper on one side of the changing table. The baby was now shrieking inconsolably, and she moved as fast as she could to get it dressed again. Her fingers were not as efficient as they might have been. She had never done this before, and was surprised at how unhelpful infants were. She couldn't help thinking that the baby's cry was one of disapproval. It terrified her to think that Anna might somehow know she was not her real mother and dislike her.

"Anna, Anna, Anna, I'll be your real mother," she whispered.

In a few awkward minutes, she managed to get the baby dressed in a light cotton gown with no embroidery on it. Then she wrapped her up in another receiving blanket, because the book she had been reading all week said newborns liked to be tightly bound. The baby calmed down a little, and Laura picked her up with relief.

"She's hungry," she said. "I bet you are, too. Would you like something to eat?"

"No, I—uh, I've got to go." Peter's nose was running. He swiped at it.

"Come, I'll get you a drink to celebrate. You can't imagine what a wonderful moment this is for me," Laura said.

She moved back into the living room, with Peter following

behind. "What do you drink?" she asked, feeling in control again.

Then she noticed the shopping bag for the first time. It was sitting by the door in the front entrance hall.

"What's that?"

"Oh, it's some things the hospital gives," Peter said uneasily.

Laura picked it up and put it on the table.

"Oh, look. Here's some formula." She pulled out the complimentary box from the makers of Enfamil. Two cans of formula and one four-ounce bottle complete with nipple. "Do you mind?" she asked, holding up the bottle.

"The bar is over there."

She pointed at a tray in the dining room with bottles and glasses on it and headed into the living room, where she put the baby on the sofa. Then she started pulling the rest of the things out of the bag: the tub, the powder, the baby lotion. On the very bottom, under the corner of the box of Pampers, she saw something sticking out that made her sick. Peter had stopped at the bar.

She put her hand in the bag and turned the object over. It was one of the tiny bracelets they put on the baby just after birth. She didn't want to see the name on the bracelet and have it always in her memory. And she didn't want Anna ever to know her real mother's name. But she knew it would be on the birth certificate. Unless she never looked at it, she couldn't avoid finding out what it was.

After a few seconds' struggle with herself, she turned the bracelet over and studied the name typed on it. "Bettina Dunne." She frowned. Was that the baby's name or the mother's name? Odd name, she thought.

Her lip began to tremble as she made the connection.

Dunne, the letter *D*. She was seized with jealousy, almost as if she had discovered Wendal with another woman. How could that girl be so cruel as to embroider her initial on a shirt for a baby she didn't intend to keep? It was worse than peculiar—it was mean and hurtful. Laura felt wounded, as if Anna's mother had meant to stake her claim on the baby even as she was relinquishing it.

Left propped up on the sofa, the baby began to wail again. Laura took her up in her arms and squeezed her tightly.

"She's mine, isn't she?" she asked shakily.

"Well, as soon as everything is formalized—" Peter chose a bottle. "It always takes a few weeks." He took a glass and looked around quickly to see if Laura was watching him. She wasn't, so he poured a double of scotch and swallowed half of it, shuddering as the burning liquid went down.

Laura leaned over and dumped the things quickly back into the bag, all except for the formula, which she opened for the baby. She fumbled putting the nipple on the bottle, then put it to the baby's mouth. Tears came to her eyes as the baby began to suck. Laura had never seen anything as thrilling. Suddenly, it was all worth it—the waiting, the uncertainty, the pain. Finally she had a baby of her own.

Downstairs, the buzzer rang.

Peter started.

"It's just Wendal," she said. "He always rings to let me know he's back." She wiped her eyes on the edge of the receiving blanket and thought of the bracelet and the little T-shirt with the letter *D* on it. The T-shirt seemed to indicate a degree of ambivalence that Laura thought it better Wendal never know about. The girl could change her mind and not sign the final adoption papers. Peter had warned her that the law gave mothers the protection of a two-month waiting period before an adoption was finalized. She thought of the Mary Beth Whitehead case: A couple had given her ten thousand dollars to bear their baby, and then she didn't want to give it to them.

But this was different. This was not a surrogate-mother case involving a mature woman who had already had two children and was married, however shakily. This was a fifteen-year-old girl who had no husband and no job, who had never held a baby, or changed one, or seen it smile. She would not know what she was giving up. She wouldn't change her mind.

Still, Laura didn't want Wendal to question the mixed message in the T-shirt. She'd throw it and the bracelet down the incinerator as soon as Peter was gone. Then Anna would be hers. She didn't know why she had the urge to take the baby and run. But she did. This adopting a baby was stranger and more painful than she had expected. She wanted Peter to go away. She didn't want to see him again. She thought of her own baby, gone in a flood on the bathroom floor.

"Wendal," she said, turning to the door with a brilliant welcoming smile. "Look who's here."

Wendal came across the room grinning, a paper bag from the supermarket in one arm. He put the bag down and knelt on the floor beside them.

"Oh my God," he said. "She's got red hair. I had red hair when I was born. Did I ever tell you that?"

"She's beautiful, isn't she?" Laura whispered.

"More than beautiful." He put his arm around his wife. "This is tremendous."

Peter watched them with his mouth twitching. "Well, I've got to be going," he said. "I'm glad you're pleased. It's always nice to see a baby so well placed."

Wendal stood up. "Oh, stay for a drink," he said. "Celebrate with us."

Peter held up his empty glass to show he'd already celebrated. "I think I'll leave you alone. It doesn't look to me like you need any help celebrating."

"Well, in that case, I'll be in touch with you next week," Wendal said.

"Now, wait just a minute," Peter exploded. "We made a deal. You were going to settle in cash today."

"Hey, calm down. We didn't hear from you until today. Noon, to be precise. I didn't think you expected to be ready with the papers today."

"What?" Peter yelled. "Why do you think I hurried over?"

"It's not a car deal," Wendal said. "Look, have a drink. Calm down. We'll sort it out."

"When? When will we sort it out?" Peter flushed purple. "Look here, if you think you can give me the runaround, you'll have more trouble than you dreamed possible. I need the money now."

"What's the matter, Peter? Why are you doing this?" She turned to Wendal. "Why is he talking like this? How much money is it? Can't we give it to him?"

Wendal raised his voice. "You're upsetting my wife. I won't put up with this kind of behavior."

"If you're good for the money, where is it?" Peter insisted. "Don't jerk me around."

"What money?" Laura said anxiously. "Wendal, you didn't say anything about—"

"It's not a goddamn car sale. Call me on Monday. I'll take care of it." Wendal bunched his fists.

"The hell I will. I thought you were honorable people."

"You're out of line; stop it." Wendal's face reddened.

"Isn't there some way we can get it?" Laura cried.

"It's all right, sweetheart." Wendal turned to her. "We'll take care of it." He moved to where Peter was sitting.

"Look, Peter, come on."

Peter flinched as if he expected a blow.

Wendal's mouth dropped open in surprise. "This is all getting out of hand," he said.

"All right, I'll go," Peter conceded finally. "But this is not a joke. I need the money for that baby's mother in forty-eight hours, or she's getting it back."

"Fine," Wendal agreed, and opened the door.

"What's the matter with him?" Laura whispered. "Is he crazy?"

Wendal double-locked the door. "I don't know," he said, uneasily. "He's always been kind of crude. He likes to scare people. But I'm not going to let it bother me."

He turned away from the door, shaking his head. "A helluva way to start."

"I'm scared," Laura said.

"Forget it. I'll take care of it. Let's see her." He held out his arms for the baby.

34

The house had gone completely dark by the time Bettina began to come around. If she had been awake while it was happening, she would have seen the tiny crack of light around the door frame of the closet fade bit by bit as the sun receded from the master bedroom window.

She was wearing the same flowered smock she had worn to

the hospital four nights before. Now it was streaked with dirt and blood. As the hours passed, the pressure on her bladder became more and more intense. The blood of afterbirth seeped out and soaked her. Her breasts filled with milk, and she needed to nurse. She'd had nothing to eat since breakfast. Hunger gnawed at her stomach like an animal trying to claw its way out of a box.

Pain and discomfort everywhere in her body finally brought her to the surface—disoriented and hallucinating. A pneumatic drill like the kind used for breaking up streets seemed at work on one spot in her skull, tearing it open, as a long column of tanks rumbled over her body on the way to war. All around were bodies, parts of bodies. Hands, feet, disemboweled torsos. A whole landscape of bloody remains left behind. They stank and rotted in the dirt. It was dark, but the sky was alight with rockets. The road was deeply pitted where land mines had exploded, and the screams of the injured and dying joined the whine of the bombs as they streaked to earth, splitting the ground apart.

A shroud covered Bettina's head, preventing her from breathing. She was in a plastic bag, zipped up to the top. There was no way out. She was zipped in the bag, and thrown on the ground in a place where a little hollow had been dug. A pile of dirt sat on one side, waiting to cover her up.

She writhed on the gritty floor, shoving her body around from one side of the closet to the other. She had to get out of the grave and stop her brains from leaking out of the hole in the side of her head. She could feel them getting away. Warm, wet, slimy on the floor, slithering out of her reach.

No, no.

A keening rose from deep in her throat as she struggled to get out of the bag, out of the grave. She had to get away before a bomb made a direct hit on the place where she was trapped. A lizard was holding her down. It was the size of a man, had teeth and hair. Its mouth was open.

"Ahhh." The whimper rose to a shriek, and finally she opened her eyes, terrified most by the sound of her own voice.

All was black. The black was total. There was not the slightest reflection, not a pinpoint of light anywhere. Bettina's body convulsed with terror. Nothing moved. After the war, there was nothing. The earth was destroyed, just the way her first-grade teacher always said it would be if people didn't look out for it right. Nothing was left. Nothing to be seen anywhere. Her eyes and ears were gone, burned by radiation. She couldn't see, couldn't get out. Her eyes closed, and she panicked.

Bring it back. Bring the world back. Then it began again, different from before. A rasping noise. A ghost breathing heavily. She started thrashing to get away from the new sound, which seemed to come from everywhere. Her hair whipped against her neck. It was alive. She screamed.

Her eyes opened, and there were a thousand eyes staring back. She shrank back into the corner, trembling all over. Pain grabbed at her from all sides. Cluster pain in her head, engorged breasts so tender the slightest touch was agony. She had to urinate.

Hold on. Hold on. The eyes stared. *Hold on. Don't let go.* For a long time she huddled in the corner, her back pressed tightly against the angle the two walls made. *Hold on.* Her own eyes popped out of her head and danced across the room, then hopped back in. In and out. *Catch them.*

There was a faint scratching in the ceiling over her head, but she couldn't move without her body breaking up in little pieces. *Hold on.* There were a thousand eyes watching. When she moved their teeth showed. The eyes slithered across the ceiling. They skittered down the walls. Some started dropping on her from above. Others flew, humming, screeching around her head in formation, like fighter planes. They filled her mouth, choking her.

A river flowed unexpectedly out on the floor. It was hot. Hot lava from inside of her. She let go, and thought it was a bloody volcano. It went on forever. Then it stopped.

She stood up to get away from the wet and hit her head on the shelf above. The shelf was loose and tilted over. A dead bat that had been trapped in there months ago fell on her shoulder.

The eyes turned into teeth. She could not hold on. Out of her throat came animal noises, piercing shrieks. She could not hold on. She banged her head against the door. *Let me out.* The snakes in her hair twisted around her neck and strangled her.

35

It was nine o'clock Saturday morning when Isobel stood there tight-lipped and tense as Peter struggled to open the closet door. She was not surprised when he recoiled, gagging. Her own stomach churned, and she was a nurse.

"Go away," she said sharply.

She didn't like him so much today. Even with people all around, he almost hit her yesterday when he found her in the playground, not the car. He made her spend the night alone. And he hadn't apologized since. She looked down at the hostage with distaste. She had a headache and no longer remembered why they were doing this. When she looked up Peter was gone. Just like a man.

Bettina lay with her cheek against the dirty floor. Her eyes were open, but she didn't blink or look toward the light. Her pupils were dilated and her mouth was slack. The floor was wet and her hair was matted with dried blood and dead spiders, and something else. A patch of hair—no, a bat.

Isobel shuddered and kicked it out of the way.

The hostage didn't move.

After a minute, Isobel knelt down, bringing her Frankenstein face close to Bettina's.

"I brought you something to drink," she said softly. "Want it?"

Bettina's eyes narrowed, but she showed no sign of having heard.

"It's coffee." Isobel unscrewed the top of the thermos and held it as close to Bettina's nose as it would go. Steam came out of the top. Bettina's hand clenched.

"Ordinary old coffee," Isobel said. "And not bad. I made it myself."

Bettina's eyes closed.

"Would you like to sit up?" She put the thermos down to help Bettina up.

"All right. You can stay there. I'll just have some coffee. Aren't you hungry? I bet you're hungry. I bet you'd like to go home and get those wet things off. I'm here to take you home."

Isobel poured some of the coffee into the cup that was the top of the thermos and put it down next to Bettina's nose. There were a few contusions on her forehead, but they weren't as bad as they seemed at first. As long as Bettina lay in that position, though, Isobel couldn't tell if there was any other damage. Physical damage, that is. She didn't look too good mentally.

"Well," she went on brightly, "I don't believe for a minute you're not hungry. You haven't had a thing to eat since yesterday. I have a muffin here; would you like it?"

Bettina's eyes opened and looked unblinkingly at the Frankenstein mask.

Isobel stared back through the holes. She felt like an idiot.

"Come on, we haven't got all day. You have to go home. Show me you're all right."

Bettina didn't move.

"I have a shopping bag right here with a lot of things in it. I brought them for you. You want to see what I got?"

They had stopped at Bettina's house earlier. Isobel had taken Bettina's key and gone calmly into the house, with Peter following behind. She needed a pair of underpants, a dress, and a wet towel. She was thorough in every respect, wanted to get it over with so she and Peter could get married. She had to keep that in mind. They were going to Paris and getting married.

She reached into the bag and held up a dress similar to the one Bettina was wearing. Bettina's eyes flickered for the first time. She tried to retreat into the corner and knocked the cup of coffee over with her knee.

Isobel swore, reached for one of the now-grubby Pampers to swab up the mess.

"Christ, Bettina, don't you want to go home? You can't go home like that," she said severely, as if Bettina might really care how she looked.

"Now come on. I'm going to clean you up."

Bettina shrank back farther into the corner. "Bees, bees, bees," she said.

Isobel advanced into the closet on her knees.

"Come on," she crooned. "Be reasonable. Nobody wants to hurt you. All I want to do is get you dressed so you can go home."

Bettina lifted her feet when Isobel got close and kicked her sharply in the stomach.

Isobel gasped and fell backward.

"You bitch!" She sat on the floor for a minute trying to catch her breath. "I was just trying to help you."

Bettina's face, which had been empty and slack, pulled together for a second. She moved forward, crawling on her stomach, and reached out for Isobel's mask.

Isobel reared back, freeing both of her hands. Without even knowing that she was going to do it, she reached out and slapped Bettina hard in the face. Once, twice, three times. Bettina's head rocked to the side with the blows, and the sound echoed in the empty room.

She raised her hands to strike back. Isobel grabbed one arm and twisted it until Bettina yelped in pain. Both of her cheeks were red and swollen. Her eyes were wild. She looked like an animal that could kill.

"Listen to me, Bettina. I'm going to change your clothes. You can't go home like this. Do you hear me? If you try anything, I swear I'll beat you bloody. I'll maim you. I'll pump you so full of shit, last night will look like paradise in comparison."

Isobel moved closer. Her hand stung from the slaps, but she was beyond caring about that now.

She raised her hand to strike again.

"What the hell is going on here?" Peter's voice hit her like a hammer. Isobel hadn't heard him come in.

"What are you doing? Are you crazy?" He looked at them with disgust. There was a blister on one side of Bettina's face that looked like the shape of a hand.

Isobel's expression changed instantly. "Peter, she kicked me," she said contritely. "I had to or she might have—"

"Oh, Christ. Can't I trust you to do anything?" he said furiously. "Everything you touch, you mess up."

Isobel got up quickly to go to him, but he pushed her away.

"You're a mess. You stink."

"Oh, Peter!" she cried.

Bettina looked from one of them to the other.

"Idiot," Peter said, sneering.

"Idiot?" Isobel's voice rose to a shriek. "Don't you dare call me that. You couldn't handle this in a million years. You haven't a clue what to do."

"Okay, okay." Peter drew her out into the upstairs hall. "Sweetheart," he said softly. "Do you remember what we're here to do? We've got to take her home, remember?"

"Yes, but she—"

"I don't care what she did. We've got to get rid of her. Just get her into the car, that's all."

"But Peter. She's—"

"We'll just put her in the car, Isobel," he said sharply.

They moved a few steps down the hall, talking as they went.

The door of the closet was open. Bettina reached out her hand and touched the dress with the daisies on it. A fly buzzed around her head. Slowly she pulled herself to her feet.

A few seconds later she was staggering toward the bedroom door, hugging the wall as she went.

"Christ," Peter whispered, "look at that."

Bettina was picking up each foot carefully and putting it down, moving from side to side jerkily as she slowly inched along the wall.

"Go get all the things in the closet, and let's get out of here," Peter said softly. "I'll take care of this."

He moved toward Bettina and took her arm. "You've been very sick, Bettina," he said. "But you're much better now."

Bettina let him take her arm and move her toward the stairs.

He talked all the way to the front door, telling her how sick she had been and asking her questions like what her name was. She didn't answer.

They got to the front door. Bettina blinked in the sunlight. Isobel came down the stairs behind them with the bag.

"Did you wipe off the doorknobs?" Peter demanded.

"Yes," Isobel said wearily.

"Did you take everything?"

"Yes." Isobel looked at Bettina. "What about the blindfold?"

"I don't think it's necessary," Peter said. "Put her in the back, will you?"

Bettina slumped against the car door as they drove her home. Peter had put on a big hat that came down over his hair and ears. He had a fake mustache and dark glasses. Isobel wore a huge red wig and sunglasses that covered most of her face. Bettina didn't seem to register anything, and she didn't show any signs of recognition when they reached her house.

36

Tom left Otto in Manhattan and drove out to New Jersey, feeling fine in the big limousine Axam had sent to the airport for him. He liked the idea of picking up his wife and new baby in style, and pulled up at the entrance of Chester Memorial Hospital with great pride. He told the driver he'd be about a half an hour and went inside.

Two minutes later he charged back through the double doors and got back in the car.

"Is there a problem, sir?" the driver asked.

"Uh, no. They just left yesterday, that's all."

Shit. He sat back and tried to get control of his anger at Bettina. He didn't want to be furious when he first saw her, but he was. He'd specifically told her to wait for him. "Why couldn't she wait for me?" he muttered to himself as they headed out into the country.

He had wanted to pick her up at the hospital. He had a vision of himself looking through the window of the nursery and seeing his redheaded daughter there for the first time. He wanted to be the one to bring them home, especially since he hadn't been the one to take them there.

"I'm being childish," he told himself.

It was four o'clock in the afternoon. He had left the hospital in Zurich at seven, had been on an airplane for nine hours. It was ten o'clock at night for him, on his first day out of a hospital since his accident. He was exhausted. And now he was disappointed. All he had wanted was to show up in his great fancy limousine and take his wife home. He was hurt and couldn't find any way to feel all right about it.

He kept changing his position on the black leather seat, trying to get comfortable. She was probably making bread or cleaning the house. So unnecessary. Why couldn't she let him bring her home, just that one little thing? He shook his head, feeling deprived. He shook his head at the waste, too. The car had a refrigerator with cans of soda in it, and a television set. If Bettina wasn't standing downstairs when he drove in, she wouldn't even see it.

"Here. Turn here," Tom told the driver.

They made a right turn and headed down Orchard. Suddenly Tom leaned forward with excitement. Everything was so green. Already there were fully formed ears on the corn in the fields around their house. Must be early corn, he thought. Very early corn. It was only the second of July. His spirits lifted in spite of himself. He had dreamed of this homecoming. And it did feel like home, as if he and Bettina had been living down this country road for years. They had a baby girl. He couldn't get used to the idea.

The mailbox appeared suddenly as the road dipped: 375. They hadn't gotten around to buying a new one yet. This one was black and rusted around the edges, listed to one side like a sinking ship. The numbers had been painted in white, though, and were clearly visible. The driver made the turn.

Tom gaped at the house and lawn. Once overgrown and weedy, the lawn was now neat and amazingly even. A few months ago, the windows on the first floor had been almost completely hidden by tree-sized bushes. The tiny shrubs they'd put in to replace them looked huge now. Bettina had also reclaimed the kidney-shaped rose garden from the wild and filled it with several dozen rosebushes of various sizes and colors. Everything was doing well.

But it was odd. The place looked deserted. All the windows were closed. Nothing moved anywhere. On all the other occasions when Tom returned home, the house was always very much alive. Even outside, he could smell Bettina's cooking, hear the music she was listening to on the radio. She always left her car in the driveway. He was the one who had to put it away at night. Now there was no sign of the car, no music coming from an open window, no tantalizing aromas.

He signed the voucher and got out without waiting for the chauffeur to open the door for him. He would have forgotten his luggage if it hadn't been unloaded for him. It was peculiar. He couldn't figure it out. Maybe the hospital had made a mistake, and Bettina was still there, after all. He almost called the driver back, but decided he'd go to the hospital in his own car if he had to. He picked up his bags and headed for the front door. Still no sign of life. The bandage on his head itched terribly all the time now. He felt like pulling it off.

The front door was unlocked. Tom went into the hall. The air was heavier than the hottest summer afternoon could account for. Everything was wrong. He could feel a vibration, as if an earthquake was about to open up the ground under his feet.

"Bettina?" he called out. The door was open. She had to be there.

No answer. He went into the kitchen, calling her name. It was empty. He opened the door to the hall. It was then that he heard the sound. A kind of grunting and panting. He stopped and listened.

"Uuh, uuh."

It was upstairs. Something panting, too. It sounded like a large dog in summer. They didn't have a dog, or any other animal. He took the stairs two at a time. His head pounded with the exertion. His leg muscles trembled, and sweat trickled down both sides of his face, down his forehead into his eyes.

He had a feeling the baby's room was empty, could not have said why. Maybe the stillness. He headed straight for his and Bettina's room, which lay in profound darkness. There the air was fetid, as well as still. The smell was like that of an animal living in a cave. Old urine and blood mixed with other odors he couldn't define. The skin prickled on the back of his neck.

Since his accident, he sometimes had double vision, which he had been afraid to tell anyone about. More often than he liked to admit to himself, he saw two of everything. There were two of everything now. He wiped the sweat out of his eyes. All he could see were a lot of vague shapes shrouded in shadow, more than there should have been.

The grunting and panting came from a dark and stinking corner near the bathroom. There were pillows on the floor, suitcases. Bettina's possessions were scattered everywhere. He stumbled over a pile of twisted-up, bloody nightgowns. Now there was another sound in the room as he plunged toward the light switch. It was himself, crying.

The light blinded him after the dark. He tilted his head to one side to bring his vision into focus, and then he screamed. Bettina was crouched on the armchair, like a large monkey. Her forehead was a mass of ugly black-and-blue marks. One of her cheeks was badly bruised and swollen. She was wearing a torn maternity dress that was covered with dark spots and dirt. The bedspread was on the floor, and there was dried blood all over the sheets.

"Close the door. Close the door," she shouted at him. "Get out, get out. Uuh, uuh, it's coming."

"Bettina." It was a cry. It was a moan. He was rooted to the spot. He couldn't move. Her blond hair was matted and dirty. He could hardly recognize her. She was worse than any crazy lady they had ever seen on the street in New York. She was something out of hell.

"Uuh, uuh."

"Oh, God. What happened?" He was afraid to go near her. He was *afraid*. His heart beat so hard against his chest, he thought he was having a heart attack. Pain everywhere—in his head behind his eyes, in his legs that didn't want to hold him up. His wife smelled like a swamp, did not seem to know him.

"Get out, get out, it's coming," she screamed.

"What happened? What happened?" He couldn't stop himself from repeating. "What's coming?"

"Ahh," she cried. "Get out, get out."

"Oh, shit." Tears mingled with sweat coursed down his face. What was going on? What happened?

"Owwwww." She held her head.

"What should I do?" he muttered.

Her eyes were wild and unfocused.

"Where's the baby? What happened?" Shit, why was he asking? She couldn't answer.

"He's in the coffin," she said suddenly, and started hitting herself and pulling at her hair.

"No, no." Tom moved quickly across the room. "Don't." He reached out for her hands, touched her hair, and a dead fly fell out into his hand. He reeled back.

She screamed. "Don't. Tom, don't."

"Okay. I won't." He squatted down on the floor in front of her, weeping with her.

"Don't hurt the baby. Don't touch him. He's dead. Bad girl, Tom."

"Oh, God. You're not a bad girl, Bettina," he said. "Tell me what happened. Can you tell me?"

"Tom. Don't come back."

"I came back," he said.

"Too late. They took him away in a coffin. I couldn't stop them."

She wept uncontrollably, sitting on her heels on the chair and hitting herself.

"Shh, stop it," Tom said. Oh, shit. He didn't know what to do, couldn't seem to think straight. "I think we need some help here," he said to himself.

"I'm going to get some help, that's what I'm going to do."

He stood up with his head cocked to the right. It must be the eye on the side of the injury that was damaged, he figured. If he tilted his head to the right so his ear was almost resting on his shoulder, he could focus.

"Bettina, you had a girl." Didn't she have a girl? There wasn't any boy in a coffin, was there? *Was there?* She was out of it, in shock or something.

She grabbed his hand. "Baby, baby." Her eyes were wild, darted back and forth. She held on, wouldn't let go.

"Jesus." It was like seeing his life end. He pried her loose and moved away. She stayed where she was, keening loudly. Oh, shit.

He went into the baby's room, terrified of what he might find. But there was nothing there. A blanket had been rolled up against the bumper in the crib, and there was a cloth diaper laid out on the sheet. Nothing else. He didn't know what to make of that. One tiny, soiled jumpsuit in the hamper. One wet diaper in the pail. Tom scratched his head where the stitches itched and went back to the bedroom. Bettina hadn't moved.

His inclination was to clean up, pick up the litter on the floor, put Bettina in the shower, and get rid of the bloody sheets. The stains on the sheets were particularly terrifying, and so was the way she smelled. But he had no idea what was wrong with her, and was afraid to touch anything. Maybe there were clues in the mess that could tell what had happened. Where was the baby?

He went downstairs. He found a few crumbs on the table. One clean cup and saucer on the counter. One tea bag in the garbage. He picked up the phone in the kitchen, almost expecting the line to be dead. It wasn't. He dialed 911.

"Nine-one-one emergency," a pleasant female voice said.

"Ah." His voice cracked. "This is Thomas Dunne at Three seventy-five Orchard."

"Yes, what's the problem?"

"I just returned from a business trip. Um." He didn't know how to report this. What did one say? He felt like breaking down like one of those children who shot a brother or sister with a gun left in a drawer that wasn't supposed to be loaded, and then had to call 911 and explain it. Help! He was just away on a business trip, and the gun went off.

"Yes, is there a problem?"

Nice voice on the other end of the line.

Tom swallowed. "My wife has been—um—assaulted, and our baby is missing."

"Would you spell your name, please?"

"*D-u-n-n-e.*"

"And the address, Mr. Dunne."

"Three seventy-five Orchard." Tom tried to calm down.

"Do you need medical assistance?"

"Ah." Tom hesitated. "I don't know. Yes," he said quickly, "I'll call her doctor."

"If she needs medical assistance, I'll have to send an ambulance."

"All right, yes, send an ambulance." Send it right away. Send a doctor, and a forensic lab. Send everything.

"Would you spell your name and address for me?"

"I just told you."

"It's routine. We need to be sure of your location."

"Please hurry," Tom said. "My wife is hurt."

"Your name and address and telephone number; it's important."

Tom repeated the information. He had to look down at the number on the phone for the phone number. He had forgotten it.

"All right, Mr. Dunne. Hold on. We'll have someone on the way in a few minutes."

"Thank you," Tom said. He figured fifteen minutes. Maybe a half an hour. He didn't want to think about what had happened to Bettina. There was a dead fly in her hair. It occurred to him that something might have happened in the barn. He didn't have the energy to go and look. Why would she go to the barn? Maybe she heard a noise. Maybe she was bitten by a rabid animal. Or a snake or something.

The possibilities whirled around in his head. But she never went into the barn. It was dark in there. He got up. The baby had to be somewhere. He went slowly to the back door, opened it. The land was fragrant with all the smells of summer. A pair of Baltimore orioles were busy at the bird feeder. Tom walked slowly toward the barn. When he got there he found that the double doors were padlocked, just the way he'd left them. They didn't use it, had planned to take it down someday. They had no use for it. His head throbbed. He couldn't remember the number of the combination. She wouldn't have gone in there.

He turned around and walked slowly back to the house. Bettina had once told him a story about a woman and her husband who murdered the couple next door so they could take their newborn baby. In Ohio, or Indiana, someplace like that. It had taken a long time for them to be caught. A noise made him look up at their bedroom window, but he couldn't see a thing.

37

O ver the radio the dispatcher told Deputy Sheriff John Cusick to go out to 375 Orchard on a "Six-zero-one."

"Would you repeat that, please?" Cusick asked.

"Six-zero-one," the dispatcher repeated.

"Well, what the hell is that, Caralee?" Cusick asked, scratching his mustache. "You make that up?"

"Possible assault, possible abduction, B and E. Ambulance on the way."

"Okay." He put his foot down on the accelerator; always liked to be there first.

Ten minutes later he pulled in the drive at 375 Orchard. There was no car outside and everything was quiet. He hoped this was a good sign. He had been looking forward to going home in an hour, and still wanted to make it. He turned off the engine and got out of the car. Nothing looked out of the ordinary. He paused for a second to listen for trouble. Sometimes he heard it screaming out at him long before he pushed a doorbell or pulled up to a sidewalk. Here there was nothing. He heard some birds twittering in the trees. That was all. It was hot. He walked around the car and headed up the walk.

Maybe it was just a crank call. It happened more in summer. He rang the doorbell, thinking it over. John Cusick was thirty-one years old, had been in the sheriff's office for six years, and was pretty sure he'd seen about everything. He had been on his own in the car for several years and liked it that way. He had scraped up bloody hit-and-run victims from quiet suburban streets, chased drunk drivers down 41 through red lights with his siren howling. He had been first on the scene of more than one homicide, even a double homicide. He had seen what a Mafia hit looked like after it had been stashed away for a while; had used his gun but never killed anyone. He was a married man with a two-year-old son he worshipped and wanted to get home to. He was tall and slim, had dark brown hair and a dark, bushy mustache, and wore black reflector sunglasses no matter what the season.

The door opened, and Cusick's heart sank. The man in front of him didn't look good. His blue oxford-cloth shirt, open at the neck, was badly wrinkled and soaked with sweat. His khaki pants looked like they'd been slept in. His shoes had blades of grass on them and some clumps of wet brown earth around the soles, as if he'd been hiking recently. And he had a medical dressing on his head that covered a lot of forehead and much of his ginger hair. His blue eyes were bloodshot, and his face, except for the boyish freckles, was peculiarly sallow. Like the blood had gone out of a tan. He looked the way Tarzan might, if he had a bad case of malaria.

Well, we have a head injury here for starters, Cusick thought.

"Good afternoon," he said, nodding. "I'm Deputy Sheriff Cusick. What seems to be the problem?"

"Tom Dunne," Tom said. He cocked his head to one side in an attempt to reduce the four black mirrors, two bristling brown mustaches, and many pale, unsmiling lips he saw into the correct number of features for one face. He stood back so the officer could come in.

Cusick stepped through the door and looked around the hall. Everything had a new coat of paint on it. The floors were polished to a high shine and had no marks on them. There were no greasy fingerprints on the woodwork. There was no sign the lock on the front door had been tampered with. The house hadn't been lived in for long.

That much was clear.

"What happened to you?" he asked.

Tom cocked his head even farther, squinting to bring the policeman into focus. He looked like a traffic cop. State Police or something. Good for handing out tickets. Sheriffs on TV were always the ones who didn't know what they were doing. Bungled everything.

"Um. I'm not sure where to start. My wife had a baby." Tom swallowed. "The baby is missing and she's—she's . . . I don't know what to call it."

"Where is she?" Cusick asked.

Tom sniffed. "Upstairs."

"I see." Deputy Sheriff Cusick cocked his head the way Tom's head was cocked. He took out his notebook.

"It looks like you've sustained a head injury." Cusick touched his own head.

"Oh, yeah. I had an accident in Adam Adar." Tom lifted his hand to the bandage. "It's nothing. Maybe we better go upstairs."

"Where's that?" Cusick asked suspiciously.

"Right over there." Tom pointed at the stairs.

"No, Adam—that place you said."

"Oh, it's in the Middle East. I'm with Axam Oil. I've been hospitalized in Europe." Tom spoke impatiently.

"I see."

"I just got back today. Could we go upstairs? I'm worried about my wife." He swayed a little and caught the wall.

Cusick reached out a hand. "You look like maybe you should sit down." Cusick indicated the living room.

Tom shook his head.

"Could you please come and take a look at my wife? She's the one who's been injured," he pleaded. "We can talk later."

"Sure, you want to show me where she is?" Cusick asked.

"This way." Tom took the stairs slowly, hanging on to the rail. He raised one foot and then the other, very slowly. "Oh, God." The odor assaulted them first.

"I don't know, I don't know." He tried to explain. "She was fine when I left. She was fine when I talked to her two days ago. I don't know what could have happened. My wife is— beautiful, healthy."

They stopped at the door and looked in. Bettina was now on her knees on the chair. Her tangled hair had fallen forward onto her face. Her chin was on her chest and she was completely quiet.

Cusick followed Tom into the room and stopped just inside the doorway. He took note of everything—the mess, the dried blood smeared on the sheets, on the woman's dress, on the chair, the smell of feces and vomit. He hadn't ever seen anything like this before. He took off his glasses.

"Mrs. Dunne?" he said softly.

Bettina raised her head.

He saw the bruises. He moved forward a few steps. "It looks like you've had a bad time out here."

Bettina started shaking her head. Her lips moved but no sound came out. Tom crossed the room and held his hands out to her. She pushed him away.

"Oh, God. What happened to you?" he cried. "Tell us what happened, please."

She shook her head.

Well, she's out of it, Cusick thought. Where the hell was the ambulance? Caralee said they were sending an ambulance. There was nothing he could do. This was one for the head-shrinkers.

He turned toward the door. "I'm just going to use the phone downstairs."

"It's in the kitchen; I'll show you."

"No, no, no." Bettina screamed. She started to cry again. "No, no, no. Bad girl, can't help it."

"Oh, God, Bettina, don't cry. Just stay here for a minute, I'll be right back."

"Don't open the door," she cried. "Don't ever do it. Don't. I mean it. He's out there."

"Who?" Tom said wildly. "Who's out there?"

"Frankenstein. Red eyes." She repeated it over and over.

"I have a concussion," Tom said softly. "That's what happens when you hit your head very hard."

"No, no, no." She rocked back and forth.

"I know," he muttered. "I look terrible. I'll be back in a minute."

He followed the sheriff down the stairs.

"Oh, God. What happened? What do you think happened?" He was crying. "I don't understand." Tom suppressed a sob.

Cusick didn't have any idea. "Which way is the kitchen?"

"Through there."

A shriek came from upstairs. Tom turned around and went back. Cusick went into the kitchen. He was just hanging up the phone when Tom came in shakily. "I don't understand. I just don't understand this."

"They're on their way. Do you mind if I ask you a few questions while we're waiting?"

"I don't want to leave her up there."

"We can talk in the upstairs hall," Cusick suggested. "Can you make it back there?"

Tom didn't answer. He headed back upstairs.

"You say your wife had a baby?" Cusick asked his back. He had his notebook and pen out.

Tom prickled. "I *know* my wife had a baby," he said angrily. "What do you do in the case of abduction?"

"Well, we don't know it's an abduction," Cusick pointed out. They stopped at the top of the stairs. He licked the end of the pen, an old habit from grammar school.

"The baby's not here, is it?" Tom said fiercely.

He looked in the room. Bettina was sitting in the same chair, shaking her head back and forth, talking to herself. The men stood in the hall.

"She may have been feeling bad and given it to a relative, or a baby-sitter."

"No way," Tom said. "She wouldn't do that."

"Well, there are other possibilities." Cusick looked at Tom, his pen poised.

Tom stared back. "Like what?"

"Mr. Dunne, what hospital did your wife deliver in?"

"Chester Memorial."

"That's good. We'll be going there. It'll save me a call."

"A call?" Tom said dumbly.

"To confirm the birth. Was it a boy or a girl—the child in question?"

"A girl," Tom said, biting his lips. "What are you going to do?"

"A girl." Cusick made a note, licked his pen again. "Jesus."

There was a bench in the hall. Tom held on to it.

"What do you do in a case like this?" he asked.

"A case like what? We don't know what kind of case it is. Why don't you sit down."

Tom looked in the room. No change in Bettina. He sat down.

"If it's a—kidnapping." Tom coughed on the word.

"If it's a kidnapping, then you'll have some kind of communication. Have you had one?"

"I just got here. A theft then—an abduction. Whatever you want to call it, somebody took my baby. Jesus. Can't we get some people over here?" Tom's voice rose.

"They're coming."

"What do you do when someone disappears?"

"It depends. If it's a missing person, we file a report. Punch it into the computer with a recent photo. It goes into a national network."

"She's not a missing person. Somebody took our baby.

Jesus. We don't have a picture of her. She doesn't even have a name. She's less than a week old." Tom broke down.

"You want some water or something?"

"No, I want some help."

"We're doing the best we can." Cusick drew a question mark under *girl*. "Now, what can you tell me about your wife? Does she have any history of depression, mental illness? Has she ever been hospitalized for either of the above? Has she ever taken any medication for said depression or mental illness?"

"No," Tom said vehemently. "She's perfectly sane." He looked at the sheriff standing there with the notebook and choked on a laugh because she certainly didn't look sane.

Cusick made no sign that he might have an opinion one way or another.

"What was her state of mind after the birth? I don't suppose you can tell me that. You said you weren't here, is that right?" Cusick shifted his weight from one leg to the other.

"I spoke to her. She was thrilled," Tom said. "She was ecstatic. What are you implying?"

"She was alone, I take it," Cusick went on, unperturbed.

"For one day. She knew I was coming home today. What are you getting at?"

"I'm not *getting* at anything," Cusick responded calmly. From the distance he heard the hew-haw of the ambulance. "These are routine questions. We ask a lot of them; it's our job." It was the other guy's problem when he couldn't answer them.

"Better go downstairs," Cusick said. There was a window opposite the top of the stairs. Through it he could see the ambulance careen down the drive.

38

There was a brief lull in ER between an asthma attack, a bee bite, a bad firecracker accident, and a broken leg. Helen Morgenwroth, head nurse in Emergency, was making an entry in the computer at the front desk when Cusick strode in. She finished quickly because of the noise and got up.

"What do we have here?" she asked, moving quickly toward the shrieking woman, tightly wrapped in blankets, being wheeled in by two paramedics.

"That's for you to tell me," he said.

"Nice," she said. "Name?"

"Bettina Dunne." Tom moved forward.

She turned her head to look at him. "What about you?"

"I'm her husband."

"Take her in there," she directed the paramedics, indicating a private room. She looked back at Tom.

"Do you need medical assistance, too?"

"Yes. I mean no."

"Which is it?"

"My wife does. I'd like to be with her."

"You'll have to wait in there." She pointed to the waiting room. "We'll let you know."

She pulled a chart and went into the examining room, where the paramedics were beginning to unstrap Bettina.

"Oh, my. Looks like we've had a nasty bump here," she remarked when she saw Bettina's head.

Bettina was twitching and weeping uncontrollably. Helen went out to get another nurse, someone big.

"It's okay, honey; you're all right," she said when she came back in with Alice.

Four of them started unwrapping the blankets.

"No, no, no, no," Bettina cried. "No. Don't touch. Oh, God. No."

"Bad trip and a half, it looks like," Alice said, wrinkling her nose. "Overdose?"

"She's pretty much out of it," one of the paramedics said. "Ready?"

Four sets of hands moved her to the bed.

"Poor thing. We'll fix you up," Helen promised. "Thanks," she said to the departing paramedics.

"Come on, calm down. We're here to help."

Bettina quieted a little as two sets of strong hands rearranged her on the clean sheets. Helen and Alice, who figured they were used to a lot worse, unwrapped her and then covered her again with a white cotton blanket.

"Does that hurt a lot?" Helen soaked a large gauze pad and dabbed at the bruises on Bettina's head. "Doesn't look too bad."

"No, no, no!" Bettina winced and raised her hands.

Alice moved in quickly to restrain her.

"Don't touch," Bettina cried. "Don't touch me."

"We're just cleaning you up, that's all." Alice was a big, unflappable girl, the seventh child in her family. She had a soothing voice.

"The doctor can't see you like this. Look at your hair. I can't even tell what color it is."

The two women moved Bettina around as if she were a large doll, then nodded. "That'll do it for now."

"I'll go get him. You all right?" Helen asked over her shoulder.

"Sure, we're fine," Alice said. "Aren't we, honey?"

Bettina held her head to stop it from shaking. "Oh, no. Oh, no."

Helen went off in search of Dr. Krughauser. She found him explaining to a worried woman, curtained off in ambulatory, that all she had was a very bad case of cystitis, and yes, it hurt a lot; but she did not need to be admitted. No, not even if her insurance would pay for it and she needed a rest from her family.

"Dr. Krughauser, would you take a look at this before I prep her?" Helen said as soon as she could get a word in.

"Here, you can call me if you need to." Dr. Krughauser gave the woman his card and moved out of the area.

He fell into step beside Helen.

Krughauser was a regular in the Emergency Room. In fact, emergency medicine was his specialty. He moonlighted in the Chester hospital on weekends; and when he took vacations in the summer, he often worked for a few weeks at a time at some resort area hospital or another for a change of pace.

"What do you have?" he asked.

"I'm not sure. Bad trip, maybe. Her husband and someone from the sheriff's office are in the waiting room. She was brought in an ambulance. She has some contusions on her head. There's no sign of a fracture."

They walked quickly down the hall. "I don't think her head is injured. She's a mess, though. I'd like to prep her for you."

"She in here?"

"Yes," Helen said, and opened the door.

Dr. Krughauser nodded to the patient. "I'm Dr.

Krughauser.'' He looked briefly at her head and her eyes. Her pupils were dilated and she was too agitated to sit still. "We'll get you fixed up in a jiffy.''

He lifted the cotton blanket and saw the maternity dress. He recognized it. Someone he knew had a dress just like it. "Are you pregnant?'' he asked.

Bettina bit her lip.

"Can you hear me?'' he asked gently. He had learned to ask this question after he had spent some time trying to get answers from a young girl who turned out to be stone deaf and couldn't respond to anything he said.

Bettina nodded.

"Do you understand what I'm asking you?'' He turned to Helen. "What's her name?''

Helen looked at the form on the clipboard. "Bettina Dunne,'' she read out.

"I lost it,'' Bettina screamed suddenly. "I had it, but I lost it.'' She started trembling all over.

"Maybe she had a miscarriage,'' Dr. Krughauser speculated. "Why don't you go ahead and prep her.''

"Okeydokey,'' Alice said cheerfully.

The two nurses did the whole thing. They washed Bettina from her hair to her feet. She did not stop muttering and talking and crying the whole time. She muttered about the blood on her dress. She muttered about the dark, about nurses, gold shoes, and spiders. Everything smelled bad. She wanted to be washed again, did not want the soap removed. She muttered on and on about the baby in the coffin.

"Uh-huh,'' Helen said.

"Frankenstein gave me a shot, a shot, a shot.''

"Uh-huh.''

"Too tight.'' She squeezed her eyes shut. "Can't breathe.''

They were tying her into a pink hospital gown.

"Look, it's loose. It's not tight. It's not even touching you." Helen demonstrated how loose it was.

"Looks like she's had a baby."

The two women didn't have to be experienced nurses to know a nursing mother when they saw one. Bettina's breasts were leaking milk, and were so tender she winced at every touch. The muscles in her abdomen were stretched, her stomach was soft and mushy.

"Let me see if she's got a chart here."

A few minutes later Helen had confirmed the birth of a healthy girl to Bettina Dunne earlier in the week and her checking out of the hospital—surprise, only the day before. A whole lot of things must have gone very wrong.

She told Dr. Krughauser what she'd found out. He immediately called Dr. Street, whose service said he was away for the weekend. Then he put in a call to Aaron Simon, who had been in the hospital earlier. But Dr. Simon did not respond to the page.

39

Ayub Yahya responded to the page. "Yes, yes. I am coming. No problem, I am here."

He was the temporary psychiatric resident, a former urologist from Pakistan who had come highly recommended from another Jersey inpatient facility. He was a small, eager man in his early forties, halfway through a six-week stint at Chester Memorial.

He hurricd to Bettina's room in ER to interview the patient in order to diagnose her mental state.

"Hello. I'm Dr. Yahya," he said. He frowned at the contusions on her forehead and the dilated blue eyes.

Bettina frowned back. She had been there for three hours and had not yet been given any food or medication.

He made a note that the patient was hostile.

"I can see you're having a bad time. You were brought in in an ambulance," he said in a neutral, heavily accented voice that was hard for many people to understand.

Bettina didn't respond.

"I'm Dr. Yahya. I didn't catch your name."

"Dunne." Bettina started crying again.

"No, we're not done. We just started. Can you tell me your name?"

Bettina shook her head.

"Uh-huh." He checked her chart. "Ah, Battina. Is that your name?"

Bettina shuddered. "Dark."

"I can see you're very distressed. But we have plenty of light here." He wondered if she meant his skin, which was quite dark. He worried about his skin color. There was a lot of prejudice in this country; he had to watch for it all the time. He kept his face neutral while he waited for her answer.

Bettina twisted the corner of the blanket around her hands, and her breathing quickened.

"Okee. We do some things to help find out what's bothering you. Who's President of United States?" he asked. No answer from the patient. He made some quick notes in his notebook.

Bettina hiccuped. "I can't breathe. My head hurts." She shut her eyes. "Buzz."

"Battina, do you remember who your President is?"

"Frankenstein."

"Are you sure your President is Frankenstein?"

"Bees."

"Um, what year is it?"

She waved her hand as if at a swarm of bees. He backed away in case she was violent.

"Who is the governor?" he persisted.

"Frankenstein."

He backed away a few more feet.

"Do you know what state we're in?"

"Upset," she muttered.

"I mean, New York, Massachusetts. That kind of state."

She shook her head. "Bad. My breasts—my head. Hurts."

Dr. Yahya nodded and made more notes on his pad.

"Can you tell me why a rolling stone gathers no moss?"

"What?"

"What it means."

"My baby," she wailed. "I want my baby." Tears coursed down her face. "I need an aspirin. I can't think." Bettina growled.

He nodded. He thought she needed a lot more than an aspirin. He made a note that she was aware she couldn't think.

"What would you do if you were in a house that was on fire?" he asked calmly.

"Bloody. All bloody." She shook her head and growled some more.

Dr. Yahya looked at his list. He was testing her mental status, her fund of knowledge, the degree of her contact with reality. He concluded from the animal noises she was making that her resistance was great. She had a preoccupation with blood, which meant she might be violent. Might have been violent. Had violent tendencies, anyway. He didn't know what to make of her repeated references to Frankenstein whenever he tried to get her to answer a question about a person.

"I'm going to show you three objects, and then I'm going to take them away and ask you to tell me what they are and in what order I showed them to you," he said after a minute.

Bettina stared as Dr. Yahya took a pen, a feather, and a toothbrush out of his pocket one at a time and held them up.

Her eyes went from one to the other as if they made no sense. She started to cry and held up her arms for him to stop. He called in a guard, in the form of a huge male nurse, to restrain her if she got any further out of hand, then went on with his interview.

Many questions later, as she became more hysterical, disorganized, and incoherent, he concluded that she was acutely psychotic, hostile, fearful, full of rage, and excessively agitated.

He went out to the waiting room to talk to the husband about admitting her.

"I'm afraid your wife is a very sick woman," he said, looking Tom over.

"What's wrong with her?" Tom asked.

"She's acutely psychotic. She is out of touch with reality." He shrugged elaborately. "Angry, paranoid."

"But why? What caused it?" Tom shook his head incredulously.

"This I cannot tell you. Has she ever had a psychotic episode before?"

"No, she's the most normal person I know. Something happened to her. I want to see her," Tom demanded.

"Well, you can't see her. We have to admit her. That's the first step. It will take some time to see what's what," Dr. Yahya said firmly.

"I have to see her. She's my wife. You can't take her away just like that. I want to see her. I want to know what you're doing with her."

"This is a very sick woman. We have to get her stabilized. You'll see her then."

"When will that be?"

"I can only tell you what we have to do. I can't predict how long it will take. Patience is important in cases like this."

Tom cocked his head to one side in an effort to get the doctor in focus. There were two of him. Round, plump, and rather vacant. The doctor also cocked his head. The husband seemed almost as hysterical as the wife. Dr. Yahya wondered if Tom had something to hide, because he didn't seem to want his wife to receive the care she needed. Maybe he was afraid she'd say something he didn't want her to say. Dr. Yahya took a minute or two to study the stitches in Tom's forehead. Both persons in this couple seemed to have head injuries. It looked like some sort of domestic-violence case. Nasty.

"I want to know what happened to my baby and my wife," Tom was insisting.

Dr. Yahya nodded. So did he. So did the police, he understood. Everybody wanted to know. It was a very serious matter.

"Maybe you can say what happened to her," he suggested.

"How can I? I wasn't here."

"I see," Dr. Yahya said. It was like that. Well, he was certainly not going to argue about that. He turned away.

"I want to go with her," Tom said.

Ayub nodded. Sure he did. But he wasn't going to. "There are no visitors on the eighth floor," he said.

"What?" Tom cried.

"We find it's better for the patients that way. Better for you, too," Dr. Yahya added.

"I need to talk to her," Tom pleaded.

"A social worker will get in touch with you in the morning —Monday at the latest—to take you and your wife's history."

"This is crazy," Tom protested. "This is insane. I don't believe this."

"We find it's the best way for the patient." Dr. Yahya turned away for the second time. He didn't like the look of this wasted wild man. They must both be taking drugs.

"Wait a minute." Tom caught his arm. "What about the baby?"

"Please. Not to touch." The doctor backed away before continuing. "Calm down. I'll get in touch with her doctor as soon as you let me go."

Cusick, who had been at Tom's side in the waiting room for hours, now broke into the conversation for the first time. "Dr. um, Yah-ha, did she give you any indication of the baby's whereabouts?"

"I told you, she's acutely psychotic. She doesn't even know her name."

Tom shook his head. "That's not true."

"Dangerous?" Cusick asked.

Yahya remembered the growl. "Possibly. I'll be able to tell you more in a few days."

"A few days," Tom sputtered.

Cusick took his arm. "Come on. I'll drive you home. There's nothing you can do here."

Dr. Yahya was relieved when the policeman persuaded the husband to leave the premises. He didn't want to have to take any steps to get him out.

40

Aaron stopped at the hospital early on Saturday and then took off with Sally on the shopping trip neither had gotten to earlier in the week. The challenge now was to not argue over who should have gotten to what how many days ago and to just get it taken care of. He didn't think it was a big deal. But, of course, Sally thought it was. Must be feeling guilty, he concluded, for trying to change the rules mid way through the marriage.

These days they had to be watchdogs for each other. They were almost at the state where they had to do things together or no one did anything. Aaron suspected Sally took the position she did not because she hated domestic chores so much, but because she wanted him to do them with her. It was a political thing.

She was as involved in her job as he was in his, and no longer felt it was politically correct for her always to have to think of everything and pick up all the domestic slack. He could see by the set of her jaw that she considered this late start on the barbecue his fault.

"Let's think of this as an adventure," he suggested, and sighed when she tossed her as-yet-ungraying mahogany-colored hair.

They tore the list in half and went in opposite directions in the supermarket. So this was the togetherness she dreamed of. He smiled to himself as he watched her neat figure recede down an impossibly long aisle crowded with forty-two more kinds of everything than anyone could ever want.

He went to find the butcher in the back, behind the doors in the meat department, because he wanted the widest range of steaks to choose from. Cholesterol was another one of those things that had changed life for the worse. He was sure that more than half the pleasure of eating had gone out the window with the constant worry of what was correct to eat and what would kill him if he had too much of it. Just as he was secretly convinced that some of the pleasure of marriage, of romance itself, had been cast away with the inflexible requirement of always having to say and do the politically correct thing. There was very little joy in the certainty of having to face the arch rebuttal whenever the love of his life thought he was shirking some duty or other.

Aaron had red meat and whimsy so infrequently these days, he dreamed about them the way some people dream about exotic cars. He picked out the steaks carefully, thinking of the long-ago pleasures of his reckless youth. He found Sally already in line at the checkout counter, a triumphant smile on her face. She'd managed to load a huge basketful of stuff in the time it had taken him to get one item. Women are so much more efficient than men, he knew she was thinking. Indeed they were; he couldn't agree more.

"Ready, darling?" she asked, and feigned surprise at his unfinished task.

"He cut them specially," Aaron replied, holding out the large package of meat.

"Great," she said. Big smile. "Where's everything else?"

He had to go back for the items he had forgotten.

The answering-machine light was flashing when they got

home with the bags. He didn't want a beeper. He listened to the message and called in.

"Sorry to bother you today, but we have something you better look at," Krughauser said.

"What is it?" Aaron looked at the bags on the counter. They had to be unloaded. The plates had to be counted, the steaks marinated, the salad greens washed—well, he never washed the salad. He had to make the dressing, though. He liked doing that. He looked at his watch. It was already five o'clock. Shit. How could it have taken three hours to buy so few things. He smiled at Sally.

"One of the patients in the hospital—" Krughauser began.

"One of mine?" Aaron asked quickly.

"She is now. She was an OB patient. Had her baby, was released yesterday. Today she's brought back in an ambulance, complete breakdown and the baby is missing. We're going to admit her to your floor."

"Jesus," Aaron said. He turned his back on the counter with the unloaded bags as a bridge to get back into his professional self. "What's the story?"

"No one seems to know."

"Is there a husband in the picture?"

"It seems he was out of town until today. He was the one who found her."

"Jesus," Aaron said again. "Who did she leave with yesterday?"

"Apparently nobody."

This was not the time and Krughauser was not the person to ask if there was a hospital fuck-up here. Did somebody release a postpartum borderline or depressed patient to her own care? He didn't ask it, but it was on his mind.

"I'm on my way."

He turned mournfully back to his wife.

Sally frowned but didn't ask. She was always reliable in a crisis. He stopped to kiss her briefly before grabbing a sports jacket and hurrying out.

41

Tom sat beside Cusick in the patrol car. His head throbbed even more than it had earlier in an examining room at the hospital when a young resident started probing at the stitches. He had looked so strange and felt so bad he decided to let them take off the bandage and examine him.

The surgical resident explored the tangle of strings at the end of the stitches, frowning at what he saw.

"How many layers do you have here?" he asked.

"I don't know," Tom said. "Does it matter?"

"Yes. If you have more than one—and it looks like you do —I can't take them all out. It'll put too much stress on the tissue underneath."

The resident peered at it intently. "Where'd you have this done?"

"In the Middle East," Tom said wearily. He didn't want to start explaining again where Adam Adar was.

"No kidding. Well, it looks clean, no sign of infection."

He clipped some of the stitches, left the tangle at the ends.

"Come back in three days, and we'll take a few more," he said. He gave a little yank on one of the strings and Tom yelped.

"Sorry. If it were a little further along, it might have pulled right out."

"What if it never pulls out?" Tom asked, as if it mattered.

"Just clip it down to the skin. Some of them are happy in there and stay forever. Others just come out on their own."

Tom didn't tell him he was having trouble seeing and thinking, or that he felt responsible for the tragedy that happened to his wife and baby. The thought of Bettina crazy and locked up was more than he could bear. If he couldn't get her out, he didn't know what he'd do. He couldn't live with it.

"You all right?" Cusick asked as soon as they were on the road.

How could he be all right with his baby missing and his wife insane?

"What is it like in the—" Tom hesitated. He didn't know what to call it—loony bin, psychiatric ward? "On the eighth floor?" he asked finally.

"Very nice," Cusick replied. "Nice people."

"Oh, yeah?" The shrink was a bad joke. Something out of a movie. A horror movie. Tom was overcome with fury. He didn't know what an acute psychotic break was, or what they did with people who had one. But he didn't think the guy who committed Bettina was up to fixing it.

His head pounded. In the Emergency Room, no one had even given him an aspirin. He remembered he wasn't supposed to take aspirin. He couldn't remember why. He didn't know if there was an Advil in the house. God, he wanted Bettina.

Cusick glanced over. "I mean, the staff is nice. They know what they're doing. It isn't, you know, like a state hospital. It's more like a hotel, very calm. You don't see anything terrible," he added.

"Oh, great."

Tom held on as Cusick speeded up way over the speed

limit. He had visions of the friendly staff medicating Bettina to a point where she could no longer even try to work out what had happened to her.

"Look, I have a wife and a kid—I know how you feel," Cusick said as he whipped around a car that had slowed way down at the sight of him.

Tom looked over and wondered if he did. It was night and Cusick still had his sunglasses on.

"How old?" he asked.

"Twenty-seven," Cusick said.

"Your child? You don't look old enough." Tom took another look.

"Oh, no, my son's two," Cusick said proudly. It was his wife who was twenty-seven.

"Look, what do you say to getting some burgers? It's going to be a long night," Cusick said.

It was almost seven-thirty, and neither of them had put anything more in their stomachs than a cup of coffee from the machine. He signaled for a turn without waiting for Tom's answer, circled around to the take-out window at McDonald's.

"What's up, John? Haven't seen you since yesterday," came the disembodied voice from the speakerphone.

"Nothing much." Cusick turned to Tom. "What'll you have?"

Tom shook his head.

"Maybe you'll change your mind when you smell it." Cusick got two coffees, three quarter-pounders, and two large fries. He still ate like a kid and didn't put on weight. He dug into his pocket for his wallet.

"Here." Tom held out a ten for the deputy's moment of empathy. Maybe he did understand.

"Thanks. I can put in for it later," Cusick said.

Tom was taken aback. Suddenly he thought Cusick meant

he could get the money for the hamburger back because Tom was in custody. He sank back in the seat horrified. Did they think he had something to do with this? Was he a suspect? Was that why the cop was being so nice and driving him home? Cusick said he had a lot of questions. Was that coming next? Shit, he wasn't even there. That was the whole point. He wasn't there.

Unaccountably, the memory came to him of his mother when he was very little, laughing at some mishap or another, raising her eyes to where she believed the heavens were and saying, "God give me strength." Sometimes it still made him want to cry when he thought of her.

He turned his head to the window. It was getting dark.

42

It was completely dark by the time they drove up the driveway with the bag of hamburgers and fries between them. Tom gasped. There were lights everywhere.

"Jesus, what's all this?"

Cusick groaned. "This is where the mill of the law grinds slow and exceedingly small."

"What?" Tom thought it was God who had the mill.

"Never mind." Cusick had to stop halfway up the drive because the rest of it was already clogged with a number of cars and vans, both marked and unmarked, that had gotten there first.

A young woman with perfect lipstick and hair frozen solid

with hair spray came running up to the car. She flung herself on the passenger door almost before the car stopped. Three men hobbled after her, slowed down by the weight of their bulky equipment. One had a powerful light that was not yet turned on, one had a Minicam, and one carried the sound pack.

"Is this the husband?" the woman demanded over the top of the car at Cusick, who got out first.

She protected her position with her body. No one else could get to Tom without knocking her out of the way, nor could Tom get out and escape without speaking to her. There was an overcharged, almost desperate urgency to her, as if she were the one who had lost the baby.

"Give him a break, will you? It's been a long day," Cusick said. He looked regretfully at the McDonald's bag. He couldn't very well reach for it now.

The woman opened the car door so Tom could get out. As he extended a foot and leaned forward, the man with the powerful light flipped a switch. The heat, as well as the sudden blinding illumination, caught Tom by surprise. He reacted instinctively. He recoiled as if from a blow and put his hands in front of his face. For a second he felt trapped, the way a suspect must feel: He had been taken somewhere in a police car, then assaulted by the press at the end of the trip. Only this was not the police station or a courthouse. This was his house. How did they know? His stomach churned with rage. He knew they listened to the police radio. The press probably heard him make the call.

The woman with the camera crew shoved her head through the car window after Tom closed the door on her.

"Hi, I'm sorry to bother you. I know it's a difficult time." She tried to shake hands with Tom. He turned away, making it impossible for her to mistake his refusal to acknowledge her.

She yanked her head out the window long enough to yell, "Hey, Frank, turn that light off, I'm not ready to shoot yet."

Tom took the moment to push the car door open. He got out, feeling the painful rush of blood to his cheeks. "You're on my property," he said with as much restraint as he could manage. "You'll have to leave immediately."

The woman, dark-haired, over-made-up by Tom's standards, dressed very well in a blue linen suit with red blouse, seemed surprised by his attitude.

"I'm Claudia Ravello from WRCR," she said. She smiled to show what a wonderful thing that was. "The six o'clock news," she prompted after a second.

"I don't care who you are. I want you out of here," Tom said, almost choking on his fury. "Off my property, you understand?"

"Well, sure. But I'd like a few words with you first. Do you have any leads on the whereabouts of the baby?"

"The whereabouts of the baby"? This woman was talking about his child, his little girl. Where she might be was a question Tom could not face without breaking down completely. He had to think only of Bettina and what was happening to her. He tried to concentrate on that. Only that. She needed him sane, not crazy.

He turned his back on Claudia and started walking up the hill, shaking his head. Oh, God, he wanted Bettina. He wanted to get her back and hold her tight. God help him, he was to blame for this.

At a signal from Claudia, the light man switched on the strobe again and pointed it at Tom's retreating back. The red light on the videocam was on. She was taping.

"Was the baby abducted? Can you answer that, Mr. Dunne? We hear your wife has been hospitalized. Is she injured? I see you've sustained an injury, too. What happened?" Claudia babbled at his back, hurrying along after him.

"Please, Mr. Dunne. Just give me a few words, a few shots

of your face. A picture of your wife. And I'll take off. I understand what you're going through, believe me; and maybe we can help. Think about it."

Tom stopped suddenly and turned around. Claudia Ravello banged into him.

"Oops, sorry," she said, seeing him clearly for the first time. "Oh, you did fight them off, didn't you? That's a nasty cut. Did you see their faces?"

"That 'nasty cut' is ten days old," Tom said, angling himself so that the camera could not get an unobstructed view of his face.

"Now, look, I don't know how you got here. I don't know what you've heard, but please go away. I don't have anything to tell you. There's no story here."

"Well, you're wrong about that, Mr. Dunne. In a few hours there are going to be seventy-five people out here from all over, camping on your lawn. A missing baby is a very big story. Why don't you give me an interview now, and then you'll have the comfort of knowing somebody has the facts right."

"Look, I just got back. I don't know what the facts are," he protested. "This is hell." He started walking again.

"Is it true your wife is being held for observation and psychological testing?" Claudia shot at him.

"No, that's not true," Tom said furiously.

"Are you and your wife on good terms?"

"Of course." Tom strode on, with Cusick a pace behind.

"You say you were away. Were you separated, Mr. Dunne?" Claudia Ravello's face became hard with purpose. She was known for using whatever tactics worked.

He stumbled. She pressed forward, sensing defensiveness.

"No," Tom answered wildly. "We aren't separated."

There were police all around him, and no one came forward to help.

"Cusick," he shouted. "Can't you get these people out of here? For God's sake, where are you?"

"Okay, okay, I'm right here." Cusick stepped forward and waved Claudia and her crew away. "Go on, wait by the gate, you had your chance."

"Come on, give me a break," Claudia said. "Can't you see we're doing an interview?"

"He wants you out, Claudia; don't overstay your welcome," Cusick said.

"What's your name?" Claudia looked at the badge on his shirt. "Well, thanks, John Cusick, I'll remember you at Christmas," she said, taking just one step back.

"I appreciate it," Cusick replied, attempting to move her along, out of Tom's way as he went up the steps to his house.

She hesitated before heading toward her car. "Listen, I'll forgive you if you can get me her picture."

Cusick shook his head. "Why should I?"

"Because you never know, you might need me someday. And you like my show, right?" She smiled broadly, revealing big teeth and a dimple.

"I've never seen your show," Cusick said. "I don't have time to watch the news."

"Cusick," someone yelled from the house, "stop gabbing and get up here. We have a lot of work to do."

Cusick broke away, went to his car, and grabbed the bag of hamburgers, then followed Tom into the house, where he heard him protesting.

"Can you people just walk into someone's house like this? What do you think you're doing here?"

"You had a baby, sir. We're looking for the baby."

43

Aaron Simon raced back to the hospital, hoping to get to the patient before his resident did. The temporary replacement, Ayub Yahya, was not the ideal person to handle the situation. His first choice for Ron's replacement would not be available for another month. Aaron hated this. Always having to worry about what kind of harm might be visited on the patients just by their being in the hospital. Instead of just worrying about the harm they might do themselves in their own lives. Doctors shouldn't make it worse. It was the least they could offer. But sometimes they did. He worried about Laura Hunter, who hadn't called him since her miscarriage. It had been several weeks. He was afraid she wouldn't call. He was also worried about her blood and the transfusion she had been given. "Blood all over the place" was what she said.

That's what Max accused him of not experiencing as a psychiatrist—the patient's lifeblood all over the place and on his hands. His role appeared passive, and indeed it was. He was required to let things evolve. He couldn't call Laura. He couldn't accuse Max outright. They had to come to him when they were ready. If they were ready. There were a lot of things in this world he just couldn't reach out and fix. His was a waiting game. Sometimes he hated it.

He drove too fast. He had noticed almost immediately that new patients seemed to be more agitated when Ayub was their first interview. Aaron attributed Ayub's tendency to find patients' symptoms before they revealed them to his having been focused for so many years on the other end of the body. He had been a urologist. Aaron had heard him remark that he preferred being a psychiatrist because the patients might not recover, but at least they didn't die. Very revealing, and not very smart. He hurried.

He got to the hospital in time to find Bettina still in ER. But his heart sank as Ayub galloped over to him before he reached the door to her room.

"Ah, good, you are here," Ayub said.

"I am here," Aaron confirmed.

"The patient is acutely psychotic, may be violent," Ayub said, cocking his head at the door.

"May be some kind of postpartum episode. The husband said it never happened before, but he may not be reliable. Very out of touch."

"Thank you," Aaron said formally.

"I was just going to type up my report. I will give you my notes on her mental-status tests. I will have it for you within the hour. Okeydokey?" Ayub said.

Aaron nodded curtly and turned the door handle. He could hardly wait to receive his colleague's insights.

The woman the hospital had released the day before was sitting on the bed in the examining room rocking back and forth, sobbing copiously and muttering to herself. She had used or shredded the boxful of hospital tissues that she had been given. Her face was awash with tears, bloated, and red.

"Oh no, oh no, oh no," she cried as Aaron came in. "No more."

"Hello, Mrs. Dunne, I'm Dr. Simon," he said gently.

"Gotta go now." She growled, and wiped her nose with her hand. She shook her head rapidly back and forth. "No, no, no, no. Don't hurt me."

"I won't hurt you." Aaron sat down on the stool beside the examining table and waited.

Bettina shrank away, as far as she could get without actually falling off the bed.

"Don't touch me," she cried.

"I won't touch you. I'm not that kind of doctor." He crossed one leg over the other and sat very still. He sat that way while Bettina Dunne shook her fist and her head at him and made some guttural noises. Gradually she calmed down.

After a while the only sound was her ragged breathing. But her body just wouldn't stay still. It moved this way and that, jerking out of control.

"Bees," she said. "Stinging buzz bees."

He nodded.

"Hurts. Oww."

"What hurts?"

"Can't think. Hurts so much." She looked at him piteously.

"Where does it hurt?"

"Here." she touched her breasts. "And here." She held her head, where the drill was still going. "Buzz."

"We can give you something for pain. Would you like something?"

"No, no shots," she said, getting agitated again.

"Are you afraid of shots?"

She shrank back even farther and bared her teeth, growled, then stopped, began sobbing again.

"I lost my baby." Her crying grew to a wail.

"Do you know where you lost her?" Aaron asked.

"She was in the coffin. They wouldn't let me touch her."

"Before she was in the coffin?"

"I don't know." Bettina began hitting herself. "I don't know. I don't know. Please—"

"We're trying to find her."

"Please—"

He nodded. "We're trying. A lot of people are looking. I hear you've been here a long time. Have you had anything to eat?" Aaron asked.

Bettina shook her head. "I'm so hungry."

"I bet you are. We're going to take you upstairs and try to make you more comfortable."

"Oh, God. Don't lock me in."

"Do you know where you are?" Aaron asked.

Bettina looked around. "I had my baby here." She began to cry again.

"We're going to make you more comfortable. Then we'll talk about it some more tomorrow."

"Bad girl. No, don't open the door."

"We'll get you some food. How about that?"

Aaron stood up. She was still shaking all over, limbs out of control. He didn't want to agitate her further. Now was not the time to ask too many questions or press her too hard. There would be enough of that later.

"I'll see you tomorrow," he said.

He went out to look at her chart. No one had thought to do a urinalysis. He ordered one and raised some hell about getting the patient upstairs. She needed to be fed and calmed down enough to get some sleep. Then he went home to light the grill.

44

All day Saturday, Peter hid under the sheets in his bed, tossing and shivering with a thousand complaints, afraid to go out. The van was out there. Every time he went to the window, it was there, parked down the street. It was black and had a lurid red sunset painted on the side.

The question that plagued him was how to get his head straight without some relief from the swamp of pain he was in. Saturday was so quiet it seemed there had to be a soundproof booth around him, separating him from all things human. It was a feeling he had had before. He wanted to hurt someone.

He kept a bottle of scotch by his side and drank from it. When he had to go from one room to another, he kept his body low. He had done his work, kept his side of the bargain. Isobel had failed him. Chrissie Elton had failed him. Wendal and Laura had failed him the most. They had not paid him the money when they said they would. They had to pay for that. Peter considered what he could do to them.

He could take the baby back and keep it until they paid him his money, in cash. He could wait outside and watch. The minute Wendal left the apartment, he'd take the baby and not give it back to them.

He called Angel several times, but there was no answer. He banged the phone down in frustration. Nobody should be expected to hand over money on a day when the banks were closed. Peter wanted to tell him that. He'd have it by Tuesday, Friday at the latest. That was fair.

He couldn't believe this was happening to him over a few thousand dollars. At any other time in his life he would have found the danger impossible to imagine. He would have laughed or raised the money, swatted the fly buzzing around his head. Money was nothing to him. But now his house was stripped. His car was gone and so were all his securities and assets. In the last year he had borrowed so much money from every friend he had, no one would talk to him anymore. Now he was so desperate for money he had considered stealing the silver and jewelry out of the Dunnes' house. They had two cars. The signs of their prosperity were all over the place. Isobel wouldn't let him take anything. It would have proved someone had taken the baby. Now he couldn't go back there.

Peter brooded all Saturday afternoon. He had to leave the apartment soon. Had to get the baby back. He would hide out until he got the money. He knew how to hide. If they didn't give him the money, he would leave the baby somewhere no one would ever find it. Good. He smoked the last of the marijuana and drank steadily until he fell asleep on the living room floor, his hand inches away from the telephone.

He planned to leave in the morning, early. But he was awakened by the phone at eight o'clock. It was Sunday, the 3rd of July.

"Congratulations," Angel said.

"Oh, yeah," Peter said, snapping awake with pain in every part of him. "What for?"

"You had a baby, and I'm gonna get paid. I'll be here all day. You can drop the money off anytime."

Peter hesitated.

"What's the matter? You having more problems, Peter?" Angel asked, his voice darkening with concern.

"No, it's just a holiday. The banks are closed," Peter said cautiously.

"Peter, people have babies and get paid even on holidays."

"Maybe, but there's still a lot of paperwork to be done here. It's not a simple thing."

"Hey, aren't you a lawyer? I thought you'd taken care of all that. I got lawyers. They take care of it, doesn't matter what day it is."

"Well, there have been some changes in this case. I didn't have time to get it done," Peter said nervously.

"Oh, yeah? What does that have to do with me?" Angel's voice was angry.

Peter's hands were shaking. He could hardly breathe.

"You know how it is with lawyers," Peter said. "You don't get paid until the paperwork is done."

"You know, Peter, with you it's always something. You make me unhappy. I've been very patient with you. I've tried to understand your needs. Not everybody would. And you disappoint me at every turn."

"Look, these things take time." Peter's hands were trembling with terror, but his practiced voice sounded calm.

"Oh, yeah? We have people who do papers. Tell me what kind of papers you need. You can have them in a few hours. A hundred times I offered my help. Whatever you needed. You wanted to do adoptions. Fine, I offered you babies, papers. Whatever. And you didn't want my help."

"Look, Angel, I told you I can't deal in your crack-whore babies."

"Don't make me angry, Peter. Nice girls in trouble. That's what you wanted. That's what I offered."

"They can tell the minute they're born. I told you that. I can't deal in sick babies. I told you that. My clients won't take anything but perfect. I'm legitimate. I don't do the kind of things you do."

"You turned me down," Angel said. "I offered help and you turned me down."

"I never turned you down. Never," Peter said. "You get me a healthy baby from a healthy mother, I'll place it, you know that."

"Instead you make trouble for me. Big trouble."

"I owe you a little money," Peter said. "That's not big trouble."

Angel was silent for a long time. "Lying I don't like," he said finally, "but crazy is fatal."

"What are you talking about?" Peter cried.

"You know, Peter, I have a good wife. I trust my wife. Last night she made me look at something on the news that offended me. Did you see the news?"

"No," Peter said. "What was on the news?"

"Well, it was bad. It hurt me. We don't do business like that. That kind of stuff hurts everybody."

"Look, don't start that. You got me into this—" Peter said wildly.

"Don't say that. Don't even think like that. You came to me. I didn't come to you. Do you want me to lose my patience completely?"

Peter spoke quickly. Never had he hated anyone the way he hated Angel. Angel terrified him. Angel was like a hundred vicious enemies, who saw everything and could be everywhere at the same time. How did he know so much? Peter felt like a helpless kid with a vicious father.

"All right. All right," Peter admitted. "Maybe I did come to you. But what do you want from me? I'm doing the best that I can."

"Oh, Peter, Peter, you offend me. I've been so patient. I've offered you my lawyers, whatever you need, and you abused my trust. You go out and pull a stunt like this. How can I ever trust you again?"

Peter gasped. "Look, give me a few more days. Just till Friday."

Angel sighed. "You don't understand. There's more than money here. You disappointed me. You hurt people. You put a trail out that could lead to me. You don't do that to me. You put me in a position. Now I got to fix it."

"No, I won't disappoint you. I promise. I'll work it out. Please stay out of it." Peter babbled on. It was some time before he realized Angel had hung up. The line was dead. He was cut off.

In the silence, the menace grew until Peter broke down and sobbed with terror so alive he could feel it squeezing the life out of him.

45

Laura pushed the button on the coffee machine and stepped out her front door to pick up the papers Wendal had left on his way out. The headline took up almost the whole page: MISSING BABY SPURS STATEWIDE SEARCH.

She saw the photo next. A smiling girl gazed out of a college yearbook picture. The name under it was "Bettina

Dunne.'' Laura turned to stone in an instant. Her hand extended
to the paper, but she couldn't pick it up.

A vision of her three babies in heaven, cherubs with wings,
lost in the clouds, came to her. Sometimes she imagined them
flying around her head, just out of reach. Now they hovered over
her, their wings beating at the air. She always imagined them
fully formed. They were real babies to her, as real as the one in
the other room. Bad luck came in threes. This was her fourth
baby.

She felt her throat constricting. She closed the door and
leaned against it, trying to find a way to breathe. It could not be.
It could not. Peter was crazy. She knew it when she saw his face.
Her thoughts came as wildly as her heartbeats. He was crazy.
What did he do?

A minute later she was unable to contain her need to know,
and opened the door. There were two papers on the welcome
mat. She brought them inside and read the stories. ''The husband, Tom Dunne, denies that his wife was depressed over their
separation,'' said one. ''Police say that the mother, twenty-nine-
year-old Bettina Dunne, was incoherent when found by her husband on his return from a business trip and was unable to answer
questions about the whereabouts of their three-day-old baby girl.
A manhunt has been organized to search the area in hopes of
finding the infant alive.'' Continued on B2.

Laura turned to B2, her feelings of horror growing. ''Hospital sources confirm that she is being held for psychological
testing. When asked if the mother was considered a suspect,
Sheriff Anderson said, 'Although there is no evidence at this time
that the mother harmed the infant, we're covering all bases.' ''

There was quite a bit of information. In just a few hours,
even on the July 4th weekend, a number of reporters had managed to dig up a lot of background material on Tom and Bettina

Dunne. The articles listed the titles of the books Bettina had illustrated and identified Tom as an engineer for Axam Oil. One of them reported where he had been in the Middle East and how recently the couple had moved to New Jersey from New York.

Laura read and reread them. Then she turned on the television. A special broadcast was showing the police dragging the Dunnes' pond with a net, and methodically digging up the new plantings around the house, looking for a body wherever the earth was loose.

Laura's mouth filled with burning acid as it became clearer to her what was happening. She had lost a baby, more than one. It wasn't a big step for her to see herself go mad with grief and frustration, as Bettina must have done. But then to be suspected of killing the infant because she didn't know where it was was cruel beyond belief. Laura could not bear it, rushed to the bathroom and vomited.

There must be some mistake. It had to be a mix-up of some kind. Laura could not believe that she had someone else's baby. A real person's baby, who was married and wanted it and lived not far from her. The enormity of her dilemma overwhelmed her.

When she came out of the bathroom, there was a discussion on the special broadcast with two psychologists about women with postpartum depression who murder their babies. They cited the Ferrara case, in which a woman told police her three-month-old baby had been taken out of its carriage by three men in a car. Later she led them to a garbage can where she had stuffed the baby's body, admitting that she'd killed it because it cried too much. Another woman threw her infant out a three-story window and said, "It fell."

The psychologists stressed that in both cases there were other pressures and family troubles, as well as a history of depression. "Normal women don't get severely depressed out of the blue. Nor do they murder their babies just because they're upset," said Margerie Queeg, Ph.D.

"No, indeed, Margerie," agreed Dr. Weeble. "These are extreme examples of what can happen when a mother with emotional problems is faced with more stress than she can handle."

Laura's knees were still shaking as she watched. She had to sit down. Her mouth had a sour taste. The two psychologists started talking about abortion, and freedom of choice versus legislation determining who has babies. Laura couldn't get her heart to stop hammering away in her chest. She got up to check the baby. She was still there, sleeping peacefully.

"Oh my God, she's so beautiful." Laura thought if there was ever a time she felt her heart would break it was now.

She turned off the television, but still saw the two psychologists discussing "extreme examples" and the police shovels turning over the dirt in the flower gardens. She had named the baby. Anna was hers.

Laura was shaking all over as she sat down at the table. She felt that any second they would find her, but she knew no one would ever know—unless Peter told them. This was a terrible thing to think about.

Wendal was out getting supplies for breakfast. What would she tell him? She felt herself becoming hysterical with this secret that probably only she and Peter knew. And Peter didn't know she knew. Maybe Peter didn't even know.

But how could he not know? Somebody he trusted could have given him the wrong baby, she told herself. Then where was the right one? No way to know. She remembered the look on Peter's face. Of course he knew. Now his fury made sense. He had taken someone's real baby and was fencing it like stolen silver.

She felt like being sick again. Good people didn't have things like this happen to them. How could she think about it without being appalled, sickened. It was so cruel to all of them. No worse for the mother than for her, she told herself.

"I'll have to give her back," she said aloud, with a racking sob. "Oh, God, I'm going to have to give her back."

She couldn't let another woman have a cloud over her all her life for something she didn't do. *Well, I suffered for something that wasn't my fault,* Laura argued. *My babies died. Things happen. She can have other children, I can't. Bad things happen that you can't control. I might not even know this. If I didn't know, I wouldn't be responsible.*

Laura chewed on her lip. But she did know. She couldn't pretend that she didn't know. And this was a chance to stop an evil thing. She could send Peter to jail, where he belonged. She began to cry when she thought of him. How could he do such a terrible thing to her? She had even given the baby a name, and fallen in love with her as if she were her own. She had to tell Wendal right away. Nobody else knew but Peter and her. On the other hand, Wendal was sure to know anyway, even if she didn't tell him. He would guess. He always figured things out.

She blew her nose and put the papers on the table with the headlines and the picture of Bettina Dunne prominently displayed. She was sure he would make the connection. *D* was not for duck, it was for Dunne. He'd figure it out and then it would be out of her hands. He would do the right thing.

He rang the buzzer from downstairs to let her know he was coming. If he guessed, then she wouldn't have to tell him. She didn't want to be the one who gave the baby up. She went into the bathroom to spray the air, so Wendal wouldn't know she had been sick. She put some lipstick on. Her cheeks were very pale.

"I'm going to be all right, whatever happens," she told

herself in the mirror. It was going to be all right. Maybe she wouldn't have to give her up today.

Laura went into the yellow room with the white, frilly curtains. In the white crib, the baby was still sleeping. From time to time her little lips twitched and her eyelids fluttered but did not open, as if she might be having a good dream she didn't want to end.

46

Aaron dressed with impatience, a cup of coffee on the sink beside him as he shaved. Last night's party was long behind him, even though it was only a few hours past. It was Sunday. He had spent an extra hour and a half the night before cleaning up outside and inside so he could get out of here this morning without feeling guilty. The garbage bags with the dozens of paper plates and plastic cups were neatly tied at the top and waiting for Tuesday's pickup. He had done it all mechanically—grilled the steaks to perfection, talked to wives he'd only seen once or twice since last year, been affable to colleagues he didn't like. Sally had stopped sulking in crisis and been her most excellent party self. It was times like this that he remembered why he loved her so much.

But he had been preoccupied the whole time. Women didn't just walk out of Chester Memorial Hospital and get in taxis with no car seats, no nurses standing by to help, and no one

home to make sure they were all right. They didn't go off their
rocker and lose their babies within a few hours. It just didn't
happen. The thought of a new scandal, only a few months after
the last one, was too much. And this was a bad one. This would
not be confined to Clinical Care meetings where only the hospital staff knew about it. This would be public. The media would
get in on this one. Actually, the media would have gotten in on
the last one if they knew about it. But the real tragedy was the
woman herself. Shit. He cut his neck. Great, now he was slitting
his throat.

He slapped some shaving lotion on his face. It burned.
Good, wake him up. He didn't think about being off duty on
weekends. He never thought about things like that. People were
sick. Their illnesses didn't go on vacation. He didn't even take
the time to sit down for breakfast. He didn't want to take a
second longer getting to the case of Bettina Dunne than he had
to. He looked in on Sally. She was still asleep, curled up and
hugging a pillow. Oh, well, he probably would have hurried out
and missed Sunday breakfast even for a less compelling case, and
she knew it.

Aaron liked beginnings. First meetings with a new patient
were a little like love affairs in a way. God help him if the first
sessions were the best, but they had a clarity about them he
remembered long after he knew someone very well. He tiptoed
down the stairs and put his empty cup in the kitchen sink. He
took a second to go back and check on the kids. Ten and twelve,
still out cold, the covers thrown back in the summer heat. It was
eight in the morning.

He went down the stairs a second time and slid out the
back door. There wasn't a sound of protest anywhere. He waited
in the garage, just to make sure no one was up and wanted to
speak with him. He made it to the car without anyone calling

after him, turned on the engine, and pulled out into the suburban street. Still, no one called him back. He sighed with relief. They'd probably sleep until ten. He'd be back by then.

The sun was bright and the air was still. Aaron could feel his head clearing. He always felt particularly alert in the beginning of a relationship, almost vibrant, as if every nerve ending in his body were an antenna for picking up clues and information. To him every case was a puzzle in which the pieces had a definite place and effect but no shape or name until he and the patient identified them and recognized them for whatever good or evil they represented. Searching for answers excited him.

He liked the process of getting to know new people, even very sick ones, and helping them as much as they could be helped. There was no standard for mental health. It was all relative, as intelligence and motivation and happiness were relative things. Not everyone's needs were the same. All sorts of people functioned quite well with very little.

He had discovered that sometimes the smallest step was a triumph that made all the difference in a person's life. Going to a fancy restaurant and feeling that one belonged. Taking a walk in the park after being terrified of going out. Going to the supermarket without being paralyzed over having to choose what to put in the basket. He looked forward to his patients taking these steps without impatience, but with eagerness, and savored them the way some people relished their possessions and the size of their salaries.

His mind wandered as he drove through the quiet streets. Sometime the night before he had spoken to Arthur Street, the patient's obstetrician, who was away on vacation. Arthur described the patient as healthy, competent, and in good spirits the last time he saw her. Perfectly routine and normal birth. He was mystified and appalled by what Aaron told him, had never heard of anything like it. He wanted to come right home.

Aaron wondered if he had done the right thing in telling him to wait a day. Arthur was on an island somewhere, Maine or Massachusetts, and needed a boat to get back to the mainland. Aaron told him to stay where he was for the moment. A day or two wouldn't make a big difference. He promised to call him this morning. Maybe he should have encouraged him to come back.

He switched his thoughts to the woman. What had caused the psychotic break? He'd know soon enough if it was cocaine or barbiturates. Not likely to be alcohol. Even in very large amounts, it wouldn't bring on this kind of reaction. As he pulled into the hospital parking lot, he felt confident that if Bettina knew where her baby was—even if the knowledge was deeply hidden in her unconscious—he could help her find a way to tell him. The problem was, she might not know.

He found her sitting up in bed, wearing blue-and-white hospital pajamas. There was a fully stocked breakfast tray in front of her. The blank, unfocused stare he had encountered the night before had been replaced by what looked like a keen awareness. Her body was still, her expression guarded but organized. He was shocked at the difference. It was an open face, full of intelligence and shock and pain.

"Hi. How are you feeling this morning?" Aaron came in and stood beside her bed.

Bettina stopped trying to eat the tasteless oatmeal on her tray. Her eyes filled with tears. "No one will tell me anything."

"What do you want to know?"

"What am I doing here? This is—" she lost control and wept.

"You're in the same hospital you were in before," Aaron said gently.

"No." She shook her head. "This is for—There are crazy

people here. You think I'm crazy?'' It was a question. It was a cry. "I'm not crazy."

He stood there quietly.

"What happened to me? Where's my baby? I want to see my baby."

"Do you know where she is?"

"She's in her crib," Bettina cried. "I left her in her crib."

"Do you know how you got here?"

There was silence for a long time.

"In an ambulance," she said finally. "Tom was there. Where's the baby?"

Aaron did not say.

"My head hurts so much. It's hard to think. It's"—she looked down at the tray as if she'd never seen it before—"like being in a tunnel with noises everywhere. I'm so scared."

"What kind of noises?"

"I want to see my baby. I'm worried about her. Who's taking care of her? Is Tom taking care of her? Where's Tom? Why doesn't he come to take me home?"

He made a small motion with his head that could have meant anything. "You just got here. I don't think you feel well enough to go home."

"Tom can't take care of the baby. She needs her mother." Bettina started weeping again. "Why won't you tell me what's going on?"

"Your husband came home yesterday, do you remember that?"

She nodded slowly.

"Are you a psychiatrist?" she asked, frowning. He was wearing a sports jacket, blue shirt and tie, the kind of khaki pants Tom wore. He didn't look like a doctor.

He gave her the barest nod to the psychiatrist question, in case she had negative feelings about his profession.

"I saw you yesterday when you came in. Do you remember?" Finally he took a chair and pulled it up.

"You got me some food," she said reluctantly.

He smiled. "How was it?"

She looked at him sharply. "I wasn't in any shape to tell."

"You look and sound a lot better now."

"Well, I'm not better. I need some reassurance that my baby's all right."

When he didn't say anything, she went on. "How would you feel if you were me? No one tells me anything. Everybody's watching me, but no one's listening."

She said this in a low, clear voice, and sounded remarkably sane. It was puzzling. Aaron felt fairly convinced that she had no idea her baby wasn't at home where she'd left her. He hesitated and then replied, "I'm here to listen to you."

"Ninety-three," she said, and returned to her oatmeal.

He didn't respond for a minute, waited for what she might say next. It didn't matter that he didn't know what she meant. She would explain it to him if she could. He watched her raise the spoon to her lips and take the tiniest bite of what he knew was a solid mass of glutinous mush. Her nose began to run as tears filled her eyes again. He could not ask her what she was thinking. She had to tell him herself. All he could do was try to make her want to. She swiped at her nose with her napkin.

"Eighty-six," she said, looking at him intently now. "Seventy-nine." The tears began to fall unchecked as she went on. "Seventy-two, sixty-five."

Aaron had read Ayub's notes. He realized she was giving him serial sevens. It was part of the mental-status test. The patient is asked to count backward from a hundred by sevens. A disorganized person can't do it. Bettina was doing it, slowly and deliberately. It was clear the exercise was giving her as much distress as it had the day before, when she had been unable, or unwilling, to do it. His bristly eyebrows came together with distress of his own.

"Thank you, that's great," he told her. "You don't have to do that anymore."

He passed over a box of tissues, and she wiped her eyes.

"If I give you all the right answers, will you let me see my husband?" she asked.

"Is that what you want?"

"Yes. I want a lot of things. I want to see my baby. I want to go home. I want my life back."

"Maybe it would be more useful if I asked a different kind of question," Aaron suggested.

"I'm not crazy," she said. "I know you're here to see if I'm crazy."

He smiled faintly. "We just met. I never said you're crazy."

"You wouldn't tell me if you thought so."

"How do you know what I would say?" he protested.

She shrugged. "The other doctor thought I was crazy." She swallowed some orange juice, looked away.

"We're all a little crazy sometimes," Aaron said easily. "You came here in an ambulance yesterday. You said you remember that. You had a bad time. Can you tell me about it?"

Bettina shook her head. "You won't help me."

He did the opposite of sniffing. He blew the air out of his nose, making a kind of humphing noise. He hated it when they said that, but the patient was often right. It was something he knew from his earliest days as a resident, and relearned over and over. They knew what was right and what was wrong. They knew who was for them and who was against them. They knew when they had been hurt and why. He had to listen very closely to find the truth about a lot more things than their illness. He realized he liked Bettina Dunne. The things she said might very well be the kind of things he would say in the same situation.

She didn't seem to know what had happened to her, and she was right to doubt him after the perfectly correct, but not very sensitive grilling she had gotten from his colleague the day before. Why should she want to tell him anything? Ayub meant well, but his approach would not work for a sensitive and intelligent patient like this. Try as they might, they couldn't teach sensitivity to doctors.

He sat in the chair and crossed his legs. He thought it was very puzzling indeed that a person who was so disoriented yesterday could seem perfectly rational and coherent today.

"Try me," he said.

47

Isobel held the phone to her ear and swore. "Sorry, I can't come to the phone right now. But if you will leave your name and a brief message, I will get back to you as soon as I can. Please wait for the beep."

She hung up. Damn. She knew Peter was there. She switched the television back on with the remote control button, watched a bunch of reporters get the story all wrong again.

She hit redial. Peter's number rang two times and was picked up by the machine. "Sorry—" she hung up before the message went any further. She wanted to know just how long he expected her to sit there and be normal. They were supposed to be a team, weren't they? She didn't like this at all. She dialed again, hung up when she heard the click of the answering machine about to play the message.

The problem was she couldn't sleep, couldn't eat. It was ten in the morning and she had been up since four-thirty. She poured herself a glass of cooking sherry from the bottle beside the stove, which was all the alcohol left in the apartment, and went into her bedroom. The pink sheets were all tangled on her bed, a testament to her restlessness during the night.

The other problem was she didn't like Laura Hunter, didn't like her at all. "I don't know why that makes a difference to me," she thought.

It made a difference because Bettina's baby hadn't gone to some unknown person she'd never see. It had gone to someone she knew, a nose-in-the-air bitch she'd known for years. Laura was the kind of patient who complained about everything. It was always too cold or too hot. She never thought the examining room was clean enough, didn't like to be kept waiting. This was the kind of woman who would come in with baby pictures. She might even be there someday at the same time as Bettina—if Bettina ever recovered. They'd be in the same office. Two different doctors, maybe, but the same office. Isobel couldn't even stand the *thought* of this possibility.

She looked around and was distressed by the messy room, even more so by the knowledge of what was hidden in the bottom of her closet. She wanted to clean up, make her bed, leave a clue somewhere. Laura Hunter. Laura Hunter had the baby. She turned around and left the room. She just didn't have the energy to do anything about anything.

What she wanted was to see Peter and be reassured that he still loved her. She drank the sherry in one gulp, unmindful of its roughness around the edges, and paced around her tiny living room.

How could he expect her to just sit there? It was terrible. She didn't mean to do everything he'd told her not to do, but she couldn't help it. He'd told her to forget the whole thing, put it out of her mind and think of something else. But now that it was done the little mistakes played over and over in her mind. How they had handled Bettina, the needle mark on her thigh. She didn't know how Bettina would respond to the drug. She knew it would be gone from her system in twenty-four hours. If they didn't give her the right kind of blood test, and very quickly, they wouldn't find anything. That didn't comfort her, though. She didn't know what she wanted. Bettina crazy forever and herself safe? But that would mean Laura Hunter would have the baby. She hated the idea. But what about if Bettina recovered? What then?

Isobel considered the moment she had diluted the drug in the vial. She'd squirted some in the air before Peter caught her arm. But she had no idea how much Bettina got and what it would do to her.

The bottle of sherry still had one glass in it. Isobel knew she'd have to go out and get herself something to drink soon, wondered what would be open on Sunday. She wanted to ration herself, wait a while for her next drink. She thought about that for a second, then poured the last of the sherry and punched redial. She hung up when she heard the click just before the message started. Shit, this was too much. He wasn't going to answer. Maybe he had already taken off.

Okay, she could admit it. She was scared. Her imprint was all over everything. Her name was on the job, just like the surgeons she worked with had their names on every cut they made. Mistakes like this were traceable back to the source. She had gathered up all the stuff, but how could she be sure they hadn't left something behind?

She didn't want Peter to be mad at her, needed to talk to somebody. She didn't do what he'd told her. She was racked by that—as she was by the possibility that he had taken off, gone to the Caribbean or somewhere without her.

"Peter, Peter, I need you," she cried to herself. "I couldn't get rid of it." She just didn't know where to drop the masks, the syringe, the vial, the dirty rags, the dress Bettina had worn home from the hospital, the rubber gloves she knew had their fingerprints on the inside.

She had been considering the question for hours and had decided the best place for it was the hospital garbage, in one of the bags with AIDS' patients fluids, specially tagged and separate. But she didn't want to go back there, ever. In fact, she didn't want to move at all. Initially, she put the items in a plastic bag, and that in an old suitcase, then returned it to her closet, under a pile of clothes she didn't wear anymore. Now she didn't want it there and needed Peter's advice on where to dump it.

She fought with her temptation to turn the television on again. That was another thing Peter told her not to do. But she had to know what was happening, didn't she? At first it was garbage as usual. The Mets lost another game. The police shot the berserk mother of two as she was stabbing her three-year-old with the knife of her out-of-work butcher husband.

At eleven o'clock on Saturday night, the story she had been waiting for popped up on the screen and grew from there like a virulent disease. The story of the dead mother and the child in intensive care was quickly eclipsed by the story of the living mother and her missing infant—proving to Isobel yet again that the press cared more about the misfortunes of the affluent than those of the desperately poor.

And of course they had it all wrong. But that somehow

didn't make Isobel feel any better. As long as they had it wrong, she was safe. But it worried her that the story on television was so distorted and false. Somehow she wanted to set it right.

She thought about it a lot as the hours passed. Justice was never done. People were hurt all the time, and no one ever paid. She drank steadily, remembering all the men who had hurt her and gotten away with it. Just thinking about being married and cooking dinner and having a house, a real house with a garden, made her cry. She knew she could put Peter away. If Hedda Nussbaum could get immunity from prosecution in the Lisa Steinberg case in return for testimony against Joel, then she could get immunity in this case. No one was dead. What should she do?

Her grief at the possibility of losing again was monumental, greater than anything she had ever felt before. How could she grab it back and make it right again?

She turned back to the television. More news was spewing out. Now there was a videotape of the farmhouse, with areas roped off where they were digging. Volunteer firemen, the sheriff's office. There were several men in rubber suits in the pond.

Isobel needed to talk. If the baby wasn't found, could they still prosecute the mother? She didn't think so. Bettina was on the eighth floor of the Chester hospital, "for observation," said the news. She had to hand it to Peter. He knew what he was doing. Still, it was awful to watch.

Unaccountably, she started thinking of food. Her mother had been a terrible cook, couldn't do anything right. Her failures had been the source of many bitter fights when Isobel was a child. Her mother couldn't hack it, didn't care. Whenever she was hurt and disappointed, Isobel always told herself she was all right as long as she could think of her next meal. Depressed people couldn't eat. Helpless, drunk, sick people couldn't cook, couldn't go to work. She decided to pull herself together and cook dinner for Peter. They'd talk the situation over together and decide what to do. Having made the decision to take action, she felt a lot better.

48

Bettina was on the little metal-and-plastic sofa by the window. Aaron sat on the only other chair. He pulled it over so it was facing her. He noticed that she kept moving into the ray of sunshine that streamed into the room and was slowly inching across the room. Must like heat and light, he thought. So did he.

"You remind me of my husband," she said suddenly.

They hadn't made much progress up to now, but this seemed to be a step forward. "He must be a great guy," Aaron said hopefully, with a smile.

"He is." Her face clouded. "He told me not to leave the hospital. He wanted to take me home himself."

"Why did you?"

She lowered her head until her chin was resting on her chest. The pain was still unbearable in her breasts, but she would not take the medication to stop her milk.

"I left a mess," she murmured.

Aaron frowned with concentration. "What kind of mess?"

"I was in labor." She wouldn't look at him. "It was the middle of the night." Her breathing quickened.

"Yes," he prompted.

"My waters broke. I was sick." She hesitated for a long time.

"So?" Aaron said so softly it was barely audible.

"I wanted to clean it up before Tom got home."

"Do you think he would have been angry at you if he found it?"

Bettina shook her head. Her lips trembled. She chewed on them and wrung her hands. "He wouldn't have cared. Only I cared."

"What happened then?"

Bettina thought of the ride back in the taxi, how serene the house looked. It didn't seem wrong to go home. "I put the baby in bed. She was sleeping."

There was a long pause. "I had a cup of tea."

He wrote it down. "Then what?"

"The doorbell rang."

She couldn't help getting hysterical. She shook her body like a wet dog to make it go away. Saw the pictures and couldn't describe them. There was no peephole in the door. She opened it. There were two of them. They wore Frankenstein masks. She saw it all in slow motion and then screamed out loud at the vision of them holding the towel over her mouth.

"It's okay," Aaron murmured.

"I can't breathe," Bettina cried.

"Yes, you can breathe now. Look at me. You're here with me. See? It's safe here."

She gulped and looked at him. His face was creased with concern, eyebrows beetled into a single bristly line.

"Try to put it in words," he said gently.

She looked at him, and held her breath to stop the tears. "I was expecting the man from Rappaport's. That's why I opened the door." Her tears turned to hiccups.

"The baby store?"

"He was bringing me the sample book of the baby announcements."

"Hmm." Aaron scratched his head. "Did you ask him to do that?"

"No, I tried to talk him out of it, but he said it was a service of the store." Bettina blew her nose and unconsciously shifted into the patch of sun.

"Did you call him?" Aaron asked casually.

"No."

"Did you call anybody?"

Bettina shook her head. "I got home and the phone rang almost immediately."

"Did anybody else call you?"

"No. I didn't talk to anybody. Just him."

He started the list of facts. "Who released you from the hospital? Was it Dr. Street?"

"No, he didn't come that day. I called the office. The nurse said she would arrange it."

"Did you tell anyone on the outside you were leaving?"

Bettina shook her head. "I wanted it to be a surprise."

"Did you call anybody?"

"I told you that already. I had just gotten home. I hadn't done anything. I didn't even go to my room." She sniffed. "The mess is still there."

Just double-checking. "Okay," he said.

"It was a nurse," she said suddenly.

Aaron sucked in his breath without realizing it. "Who was?"

"One of the people who—" She started crying again. "They locked me in a closet."

"Where?"

"I don't know. Why did they do it? Did they take my baby?

Is that what happened?'' Her body began to twitch uncontrollably again. "Oh, God, did they take my baby?''

"Let's talk some more about these people. How do you know it was a nurse?'' Aaron said gently.

Bettina shook her head, trying to remember. "I don't know. Talked like one.'' Her head went back and forth as she regressed into the terror. "No, no, don't do it.''

"Was it somebody you knew?''

"I don't know,'' she said wildly.

"Was it somebody from the hospital, one of those nurses?''

"I don't know. I was sick. They made me sick. I heard things. It was horrible,'' she cried. "Did they take my baby? Will you find her?''

"Well, thank you for talking to me.'' Aaron knew he had to stop now. He got up and stretched his legs.

"Where are you going?'' Bettina cried. "I want to know. You can tell me.''

"We don't know where your baby is, Bettina. We're trying to find her.''

"Oh, God. I knew it.'' She took herself out of the sun and curled up, crying and hugging herself. "Oh, God.''

"I need your help, Bettina, to find her. You have to tell me everything you can remember. But you don't have to tell me everything at one time. We'll talk about this some more later. Try to rest a little.''

"I don't want to rest. I want to see my husband.''

"We'll see. Do you want some medicine to help you relax?''

Bettina turned away from the sun, which had begun to inch closer to her. "I wish I were dead,'' she murmured.

"Everyone else is glad you're alive. I'll be back later,'' Aaron said gently.

He told the nurse on the floor to keep an eye on her, to

look in every five minutes and call him in his office if there was any change.

He headed back to his office, but once in the elevator, he pushed the button for the maternity floor, shaking his head in perplexity.

Psychotic yesterday, sane today. This was certainly unusual. The urinalysis was negative for alcohol, barbiturates and cocaine, but that didn't mean she hadn't been poisoned with some other toxic substance. Should have done some blood tests. He shrugged. They could do some now, but it was probably too late to find anything. Well, he'd try anyway. What else could explain how an ostensibly healthy woman had gone off her nut in the space of a few hours?

If she murdered her baby, as the police seemed to think at the moment, this would be a hell of a story to cover it. He pondered that possibility. She said two people came to her house, drugged her, locked her in a closet, took her baby. If she were a psychopath, this might very well be the kind of story she would invent, and embroider, and stick to, even when faced with proof it didn't happen that way.

He nodded at a colleague who was passing in the hall. On the other hand, he had seen many psychotics. He had seen the criminally insane. They did not look like this. He knew they could be plausible, entertaining, convincing, persuasive. There was no question Bettina could be out there in cuckoo land, stringing him along with her honest eyes. He had no reason to believe at this point that she wasn't a psychopath. But he had no reason to doubt her either. The doors slid open on the OB floor. He didn't come up here very often, but there were a number of babies in the nursery and a whole lot of nurses to talk to.

49

Tom looked around Dr. Simon's office. He noted the brown leather couch, the framed diplomas on the wall. A lot of books in bookcases that covered two walls. A computer and piles of unopened letters and medical journals that had accumulated during the last few days. There was nothing of a personal nature, except a small carriage clock that looked like it might have been a gift.

"Thank you for seeing me," Tom said. He had been leaving messages for him since early that morning.

"I've been jerked around quite a bit. I was afraid I'd never get to talk to anybody who knew anything," he added.

He had been besieged by reporters when he left the house and was followed by the police everywhere he went. He was still reeling from the aggressiveness, the violation of it all. Even now they were waiting for him downstairs, wanted pictures and background information, wanted his blood. The police didn't want him to leave town. It was appalling. Early in the morning an agent had called wanting to represent him. The man said there was big money in his story. It could be a book, a TV movie.

Tom felt like weeping and didn't have the privacy to do it, hadn't been allowed freedom of movement in his own house. He had been forced to watch people track up the place, leave their garbage in his kitchen. He had been questioned unmercifully for hours, though he had no answers to give. And he had slept not at all, wanting desperately to be with his wife.

"We try to do the best thing for the patient." Aaron pointed to a chair with a vaguely apologetic air. "Have a seat."

He could see why Ayub was not impressed with the husband. Half of his head had been shaved and there were a number of black strings crisscrossing an ugly red line that had obviously not been sewn by a plastics man. His color was not good and one eye was still quite bloodshot. He also looked like he hadn't eaten any solid food in a while.

"Have you seen her?" Tom asked, swallowing.

"Yes. I saw her late yesterday afternoon and this morning." He paused. "She's doing remarkably well," he said slowly. "Yesterday she was very disoriented, distraught. Now she seems quite coherent. Very upset about you and the baby, of course."

Why had they shaved so much of his head? The wound was hardly in his hair at all.

"Looks like you've had a hell of a time. What happened?" Aaron asked.

"This is the reason I wasn't here when the baby was born." Tom tried to control the anguish that overcame him every time he had to explain it. "I had an accident in the Middle East. Stupid freak thing."

"How are you doing?"

Tom shook his head. "They won't let me go into our room, questioned me all night, won't let me touch anything. It's —" He shook his head again, couldn't say how bad it was. And Bettina was locked up. The police, who were supposed to be helping her, thought she murdered her own child. It was insane.

"I'd like to see her," he said after he regained control of himself.

"It's very important to get the patient stabilized before we can start thinking of that. Any kind of pressure from the outside world can cause a relapse."

Normally Aaron did not speak with the spouse of a patient.
It was both hospital policy and his policy for family members to
communicate with him through social workers. That way there
could be no compromise of the patient's best interests. Family
members could be helpful, but often they were demanding and
difficult and did not want to leave their loved ones in the highly
structured environment they needed. In many cases patients did
not *want* to see their families and had no wish to return home.

This was different. With Bettina, everything about the
treatment—indeed her whole future—depended on establishing
reality. What mattered was not how the patient perceived the
facts, but the facts themselves. Aaron had spoken in an even,
unemotional tone. But Tom seemed like a nice fellow. He
watched Tom sweating with real distress and suffered with him.
This was a major bad day. This was the kind of thing Aaron
didn't go home and forget.

"What about your head?" he asked gently.

"I had an MRI scan in Geneva." Tom shrugged. "I'm
seeing double sometimes." He hadn't admitted this before. He
wondered what made him say it now. Was that what happened
with psychiatrists? You just took one look at them and your
secrets came out involuntarily?

"You might have an injured muscle. Do you have a doctor
here?" Aaron asked.

Tom shook his head.

"Maybe you should see an eye doctor," he suggested.

"I'd like to see Bettina." Tom didn't want to talk about
himself. What difference did it make?

"Are you angry?" Aaron asked suddenly. Bettina had said
several times that she was afraid of his anger.

"I don't think that covers it." Tom's pale cheeks reddened.
"They're digging up my wife's gardens. There are reporters all

over the place. They're trying to bribe the police to get pictures of her from the house. Wedding pictures, anything. I locked them up, but nothing is out of bounds for them. They can go where they want. They're eating in my kitchen." Tom stopped, unable to go on.

"Who's the criminal?" he asked after a minute. "Is the victim a criminal for having it happen to her? To me?"

Aaron sighed. "It's an agonizing situation. It's very painful for you, but we're trying to find out what happened. I guess this is the only way we can start answering the questions."

"They think she killed the baby." Tom was afraid to ask what kind of crazy things Bettina had said during the two times Dr. Simon saw her, and if he, too, thought she was capable of murdering her own child.

"Who does?" Aaron said sharply.

"The police do. I hear them talking. There was no sign of anyone breaking in, no fingerprints anywhere but hers. There weren't any of mine." He smiled ruefully. "She kept the place clean. Except our room." His lips twitched with the memory.

"There was blood all over the place. You've seen her. She has no injuries. They think it's the baby's blood. They're looking for a *body*."

"It's not the only thing they're doing. It's only what you can see. They're looking for other explanations, too."

Tom did not believe that. He put his hand to his head as the pain attacked and spread, taking over like an invading army.

"Are you all right?" Aaron asked.

"No. Should I be?"

He was like his wife, Aaron thought. Both said what they thought. He liked that. "Are you in pain is what I meant. Not psychic, physical."

"Both," Tom admitted. "I'm supposed to take Advil, but

there wasn't any at the house. I forgot to buy some on the way here.''

"Are you angry at your wife?" Aaron asked. He opened the bottom drawer of his desk and rummaged around in his supply of over-the-counter antihistamines and analgesics. "That's the second thing that seems to be frightening her.''

"Me?" Tom was bewildered. "What do you mean?''

"I don't know. Do you get mad at her a lot?''

Tom cocked his head to try to get this doctor with four huge eyebrows into focus. "I adore her. I think she's a—I don't know, a saint. A paragon. I've never met anybody else like her. But you wouldn't know. You don't know her." He looked away.

Aaron found the Advil. "I'm not supposed to do this," he remarked, "but take two." He held out the bottle. "You're not taking anything else, are you?''

"Thanks." Tom took the bottle gratefully. "No, I'm not taking anything.''

"I'll get you some water." Aaron left Tom in his office and went down the hall to the water fountain. He came back in a minute with a cone-shaped paper cup filled with cold water, handed it over. He thought about what Tom had said, and on the way back to his office decided he did know Bettina—had a sense of her, anyway.

"So, what about her makes you angry?''

Tom swallowed the two pills. "I don't know what you're talking about. She never makes me angry. Well, she *does* too much. Puritan ethic—do you know about that?" He peered at the man.

Aaron smiled. "I have it, too.''

"But it didn't make me *angry*.''

"She went home," Aaron pointed out. Maybe that made him angry.

Tom gulped. "She went home."

"Were you afraid something like this might happen?"

"How could I know? I didn't want her to be alone, that's all," Tom said wildly.

People often knew things. He didn't want her to be alone. Was there any particular reason he didn't? Aaron sat back in his swivel chair and waited. He didn't speak again until Tom had been silent for a long time.

"Was she depressed a lot?" he asked finally.

Tom shook his head. "I'm telling you, she's a sunny person. Look at her work. You're a shrink—look at the pictures she drew. They show how she saw the world. She wanted this baby more than anything."

"Did she ever have days when she couldn't get up?"

"No, she didn't even have premenstrual tension," Tom spit out.

Aaron snorted. Lucky fellow. "Is she a person who frustrates easily?" he asked neutrally.

"No."

"Has she ever had a psychotic episode?"

"I don't know what that is," Tom said honestly.

"The way you saw her yesterday. Agitated, incoherent, paranoid."

"No. I don't think she got like that on her own."

Aaron tended to agree with him. He paused.

"Do you know of anything very traumatic that happened to her? Either during your marriage or when she was a child. Or even when you were gone."

"No, I can't think of anything." Tom thought about it. "She has her fears. Everybody does, I guess. But nothing happened. She wasn't beaten or abused, or anything like that. Is that what you mean?"

"Well, there are other kinds of traumas, too. Losses, humiliations, verbal abuse, someone's dying she loved a lot."

"Her parents are not very warm people. They're like this." Tom gave the doctor his mother-in-law's steely, thin-lipped stare. "But they weren't *mean* to her. Her baby brother died when she was three, or four. I don't know how that affected her. Her parents didn't have any more children."

Aaron sat up and swiveled the other way. Interesting.

Tom frowned. "Why are you asking me all this if you don't think she did it?"

"I don't think she did it," Aaron said suddenly. He didn't mean to say it, but he felt for Tom and wanted to help him. He would worry and worry over having said it. Wrong thing to say at this point. Unprofessional. But the damage was done. And it was what he thought.

"You don't?" Tom said, surprised.

"No, I don't. This would not be the first time in history that someone tried to take a baby that wasn't hers. You can find it in the Bible." He was silent for a moment. Too bad Solomon wasn't here to settle this one.

"Bettina feels a lot of guilt," he said finally. "This was the second baby in her life that was lost."

"What about my . . . our baby? Do you think they can find her?" Tom said, clearly relieved by the doctor's belief in Bettina's innocence.

"You know I can't answer that. I wish I could." Aaron shook his head at his helplessness.

If Bettina's story was true, they would try to find the baby. At least it was a closed circle. There were a limited number of people in the community who knew she was vulnerable, and where to find her. What happened to the baby after that was another question.

Aaron talked to the distraught husband a while longer. Then, after having a very late and insufficient lunch, he went to see Bettina again.

50

It was dark when Peter arrived at Isobel's apartment. He had gone out the back way, along the row of town houses, and had come out at the end of the street behind where the van was parked. He didn't think he was followed. He walked a long way and then called a taxi. He had about a hundred and forty dollars left in the world and the same desperate feelings he had when he was young and poor and worried about there being enough to buy food.

He walked the last few blocks to Isobel's apartment and circled around it two or three times before he went inside. He put his finger on the buzzer and didn't let up until she opened the door. She was wearing a low-cut, slinky cotton knit that was tight around her hips and tied with a gauzy cotton scarf. The scarf was familiar. She had worn it many times before.

Her bright red mouth was open in surprise. His ring had been so insistent she thought it was the police come to get her. She had no thought of running away. The smell of roasting chicken drifted out into the hall.

He pushed past her and slammed the door.

"You got me all the way over here for this?" he said, gnashing his teeth at the table set for two, the daisies, and her irrepressible domesticity, which had disgusted him at the best of times.

Isobel backed into the room.

He went quickly to the window and looked out. "I thought you had something to tell me."

"I do, but we have to eat, don't we? I thought—"

"I can't eat," he spat at her. "I have to get out of here."

A muscle in his cheek jumped. He clenched and unclenched his fist as if it had a muscle-strengthening spring in it. He was crazed with anxiety. After he had talked to Angel that morning he turned on his answering machine, because he didn't want to be bothered by Isobel. It was no easier to get away from her than from Angel. He was trapped.

She left a message on his machine. "I have to see you. Come to my apartment tonight. It's urgent."

Then when he tried to call her back a few minutes later, there was no answer. He tried calling again and again, but she didn't pick up all day. He knew she was manipulating him. She was capable of doing anything to hurt him. He couldn't risk not going.

Isobel turned away from him. "I didn't want to talk on the phone. You told me it's bugged."

He peered out the window, still saw nothing, and swung back to her furiously. "What's the matter with you? Are you trying to get us killed? Don't you know they're after us?"

"I'm scared." Her eyes filled with tears. "I had to talk to someone."

"I told you to be a piece of the furniture. Don't think, don't make a move. Don't *talk*."

"I'm scared," she said again.

Convulsively, his fist clenched. He scanned the street a third time. He didn't know whether he had been followed or not. He had gone out the back way, after dark. He hadn't seen anyone around all day, but he couldn't be sure with them. They could be shadows. They could be less than shadows, not seen at all.

Isobel put a hand on her hip.

"Why are you dressed like that?" she asked. He had black denim jeans on, a black T-shirt, and black sneakers, not usual for him at all. When he didn't answer that question, she asked another. "Did you see the news? They're looking for a body. They think she killed it."

"Oh, yeah?" Peter laughed suddenly, pleased by his success. He was really brilliant.

"And the husband came back."

"Really?" Peter didn't know anything about it. He hadn't turned on the television, because it was long gone. And his newspapers had stopped coming to him more than six months ago. He had been afraid to go out for one all day.

"They're digging up the place." She shuddered, as if they might really find something. "It's horrible."

He grimaced. She disgusted him.

"Oh, Jesus, Isobel. What did you expect?"

"I don't know." She bit her lip.

"Did you want everyone to believe her and start looking for us?" Peter demanded.

"No, of course not." She hesitated. "But I don't want her to go to jail, either." She began to sniffle. "She's a nice person. I *know* her."

"Look, Isobel, you've got to shape up."

"What if she goes to jail?"

"She won't go to jail. She can't be tried for homicide without evidence that a homicide has been committed." Peter was trying to be patient, but he hated her. Hated the dress and the dinner.

"What does that mean?" Isobel asked.

"It means they can hold her for a while in the loony bin, but they can't indict her without a body." He leaned back in the chair and stretched. He needed something badly.

"Can you at least give me a drink?" he said.

"Oh, sorry." Isobel rushed to get him one. "Is scotch all right?" She brought out the bottle.

"Leave it here," he said smoothly.

She rolled her eyes, but did not protest.

She poured him an inch and went to get some ice, leaving the glass behind. He drank down the scotch in one swallow and poured some more.

She came back with the ice, and put three cubes in the glass.

"I can't tell you how awful it was," she said.

"What was exactly?" Peter drank what was in the glass and poured himself some more. It was in no way as satisfying as cocaine. He felt no high, no buzz, no relief or happiness at all. But alcohol helped a little. It was like letting some of the steam out of a radiator about to blow. He felt like smashing her face in. Then he began to take an interest in the sash around her hips. This was a familiar situation; they'd been here before. Every step was an invitation. She wanted it. He knew she did.

"Seeing the news and knowing it's wrong," Isobel said. "It kind of makes a person lose faith in everything."

Peter laughed loudly, and then looked toward the door. "Didn't you know that's what faith is for? The world's a piece of shit."

"I don't feel that way. But I don't want to go back to my old life. It's finished for me," Isobel murmured.

"Boy, you put a twist on everything, don't you?" Peter reached for the bottle.

"I want to go away," she said, frowning at him with disapproval. "Let's go away." Her eyes were sly, like a cat's.

"Go away? Are you crazy?" He didn't want to look at her eyes.

"I don't want to see any of those people again, sit at that desk. I don't want to hear people talking about it. And what if they start questioning me? What will I say? I don't think I can take it." Isobel let it pour out hysterically.

"Something's burning," Peter said suddenly.

"My dinner——" she cried, and ran into the kitchen.

She pulled the blackened remains out of the oven. "What a night," she cried. Everything in her life was going wrong all at once. "I put it on too high. What a mess."

He was laughing in the other room.

She came into the living room. "What's so funny?"

"You're a menace," he said, but not harshly now. "The wife's bonkers; the whole situation is made to order; there are no clues—none—and you want to leave town." It made him worry about her.

"But, Peter," Isobel said. "You always said you wanted to take me to Paris. Why not go now?"

"With what?" he asked. She didn't seem to understand.

"I don't know. Didn't they give you the money?" She frowned.

He shook his head. "No, they didn't."

Isobel sank to her knees at his feet. Her hair, which had been carefully curled two hours ago, now hung limply around her face. Her eyes were dark and smudged. Her makeup had melted from the heat in the kitchen. The facade of the confident vamp was gone. On the floor at Peter's feet, she was nothing but a plump tabby begging to be kicked. He knew why she wore that dress and that sash. He knew what she wanted.

"When will they give it to you?" she asked.

He shrugged. "A few days."

"We could take the money and go then." She stroked his knee.

He shook his head. "It's not so simple."

"Well, I'm scared. You don't have to see them. You don't have to go back there every day. I can't do it."

Peter moved uneasily in his chair. There was the smell of burned meat in the room. It was hot; he could see tiny beads of sweat between Isobel's breasts. She was stroking his thigh in a persistent way, her head lowered like someone on the dock, awaiting sentence. She wanted sex and security. He knew the way her mind worked. If he gave her a pop, she'd feel safe for a day or two.

"Peter," Isobel whispered urgently. "Let's give the baby back."

Peter stared at the ceiling, trying to hang on to his feeling of control over her. "How do you propose to do that?"

"You could think of something." Isobel's head was lowered almost to his ankle. His sneakers, which were old and worn, seemed all wrong for him. But she wouldn't allow herself to focus on them.

"It will never be right between us if you don't," Isobel said.

He realized she was on her knees, begging him. He felt the energy go. She was not a safe, passive tabby. She was all over the place, like a bird hopping from branch to branch. She had a new thought a minute, couldn't be relied on for anything.

"Don't you want it to work out between us?" she asked.

He concentrated on not losing his patience. She was pathetic. Even now, all she could think of was the relationship. She did not seem to understand anything. She was like a living Barbie doll that repeated the same things over and over no matter what was coming down around her.

"I risked everything for you," she was saying. "Don't put me off."

"Do that again," he said.

"What?" she looked up.

"What you were doing before."

She moved over and nuzzled him in the crotch. "What about the baby?" she asked.

"I'm giving it some thought," Peter murmured. He had, in fact, been thinking all day about the two cars in the garage, the large property, the guest house. The silver and electronic equipment. The Dunnes were not poor people.

He liked thinking of the Dunnes' stuff. They were affluent. He might be able to profit from both ends. He felt better, felt even better when Isobel crawled between his legs and rubbed her round, moist breasts back and forth across his crotch while her hands fumbled with his zipper.

"Nice," he murmured. He reached down and stroked her bare shoulders.

"Yours," she said.

He reached lower to where her dress went in and hugged her waist. She had a slender waist. His fingers almost met when he put his hands around it. She sucked in her stomach so he could feel how small she was, how feminine. She had his pants unzipped and her sharp little tongue darted into the gap of his boxer shorts.

"Oh," he groaned at the touch of her tongue on the tip of his penis.

"All yours," she said. "To do whatever you want."

His hands traveled down farther. He squeezed her round ass, like two ripe peaches. He untied the sash, took it off, and pulled up her dress, gathering it in his hand.

"Not here," she said suddenly, though she herself had started it here.

One hand burrowed between her thighs. She wore no underpants and was wet, open to the probing of his fingers. She really wanted it. He felt gratified, strong.

"Oh, Peter, stop," she said.

Her switching gears again annoyed him. He wanted to shut her trap, make her carry on without protesting about this and nagging him about that. He had her by her pulsing little crotch and held her tight that way. She began to pant.

"Let me close the curtains, will you?" she demanded.

"Oh, shit." He let go with disgust.

She was back in a minute, pulling him off the chair. "Come in here," she said.

He picked up the sash and followed her into her bedroom, where she had an old-fashioned brass bed that was high off the ground. She turned to embrace him before taking her dress off. He squeezed her breasts with both hands, pulling the sash back and forth across them.

"Nice," she murmured. She turned toward the bed and he grabbed her hips, pulling up her dress.

She wiggled her behind, knowing what he liked.

He pressed against her bare flesh with his jeans half on, just the way the boys in high school used to do in the back of cars. Only this was safer, more comfortable, more sophisticated by far. He pulled up her dress, higher still, until it was around her waist. His hands were all over her, reaching from behind, fondling her flat stomach, her heavy breasts. His fingers caressed her throat, pressing gently.

She sighed. He pushed against her from behind until she was resting against the bed. He drew back for a second to pull more of her dress away and to wrap the ends of the scarf securely around his hands. She closed her eyes.

"Hurt me," she said.

He entered her, holding her tight, with his legs braced

around her, while she moved against him. "Okay," he said.

"Ah." The sound turned to a gurgle as he wrapped the scarf around her neck and pulled it tight.

For what seemed to be a long time, she struggled, pushing and pulling against him while he had her pinned like an enormous frog. Pronged below and garroted above. Each thrust of her hips brought her closer to death and him closer to orgasm. All the frustration and pain he had felt, the fury at Angel, and Wendal, and Isobel herself, was released in this great surge of exquisite power. She could not get away, neither below nor above. He had all of her, just as she said he did. And the more she struggled, the more the pleasure he felt. He enjoyed the tension in his arms, the cramps in his hands, and he held on with all his strength, ramming away at her long after she was lifeless on the bed.

Afterward, he was almost surprised when she didn't get up. All the time he was cleaning up, wiping away his fingerprints, he was amazed that she had been dispatched so easily. He was almost convinced it was the way out she wanted, that she might have helped him, even enjoyed it. He went down the fire stairs and sat on the first step, the scarf bunched in his hand. As soon as he got to the bottom he started shaking all over with a desperate craving for the rest of the bottle of scotch that he had left upstairs. He sat there for several hours before he calmed down.

51

Laura was up at three-thirty in the morning, waiting in anguish for the baby to cry. What she had expected to be the best weekend of her life had turned out to be the worst. Now it was Monday, the Fourth of July. She was faced with a day by herself to take care of a baby that wasn't hers and agonize over what to do about it. Wendal had a golf date, and afterward there was a picnic, tennis matches, dinner, and fireworks at the club. They always looked forward to it all year. She knew Wendal wanted to go.

She got out of bed before dawn and looked in on Anna. She was asleep on her stomach, the way Laura had put her down, breathing softly. Her soft red hair fluffed out from her head. This was no agitated, squalling baby. Laura stroked her head with a finger. The baby stirred but didn't open her eyes.

After a few minutes of quiet adoration, Laura retreated to the armchair on the other side of the room and there waited for the baby to wake up. An hour later, when Anna began to squirm a little, Laura picked her up before she had time to make her first cry.

"Hello, baby," she crooned. "How is my little angel today?"

She was wet. Laura changed her, powdered her against the summer heat, and washed her face with cool water. She performed these tasks with reverence, knowing with every caress that Anna was not really Anna and would have to be returned.

This gave a bittersweet poignancy to the ritual. How many times would she be able to touch this skin, kiss these pink cheeks? Not many. Anna kicked on the changing table, waved her tiny hands in the air, unused to having space around her to move. For Laura each hour was exquisite torture, full of the quiet intimacy mothers have with their children only at this time in their lives, when each is everything to the other. No one could love this child more or take care of her better than she did. No one needed her more.

Wendal dragged himself out of bed at eight, helped himself to a cup of coffee, and looked for Laura. She was sitting on the terrace holding the sleeping baby, watching the sprinklers water the gardens. He was touched by the picture and went for his camera.

"No," Laura said in alarm when she saw him with it.

"Why not?"

She shook her head and grabbed at a reason. "Her eyes are closed."

He snapped the picture anyway and went to the front door for the newspapers. As he read and drank coffee, and later when he went to shave, Laura willed him to stay home and not leave her with this unbearable burden. His acting as if everything were normal made her furious. Why didn't he know? He didn't seem to know. She couldn't believe it.

Finally she put the baby down and dressed in a mint-green sundress he particularly liked. By now he was nattily dressed for a morning on the course with two important business clients. He was sitting on the sofa with his third cup of coffee, passing the time by reading the second-string articles he had only skimmed the first time he took up the papers. It was a Monday on a holiday weekend. There wasn't much in them.

Laura sat down next to him. "Honey, do you have to play

golf today?'' she asked, trying not to sound as pathetic as she felt.

"Yes," he said firmly, "I do."

"Why, today of all days, do you have to?" she asked.

"Because I promised a long time ago," Wendal said, "before I ever knew I was going to be a father."

"I wish you wouldn't go," she said.

"Look, Laura honey. I can't sit with you every minute. You wanted a baby," he said wearily, "you knew it would tie you down. I won't be able to be with you all the time. I have to go back to the office tomorrow. I don't get paternity leave." He smiled at the idea.

"I have a bad feeling," Laura murmured. "Please look at me. I'm suffering." She had some other lady's baby in her house and couldn't give it back without help. She wanted Wendal to know, and do something, make a decision for her. But she didn't want to *tell* him. If he wouldn't talk to her, she didn't know how she could solve her problem.

"If I had a dollar for every bad feeling you've ever had about something, Laura, I'd be a very rich man," Wendal replied.

"This is more important than anything that's ever happened to us before. We have to face it," she said urgently.

"I understand, believe me. I know you're an unusually sensitive person. I know you were scared by Peter's behavior the other day. I also know this story on the news has got you all upset."

"How do you know that?" Laura prickled all over, feeling he had found the way in.

"How do I know? Honey, I know you. You've got all the newspapers here. You've watched the news more than you have since that little girl fell down the drain in Texas.'' Wendal shook his head. "It's all over you. You're just—''

"Just what?'' She pointed at the paper he was holding, where there was another article on the "Missing Jersey Infant'' facing her.

"Don't you think this is odd, horrible? It's right here. It happened *right* here. Doesn't that mean anything to you?''

Wendal sighed again. "Yes, Laura, it's horrible. But a thousand horrible things happen every day. You can't break your heart over every one.''

"It's so close, Wendal.'' Laura couldn't believe he was so dense. "It could be us,'' she said. *It is us.*

"Anything could be us. Anything I deal with every day could be us. Men my age drop dead of heart attacks. People die in plane crashes; other people in the same plane live. You can't explain it. People die right here in car accidents, in bicycle accidents. All these things could be us. But they aren't us.'' He closed the paper and put it down.

"You just have to stop thinking that way.'' He pushed the coffee cup away from him. "You have to look around and say, 'The sun is shining, and everything is fine.' '' He finished his lecture and got up to void all that coffee he'd drunk.

He didn't get it. He didn't want to get it. Laura raged at him for making it so difficult for her. She listened to him urinate long and noisily, hating him because he wouldn't make the leap himself, wouldn't think the unthinkable. Maybe men couldn't do that. They weren't subtle. Before he flushed the toilet, she went into the other bathroom and closed the door.

When the phone rang, Wendal jumped to get it. "Hello?''

"Wendal, this is Peter Balkan. You put me in a bad spot about the money. I promised it for Friday. Now it's Monday, and the girl's family is all upset. They're beginning to think . . .''

"And you agreed to get me the papers first. Do you have them?" Wendal interrupted.

"I told you it would take several weeks. And let me remind you that anytime until they're formalized, the girl can change her mind. I'm doing you a favor. Usually it takes three months."

"And let me tell you something," Wendal said furiously. "I'm not going to be intimidated by you. You've upset my wife terribly. What kind of behavior is this? Why are you threatening us? This isn't a used-car deal, this is an adoption. Everything takes time. If it's on the up-and-up, fine; it'll work. You give me the papers and I'll give you the money. If it's not, you better tell me now. Either way, we're not some sleazy clients who found you in the yellow pages, so don't think you can threaten us." It couldn't be them, he kept saying to himself. But what if it was? No, it was too big a leap. If Peter was going to steal a baby he would have done it three months ago, somewhere far away. This was a coincidence.

"Wendal." Laura came into the living room. "Who is it, sweetheart?"

Wendal put his hand over the phone. "Go in the other room, Laura. And close the door, will you? It's just a business call."

"Wen." Laura's hand flew to her mouth.

"Go. I'll be in in a minute."

He waited until he heard the door click.

"Wendal," Peter said coldly. "You are—well, I think I'm just going to have to take the baby back."

"Not if you don't want a great deal of trouble, Peter. If the mother is disturbed, why don't you give her our number. I'll be happy to talk to her. Otherwise, get to work on the papers. If there's anything else wrong, you better tell me now."

Wendal paused to let Peter say something.

When he didn't answer, Wendal added, "And if you try anything funny, if you come around here and bother Laura, so help me God, I'll break your neck."

There was another long silence on the other end.

Then Peter said, "You're going to be sorry for this. We'll see who can cause whom the most trouble."

"Don't give me that," Wendal said. "I won't take your threats."

"This isn't going to end well for you, Wendal," Peter said angrily.

"If you treat this like a cash sale, Peter," Wendal replied, "maybe your practice could do with some investigation."

Peter slammed the phone down.

There was a bang and a click as the line went dead, then a second later the dial tone. Wendal replaced the receiver angrily. He had dealt with people like Peter before. They liked to yell and scream and use abusive language. They liked to threaten people. Anybody who was frightened by it got run over. No way was he going to take it. But there was no question that he was very disturbed. This was feeling very ugly and wrong. He wasn't sure what to do. Who did one go to about things like this? How could they investigate?

Laura came out. "Who was that?" she asked suspiciously.

"It was Arnold, crazy about something we're working on," Wendal said quickly. "You know how he is." He didn't want to scare her now.

Laura nodded, unconcerned with whatever business question was bugging him now.

"You look great," he said, trying to placate her for going off on his own. "I like that dress."

"Thanks a lot," she muttered.

She was still mad. He picked up his golf bag. He was sorry, he really was, but it was better that he go. She had to learn to leave the worries to him. He kissed her on the cheek and assured her he'd skip the picnic lunch and be back by noon. It was the best he could do.

52

Bettina had had the baby some days ago. She didn't know how many. She didn't know how long she had been here. She had lost her sense of time. Sometimes she stood at the window thinking about jumping out. A thousand spiders crawled across the sill. She drew back screaming, but only in her head. She knew she shouldn't scream. The window was locked. She tried it over and over. It must be screwed shut. From where she stood she could see the front door of the hospital. If she jumped, she'd land on the sidewalk, where people were coming in and out. Nobody she knew came in or out while she was standing there.

She was where crazy people were and she wanted to scream until there was no sound left in her. But if she did what she felt like doing, they might keep her there forever. She told herself not to scream.

Dr. Simon told her she had to think, think all the time about what happened. She had to tell them what happened. Remember everything and make them believe her. It was hard to do that. Her head was foggy and her body hurt from childbirth and other injuries she had no memory of getting. But she didn't feel like lying down and putting the covers over her head. She was a strong woman. She thought of the peasants in the field who gave birth and went to work the next day. She had to pull the pieces of herself together.

The army of spiders crawled down the wall and headed toward her. Bettina resisted the impulse to scream. Why wouldn't they go away? She went out into the hall to get away from them. Her legs were not so shaky now. She could walk. She walked from one end of the hall to the other, counting the rooms. Twelve on each side of the hall. Hers was right next to the nurses' station in the middle, across from the locked doors that distinguished this floor as the psychiatric unit. She couldn't get out. Don't scream, she told herself. Don't do it. Look around, think about where you are.

In the room on the other side of Bettina's was a cadaver of a person, a girl so emaciated it didn't look as if she could possibly get out of bed. Her head was a skull from which her lips and cheeks had retreated, leaving a face that was all jaw and teeth. Her neck was the size of Bettina's wrist. Her body was a stick figure, dressed in a light bathrobe that was tightly wrapped and tied around her waist. Her arms and legs protruded like an exhibit of a mummy in a natural-history museum.

The mummy wandered slowly up and down the hallway all day long, pushing a hanger on wheels with IV bottles that were attached to her. Bettina watched her progress as she neared the lounge. It was a large TV room with vapid prints on the wall and a number of cheap plastic chairs placed at random. At one end was a pool table no one was using. This room scared Bettina. It looked like a community center lounge, but everyone in it was doing something weird and was in pajamas. She passed it quickly.

The television was on, showing the French Open. A young man who didn't look more than eighteen sat in front of it, completely motionless, his eyes fixed on the screen. Two young women intently analyzed each point. A middle-aged woman, strangely made up, talked quietly to herself in the doorway, arguing as if to another person. Everything was subdued, ghostly. Don't scream, Bettina told herself.

The girl with the IV stopped to speak to her.

"How are you today?" she asked.

Bettina jumped at the voice. It surprised her that the grotesque thing addressing her sounded normal, even cheerful. She swallowed and raised her shoulders a little in a modified shrug. Not very good.

"You're new," the girl said matter-of-factly. "Are you going to watch the parade?"

Before, when crazy people talked to her, Bettina had never had to answer. She struggled to find her voice. "What parade?"

"Fourth of July. I like the bands."

The Fourth of July? It felt like months had passed since she left this hospital with her baby and a happy life in front of her. How had she gotten up here with schizophrenics and people who wanted to kill themselves? Don't scream, she told herself.

Across from where she was standing, there was a man in his room shaking all over.

"I'm Emily," the girl said after a second. She held out the bony hand without the IV sticking in it.

"I'm—Bettina," Bettina said slowly, not sure she still was.

"Strange name," Emily remarked cheerfully, and shuffled off down the hall. "I have to finish my exercise."

Another wave of grief washed over Bettina. Her strange name was the reason she'd wanted to call her daughter Katie or Elizabeth, something regular. She leaned against the window at the end of the hall. The glass was cool against her bruised forehead.

Downstairs there was a lot of activity. The police were putting up barriers, and there were people with cameras milling around. What was going on? She couldn't bear not knowing. She hurried down to the other end of the hall and back two or three times, looking for a telephone. There wasn't one. Had they found her baby dead? Was that it? Oh, God, why didn't Tom come to see her? He must hate her to leave her in here where she didn't know what was happening and couldn't use the phone. Don't scream.

She stopped by the window at the end of the hall, watching people come and go through the front doors. She was concentrating on not screaming. Telling herself over and over not to let go of the hyena inside. She saw Dr. Simon walk through the locked doors. He looked unperturbed. He stopped and talked with the nurses at the nurses' station for several minutes, glancing over a chart or two. Bettina watched him.

Finally he turned toward her and nodded, started down the hall in her direction. He hadn't changed since yesterday. He was still tall, hunched a bit around the shoulders as if he wanted to be smaller, or was tense in his muscles. He wore a white coat with his plastic name tag on it. He stopped to talk to Emily.

Bettina went into her room and sat in a chair to wait for him. She spoke first when he came in.

"I have to go home," she said. "You can't keep me here, I'm not crazy." Could they keep her here? Was she crazy? She didn't know.

The furrow between his eyes deepened. "Hello," he replied. "How are you, Dr. Simon? I'm fine, thank you, Mrs. Dunne." He sat in the other chair and crossed his long legs with a smile.

Her eyes narrowed with suspicion. "What was that for?" she demanded. Was she crazy? Was she?

"Just being friendly." His smile grew a little. "I'm glad to see you up. It's good for you."

"I don't feel friendly," she said. "This is a terrible place. I can't stand it here. I'm not crazy," she said.

"It's not so terrible," he said. "I talked to Dr. Street this morning."

"Where is he?" Bettina demanded.

"He's on a fishing trip. He'll come and see you on Wednesday when he gets back."

Bettina frowned. "I'm not staying here until Wednesday."

"He likes you," Aaron remarked. "He says that from what he knows of you, you're an attractive, intelligent young woman, who delivered a healthy baby and gave every indication of being fully prepared for a normal life."

He crossed his legs the other way.

Bettina took a deep breath and exhaled slowly. Don't lose it. "Will they find my baby?" she asked.

Aaron did not change the expression on his face. "I hope so," he said.

Bettina accepted this answer for a moment. It was better than "I don't know," which would have seemed hopeless to her. Or, "How do you feel about that?" which would have enraged her. She felt anguish. She prayed that her baby was alive. As long as she was alive, they had a chance of recovering her.

"Why can't I go home?" she asked.

"If you and your husband both want you to go home, we can't hold you here," the doctor said slowly. "You're not a prisoner. But we want you to stay until you feel up to the stresses you're going to face."

Bettina blew her nose. "Doesn't he want me to come home?"

"He loves you very much. You're his whole world." Aaron watched her face as he said it.

"I know," she said, sad that she had failed him.

He paused, waiting for her to add something. She didn't.

"I know you feel better today, but you've been through a

lot. You've had a baby. You were in shock when you came in. Do you remember?''

"Yes," Bettina said meekly.

"You were dehydrated, disoriented."

"I remember."

"It takes time to recover from all that."

Bettina blew her nose again. Is he telling me I'm crazy? she wondered. What was the truth?

"I feel uncomfortable here," she said after a minute. "I want to see my husband."

"I know." Aaron gave her his most sympathetic face.

It was an environment that made sick people feel better, and healthy people feel nervous. It was not a bad sign that Bettina wanted to be out of it. But that didn't mean it was a good idea for her to go.

"Bettina, have you seen the cameras and reporters downstairs?" he said seriously.

Bettina nodded.

"Do you know they'll converge on you the minute you show your face? They want to hear your story and take your picture."

"Oh, God. Poor Tom," she cried.

"If you go home, you'll be mobbed by reporters and questioned for hours by the police. I don't know if you're ready for that."

"Oh, God. They think I killed my baby. Does Tom think that?"

Don't scream. Don't scream, she told herself. The scream rose from deep inside. She could feel it coming like a volcano erupting. No, no, they'd keep her here forever. She had to be strong. She pushed the scream and the spiders back.

"How do your breasts feel today?" Aaron asked after a minute.

"They gave me hormones or something. It's drying up my milk." She started to cry quietly. This seemed especially cruel to her.

The resident on Saturday had refused to give her a breast pump because she was in no condition to use it. Then later, Dr. Steadman prescribed the medication, after examining her and talking with Dr. Street.

Aaron was silent as she explained how much she had looked forward to breast-feeding. This medication meant she would never have a chance to do it.

"We want to make you comfortable."

If the baby is alive, Aaron thought, she will be bottle-fed and probably won't return to the breast even if Bettina gets her back. Formula is sweeter than breast milk. An infant might take both if they were alternated. But if it had one exclusively from the beginning, it might have problems changing. These facts, however, wouldn't alter Bettina's fear that the loss of her milk meant she'd never see her baby again.

Aaron passed over the tissue box that had been lying on the end of Bettina's bed, and crossed his legs the other way.

"I know," she murmured. "They said that. It doesn't help."

They sat in silence for several minutes. The silence was terrifying. Bettina fought off a cloud of blackness that was trying to enter her head through the window above where the reporters were. The people with the cameras were there for her. They thought she killed her baby. What if her baby were found dead? Could they keep her here forever? Or put her in prison? Could they do that? What was the truth? Could she have gone crazy and killed her baby without knowing she was doing it, or remembering it afterward? She didn't know.

"Bettina?"

Bettina turned her head to the doctor. She realized that she was crying. Sounds were coming out of her that she didn't want to escape.

"Tell me about the nurses."

Don't scream, she told herself. Don't jump into the black. Wake up. You can do it.

"What nurses?" she asked blankly. She didn't remember any nurses.

53

The phone rang constantly. There was no relief from it. All of Tom's relatives called. Bettina's mother and father called. Everyone in the whole world, it seemed, suddenly wanted to get on a plane and add to the turmoil in Tom's house. His sisters, who as long as he could remember never bothered about anything but their own needs, wanted to drop everything and pay him a visit. Bettina's father, who claimed that going out to the movies might give him a stroke, was insistent that he be there for his baby.

"You can't stop me from coming," he said.

"I wouldn't want to stop you if it would help." Tom tried to talk calmly and sensibly, following Dr. Simon's example of talking reasonably about unreasonable things.

"But there's no place in the house to stay, no food, and no one to take care of you. They won't let you see Bettina," he added, which was just as well. "I'm sorry, the police need the telephone line to be open."

He said it over and over. His outrage was intense when his

sisters asked, his parents asked, George Highgate and any number of people from Axam, and even *her* own parents asked, if Bettina was capable of murdering her child.

"No, we know she didn't do any such thing." He said it a hundred times.

Saying it gave the question a credibility he resented. He was now grateful that Bettina was not permitted a telephone or the newspapers. She did not know what was going on at the house. She wasn't the one who was receiving the crank calls. Four or five people called to tell Tom they hoped Bettina would go to the electric chair. A psychic called, offering her services to locate the baby, dead or alive. Several other people wanted a ransom for her return. The police told Tom this was normal and to ignore it if he could.

In fact he was glad many times over that Bettina was not there to see the destruction of her yard, the curiosity seekers and reporters outside on the road and in the woods. He was particularly glad she missed the drama when a volunteer in waders drew the crowd to the pond.

He suddenly yelled, "Got something here," and everyone went running.

Even Tom's heart stopped when the ancient, muddy boot, caught in the wader's net, was slowly raised out of the water.

New police faces joined Cusick's. He was questioned by a detective from the Chester police, and by Sheriff Anderson, who wanted his men to keep on the case because it had happened in the county. Cusick hung around. Tom did not like going outside without him, so the reporters now called Tom on the phone as well as rushing him when he came out the door.

Claudia Ravello was the only one who got anything at all from him. He was only able to respond to the people who remembered he was human. There didn't seem to be more than one or two.

"It's Claudia Ravello," she said when she got through to him on Monday.

"The police need the line," Tom said flatly.

"Look, I'm sorry I was so rough on you Saturday. I want to make it up to you. Could we talk?"

"We are talking. What do you want?"

"I meant face-to-face. It would be easier."

"Uh uh. Say what you have to say. I have to get off the line."

"All right. I thought you'd like to know that the D.A.'s office has gotten involved."

"What does that mean?" Tom asked in alarm.

"He's got investigators running all over the hospital, interviewing everyone who had access to her, or her files. They've subpoenaed all the tests they've done on her in the hospital. That means all of them, everything from both stays."

Tom was silent for a minute. Then he said, "How do you know?"

"I know the D.A.'s office has been concerned about certain improprieties at Chester for a long time. This gives him the opportunity to open the whole place up. It won't hurt his chances for reelection in November, either," Claudia reported with relish.

"What improprieties?" Tom asked.

"Oh hiring practices, a certain laxness about security procedures. Drugs have disappeared. They had a former mental patient on the nursing staff last year. That kind of thing."

"Oh, God, why are you telling me all this?" Tom asked.

"I thought you'd be glad to know the police have broadened their investigation. They're looking for a link at the hospital. Maybe someone who took care of her, or knew her."

Tom didn't know what to say. It was as if a door was opening.

"Do you have any ideas?" Claudia asked breathlessly.

"No," Tom said. "The police have already asked me this."

"Well, have you seen your wife? I know you've been to the hospital several times. Can she talk yet? Has she told them anything?"

"You seem to know more about it than I do," Tom said. "You tell me."

"I can't get anything from that end," Claudia said honestly. "I did a negative story on Chester last year, and no one there will talk to me now. Is she in isolation? What's the story?"

Tom heard the call-waiting click. "I don't know the story, Claudia. I have to take this."

"Yes, you do. You know where she is, and what her condition is. You know if she's talking. Tell me, is she psychotic, or what?"

Click. "She's what. Listen, they have to keep the lines open, sorry." He pushed the button. "Hello?" No response but the sound of breathing.

He hung up. The phone rang again instantly. He picked up.

"Give me a break. I'm only trying to help," Claudia said. "Don't you want people to know what's really going on? Maybe somebody out there knows something. You have to have more faith in the public. You could make a public appeal. Ask for the return of the child. You never know. These things can make a difference."

"I don't know," Tom said slowly. The idea was appalling to him. He had seen it before and been disgusted. Desperate parents asking for kidneys in prime time, hearts, bone marrow. It was exploitive and horrible. He didn't like seeing it, and didn't want to even consider doing it.

"Why don't you let me come in and talk about it. What do you say?"

Click. "Look, I'll think about it."

"How about ten minutes?"

"No. Let me think about it, Claudia. I'll let you know if I want to do it." Tom hung up.

Immediately the phone rang again. He didn't want to answer it. He wanted to get something to eat. He drifted into the pantry to look for something. He'd had enough of the phone for a lifetime. Looking in the pantry made him yearn for Bettina. He wondered if Claudia's suggestion made any sense. The phone was ringing persistently. He couldn't ignore it anymore. He left the can of tuna he had been considering and reached for the phone on the wall.

"Mr. Dunne?"

"Yes," Tom said.

"Would you like to see your baby again?"

"Who is this?" Tom asked stupidly. Every rational part of him told him to hang up. He didn't.

"Never mind who I am. I know where your baby is. That's all you need to know."

Tom hung up quickly, and closed his eyes. I can't take this. I don't know what to do. The phone rang again. He didn't pick up.

"What do I do?" he agonized, but there wasn't anyone around him to answer.

The phone stopped ringing, and in a second started again.

"Shit. What do I do?"

Sit tight. Everybody said to sit tight. He did not pick up the phone. What should he do, make an appeal on TV? Respond to crank ransom calls. What? He needed Bettina.

The phone stopped ringing and he called Dr. Simon. He wasn't there, but he called back ten minutes later.

"How are you doing?" he asked.

"That's the question I have for you. Is it true they're looking for someone in the hospital?" Tom asked.

"What makes you ask?" Aaron said cautiously.

"One of the reporters called me and said the investigation has taken a turn. What's going on?"

"You know Bettina has not yet been questioned by the police." Aaron was at his desk with all his notes in front of him.

"You told me that."

"Well, I asked if she wanted me to share the information she gave me with the police. I couldn't do it without her permission."

"What information? Is there something?"

"Well, she told me on one occasion that she thought one of the people who abducted her was a nurse. We're following up."

"Jesus," Tom said. "Which one?"

"That's what they're working on. We haven't come up with anything yet."

"How is she?"

"She's coming along."

"I want to see her. I want to talk to her. You can't imagine what it's like here." With all the police. They hadn't stopped tramping through the woods. And the telephone calls.

"I can't stand it," Tom said.

"Do you want some medication?"

"What kind of medication?" Tom asked suspiciously.

"Something to calm you down. We can make you feel better, get some sleep tonight."

"If I'm crazy, will you put me on the eighth floor?" Tom said. "With my wife? I could get sick very quickly."

Aaron thought about it for less than a tenth of a second. "Okay, come in and I'll get you examined. You probably need an examination anyway. I know she wants to see you. I'll talk to Bettina and see if we can set something up."

54

Marilyn could not imagine who could have done such a terrible thing. She couldn't think about anything else. She was the guardian of newborn infants. To her, parents and babies were the most sacred thing on earth. It was an inconceivable evil to hurt a new mother like this. She was hurt and frightened that it had happened here in her domain, was anxious and worried that somehow she might be to blame in some way she didn't understand. Had she done anything wrong? She didn't think so.

She knew Isobel had been there the night Bettina Dunne gave birth. She remembered the doughnuts, remembered every word that passed between them. Isobel had been so eager to see the baby that she'd wanted Marilyn to get it back from the mother, then she just took off without seeing it. But maybe she had to go, for some reason. Marilyn had known Isobel for years, knew she could be flighty sometimes. But she wasn't a bad person. No one she knew could have done anything like this.

She pondered very carefully the questions the good-looking deputy from the sheriff's office asked her. He'd made her nervous, with the gun and the handcuffs hanging off his belt. The equipment distracted her, and she wondered how much it all weighed. In addition, he exuded a powerful maleness she wasn't used to, and didn't take his sunglasses off. She wanted to be helpful, but blushed and didn't know what to tell him. A thousand things happened every night; how could she remember what everyone said and which doors they came in and out of? It seemed so trivial and silly.

She was uncomfortable and worried about what she had said. Then later the shrink from upstairs pushed open the doors to the nursery. She'd seen him around but couldn't say she knew him.

"Hi, I'm Dr. Simon," he said. "I'm talking to all the people who were here when Bettina Dunne was on the floor."

"I know," she said, tersely, and shut up. His name was all over the papers. She knew exactly who he was. She blushed some more, not used to the attention.

"She was fine when she was here. Not crazy, or depressed. That's all I know." She gave him a hopeful smile. He was more like the men she was used to; she felt safe with him, but she didn't want to go through another interrogation.

"I'd like to talk to you for a minute, if you can take a break," he said pleasantly.

"I just took a break. I told everything I know to the police. I don't know anything else. None of us here did anything wrong." She wrapped up the squalling infant she had just changed, and put it back in its plastic bassinet.

"All right, I can talk to you here." He settled back against the wall as she moved to the next bassinet.

She frowned, wondering if he could read her mind, or just looked as if he could.

"What do you want to know?" she asked.

"Do you like working here?" Aaron asked.

Marilyn nodded warily. Were they going to fire her, even if she hadn't done anything wrong? She swallowed.

"I love it here. I—don't know who could do something like this." Her eyes filled with tears. "She was nice."

Aaron nodded. Bettina was nice. "That's what we're trying to find out."

Marilyn gulped. "The papers say you're looking for somebody in the hospital. Do you have a—lead?" she stumbled over the word.

Aaron smiled. "I thought I was asking the questions."

"I know everybody here. No one would do anything like that."

"Okay, what do you think happened then?"

Marilyn frowned. "I don't know. I can't imagine."

"Take a guess."

Marilyn turned away. "I can't. I just can't. Is she really, you know—?" She went on without waiting for the answer. "I mean, maybe somebody gave her something so she wouldn't know what was happening."

"It's a possibility."

"A drug of some kind."

Aaron nodded. "Maybe."

Marilyn chewed a knuckle and her bottom lip at the same time. "Horrible." Then she cocked her head to look at him. "Why do you think it was someone here?"

"No one else knew when she was going home, and no one else knew she was alone," Aaron said.

"She could have told someone else. Check her telephone calls."

"We did." Aaron shifted from one leg to another.

He knew all too well that people often said the opposite of what they really felt. She said she couldn't imagine anything like this happening, and then imagined it quite well. He changed his tack.

"Well, maybe it was something else. Did anything unusual happen during the time Bettina Dunne was here? Anything at all? No matter how trivial it seemed at the time."

Marilyn took her knuckle out of her mouth and thought about it. She wasn't sure what to say.

"What else was going on here? Who were the other babies, the other mothers? Were there any strangers?"

"I don't know what you mean." There were always a lot of strangers in a hospital.

"Okay, what about the babies?"

"We had a death," Marilyn said suddenly.

"Oh?" That was an event. "Who died, a mother?"

"No, a baby. But it didn't die last week. It died today. Defective heart," Marilyn said soberly.

Aaron nodded. They were standing in front of the viewing window. People who passed by could see them. She wished she could hold up a sign that read, "I haven't done anything wrong."

"Is the mother still here?" Aaron asked. "I'd like to see her."

"Oh, no, she took off the day after the baby was born."

"Really? That's very unusual for a mother to leave her sick baby," Aaron said.

"Well, it was an adoption case. She was a fifteen-year-old unwed mother. She didn't want to see it anyway."

Aaron was stunned. "What happened to the adoptive parents? Were they informed the baby was sick?"

"I don't know anything about that."

"Did you know immediately how sick the baby was?"

"Of course. It had a defective heart. It was this big." Marilyn showed how big the baby was.

"The adoptive parents must have been very upset. What a terrible thing, to wait for a baby and find out it's sick."

"Well, nobody cared about the baby. The poor thing died alone." Marilyn turned away. Except for her. She was there. Her eyes filled with tears. "Poor little thing."

"When was the baby born?" Aaron asked softly.

"Um, let me see. Oh, it was the same night as the Dunne baby." Marilyn lost what was left of her color.

Dr. Simon jumped up. "Are you sure?" he asked.

"Of course I'm sure. I remember everything."

"Was her doctor Dr. Street, by any chance?" Dr. Simon asked suddenly.

Marilyn nodded, stunned. "Why do you ask? Did he have something to do with it?" Should she say anything more? What was there to say? She didn't really know anything.

"No, of course not. He delivered two babies that night, though," he murmured speculatively.

"That's not so unusual." Marilyn chewed on her lips.

"Who were the adoptive parents?" he asked.

"I have no idea," she said. "I wouldn't know that sort of thing."

"Isn't it in the file?"

"Yeah, maybe, but the file isn't here anymore, and that part of it wouldn't be in it anyway."

"Where would it be?" Aaron was in a cold sweat.

"Administration."

"Did you tell the sheriff's office any of this?" Aaron asked.

"They didn't ask, and I didn't think of it. Is there a connection?" Marilyn's mouth was dry. She hadn't lied. She answered what they asked. She hadn't withheld information.

"Well, it looks like Dr. Street's office is at the core of this."

"Um, his nurse, Isobel, was here," she blurted out. "She brought doughnuts." She started sobbing. "It's probably nothing, but she wanted to see the babies." She began to hiccup.

"What did she do?"

Marilyn sobbed on. "She didn't do anything. She wanted to

see the Dunne baby. She was upset that the mother had it. I went to get it but she left. She never saw it.''

Aaron put his hand on her arm. "You've been a big help. You've been great.'' Aaron shoved off from the wall and propelled himself into motion.

"Did I do something wrong?'' she cried anxiously as he plunged through the swinging doors. "I'd hate to think I—''

He turned back for a second.

"No, you did right. You did just fine.''

He was gone in a second, but it took Marilyn a long time to calm down.

55

Peter sat on the back stairs of Isobel's building for a long time. Nobody came by to bother him. He was shaking all over, wanted to go back for what was left of the bottle of scotch, for her jewelry. Wanted to go back and clean the place up. But he couldn't move. There was a small suitcase beside him that he had left outside her back door before ringing her bell. He had taken it with him because he knew he couldn't go back. Angel would take him out on the Fourth of July. He said he'd give him until then. "Then'' was now.

The suitcase had a peculiar array of items in it. Some ropes and hooks from his rock-climbing days. Tennis shorts and a tennis racket. His army uniform. Several pairs of sunglasses. A fisherman's hat with flies all over it. Now all those lives were over. He had to start a new one.

It had occurred to him in the last twenty-four hours that the only thing for him to do now was to get the baby back from the Hunters. The baby was his only ticket out of New Jersey. He had to sell it somewhere else, maybe California, and disappear. How he would get the baby there was not a question that concerned him. He'd get it and worry about that later.

The only smart thing he'd done when he left Isobel's apartment was to take her car keys. He congratulated himself on that. No one would think to look for him driving her car. Finally, when he had possession of his limbs again and realized he had gotten away with it, he ducked out the back way and took off in Isobel's car. He had no idea that he was followed by a van with a sunset painted on it.

He spent the night drugged out from crack he bought with the money in Isobel's wallet. When he called Wendal in the morning, Wendal's attitude sealed his fate. He was sure Wendal was going to renege on him. There was no question now that he would have to pay with the thing his wife cared for most. Peter smoked some more crack and worked out his plan to take the baby.

In the morning a different van followed him back to The Oaks, where he wandered around the neighborhood in his tennis shorts, wearing a hat and sunglasses, swinging his racket, and looking like he was waiting for someone.

56

Aaron Simon and Deputy Sheriff Cusick sat across the desk from each other in Aaron's office. Each had a Styrofoam cup with cold coffee in front of him. Aaron did not allow patients to eat or drink anything in his office. He considered it a place of business, and a psychiatrist was supposed to nurture only symbolically. Cusick was, of course, not a patient. He could have a cup of coffee.

This was their second meeting. The night before, authorized by Bettina, Aaron had reported to Cusick everything she told him about her abduction. He watched the way Cusick took the information in. Cusick, he knew, was the one who first interviewed Tom and who saw Bettina before anyone else. He was not on the top of the hierarchy at the sheriff's office, but he seemed to be the one who received the most respect. Aaron could see why. He was shrewd and methodical, might well end up a detective. Aaron had the feeling he would. For the moment Cusick seemed more than happy in his uniform, with his sunglasses twirling around a finger, his body hung with a variety of heavy, clanging objects that he had to adjust before sitting down.

Aaron had been a psychiatrist for the army. He'd treated traumatized soldiers returning from Vietnam. This was the first time since then that he had interviewed someone used to carrying a gun. It certainly was the first time he had interviewed someone who was wearing a gun. It reminded him of Max's remark that he was passive, had never been covered with blood.

He thought about that a lot. It was true that he spent his life talking to people in small rooms. It had occurred to him that having to appear passive in treatment was one of the great ironies of his life. It was his job to be as unobtrusive as possible with every gesture, every move he made. Yet he was a man who had a lot of trouble sitting still. At night he dreamed of running, of playing basketball as he had as a kid, of breaking out somehow physically and actually doing something. Now, as he tried to find a comfortable position for his lower back, he thought that this time he wasn't just waiting for an outcome. He was committed to something, to changing the course of the story. It was a first. It made him think when this crisis was over, he would return to the AIDS problem. It was not resolved, and he wanted a resolution.

Actually, it was Cusick who had interviewed him. Another first. He hadn't minded answering the questions, but he had no intention of leaving the young man, competent as he seemed, on his own with the investigation.

The day before, the sheriff's office had questioned some of the same people Aaron had, and now Cusick shook his head admiringly at the name the psychiatrist had gotten out of Marilyn.

"How did you do it?" he asked. "She didn't say a thing to me."

"Maybe you come on too strong," Aaron said.

"Me? I've got a wife and kid. I'm a pussycat," he protested.

"The phallic symbols." Aaron indicated the holster and stick.

Cusick stood suddenly, causing the paraphernalia on his belt to clank around on his hips.

They had been talking for almost a half an hour.

"I've got to go. I have a nurse I have to see."

"Do you want me to come with you?" Aaron asked.

He had set up a meeting with Bettina and Tom in her room, but he had an hour and a half until then. He wouldn't mind being there when Cusick talked to Isobel, but he also wanted to check out the name of the dead baby's prospective adoptive parents. That was the only piece he'd withheld—the possibility they could locate the home where the missing baby might have gone. He did not want Cusick charging around with such explosive information before he had a chance to tell Tom and Bettina. They had to think of the baby's safety first and the case second.

There was so much to do. He couldn't imagine why he hadn't said, "Yes, come back now," the first time he had spoken to Arthur Street. And why Arthur hadn't just returned, regardless of whether Aaron gave him permission to stay or not. If Bettina had been one of Aaron's patients, he would have returned.

Now he had to sort it out himself. It was his territory. The police could nose around all they wanted, but he knew how to find things out.

Cusick shook his head. "I'll call you after I've seen her," he said.

"Fine," Aaron agreed.

They left the office together.

An hour later Cusick called just as Aaron was returning to his office.

"Dr. Simon. This is John Cusick." There was a lot of static. He was talking on his car phone, standing on the street.

"Hi, John. Did you find her?"

The crackle got louder for a moment, and Aaron couldn't hear his reply.

"What?" he said.

"Yeah, I found her."

Aaron hesitated. Cusick's voice, even with the static and noise covering it, sounded uncertain, upset.

"What did she say?"

"She didn't say anything. She's dead."

Aaron sucked in his breath. "How?"

"Strangled. It looks like some kind of sex thing." He was silent for a second as the sound of sirens made further communication impossible.

"I don't know if it's necessarily related or not. They're starting to go over the place now. I'll have to talk to you later."

The line got quiet. Aaron held the receiver in his hand until the nagging sound of the dial tone forced him to hang up. For a long moment he sat at his desk with his head in his hands.

57

No one was around early Monday evening the Fourth of July when Tom strode into Aaron's waiting room.

"What's going on?" He had been alarmed at the change of plans, and was not reassured to find the doctor sitting in one of the uncomfortable chairs in his waiting room as if waiting for himself.

"Where's Bettina?"

Aaron had requested that an orderly bring her across the

Bridge of Sighs in a wheelchair. The circumstances had changed, and he wanted them to meet in his office, where there was more privacy.

"Transport is going to bring her down here. I thought it would be quieter. How are you feeling?" Aaron stood up and led the way through the double doors.

"Better. Did you talk to the doctor who examined me?" Tom asked. He was feeling faint with hunger. He had forgotten to have anything before he left the house. It had never occurred to him that he would be in the Emergency Room for hours waiting for a doctor. All he had thought of was seeing his wife, and now she wasn't here.

"No," Aaron said dully. He hadn't exactly had time. "What did he say?"

"He said to take it easy and scheduled some more tests next week. Are you all right?"

Aaron nodded. "Did he give you any prescriptions?"

"Where's Bettina?" Tom said. He didn't care if he slept or not.

"She'll be here in a minute. Sit down. I have something to tell you."

"What?"

"Sit down." Aaron sat in his own chair and tilted back. He had spent the last hour trying to track down Chrissie Elton's file and couldn't find it. Her baby had just died that day, so the mother's file and the baby's file were somewhere in the system, presumably en route to Central Filing, but at the moment lost.

Finally, after checking at the morgue, and not finding it there, he had gone down to the Administration Office, where he knew her vital information would be entered in the computer. Names and addresses, her parents, the lawyer who was arranging the adoption, the adoptive parents.

If it were my baby, I would want to know, he thought. He wasn't sure how Isobel's death altered the picture, but it was very ominous and tragic. There had to be a connection between the two babies, and the only connection that made sense was replacing one baby with the other.

Somebody had been desperate enough to kidnap a baby and murder Isobel. But maybe the people who had the baby didn't know anything about it. That was his hope. If they didn't know, he didn't want anyone alerting them. Better to find the baby and deal with them than have them run away with it. He was still trying to cope with the murder aspect of it. Someone had been strangled whom he sort of knew. He had never met Isobel, but he had talked with her on the phone several times.

A door opened in the outer office. Both men jumped up. The orderly parked the wheelchair in the waiting room and took off almost before they made it to the other room. Tom rushed out, with Aaron right behind him. Bettina was struggling out of the wheelchair when they came in.

She stood up shakily and looked from the doctor to Tom for a few seconds as if to check the temperature, or to decide what it was all right to say and do.

"I didn't have a thing to wear," she said finally, her eyes filling with tears. "And they wouldn't let me walk."

Tom's mouth fell open in surprise.

"Where's your hair?" she asked.

"They cut it off. I don't know why. Oh, Bettina."

"I'm sorry," she cried.

And then she couldn't say anymore. Tom made some unintelligible sounds of gratitude and put his arms out to her. She moved shakily toward them.

They gripped hands first. Bettina's breath came in gasps. "Forgive me."

"You didn't do anything wrong, Bettina. I love you. That's

all you have to think about. I love you. I'll always love you," he said.

They embraced, murmuring softly to each other.

Aaron stepped into his office to cover his own tears. He was deeply moved by seeing them give each other the one thing he could never offer his patients, no matter how much he cared about them—the healing comfort of a lover's embrace. Their physical closeness emphasized the loneliness he sometimes felt. He was at the same time so intimate and in tune with some of his patients that he could feel their moods, their hurts and frustration, as acutely as if they were his own, and yet so far away from them that they might just as well be clouds in the sky he couldn't touch at all. Sometimes when they were doing better and were back functioning in the "real" world, he missed them and felt he was the one stuck inside.

Ever since medical school he'd thought that the struggles he continually witnessed were all the drama any man could ever need, that nothing enacted in a theater or film could be more intense or involving than his daily battles to save souls. Not unlike his patients, he dreamed of freedom, of flying down an open road on a motorcycle, his head protected from the screaming wind by a helmet that nothing from the outside could penetrate. He interpreted this as castration anxiety and fear of impotence.

A long time ago he had decided that the world of action was not his forum. Now he paced in his waiting room, preparing himself. Action was the one thing he was never permitted to take, and now he had no choice but to act. For once he could not sit back in the safety of his office and wait for things to spin out as they might. It was exhilarating. And terrifying. Stepping out of his spectator role gave him direct responsibility in a way that sitting in a chair and listening never did.

There was no question, however, that Bettina and Tom had

to know what was happening and to participate on every level, in order to be able to adjust to whatever happened. He did not think anyone else could protect them or help them as he could. The problem was that the computer was down, and they wouldn't know until the morning who might have their baby.

He went back into his office. They were still hugging, stroking each other, searching each other's face for signs of forgiveness. He didn't want to end the moment, but he had no choice.

"Why don't you sit down," Aaron suggested, interrupting as gently as he could. "We have a lot of things to talk about."

58

Peter smoked the last of the crack in his empty office, where he had pumped himself up through the long night. He was beginning to think of himself as invincible. He could do what he wanted. The Fourth of July had passed, and he was still alive. Only a few hours more and he'd be out of the area, away from Angel forever. He strode out at the first flush of dawn, got in the car he had rented after ditching Isobel's, and drove off.

By seven-thirty he was back at The Oaks. He had changed his clothes since casing The Oaks the day before and was now dressed as a fisherman, wearing the hat with the flies, a light jacket, and nylon running pants. He parked the car and walked slowly across the lawn to the back of the building.

The back door was still open from the morning's garbage collection at seven. Peter went inside. He climbed the nine flights of stairs without being seen because the service elevator was outside, in the hall next to the regular elevator. The smell of bacon drifted out from under the Hunters' back door.

At eight-fifteen the front door opened, and Wendal called out that he was leaving. The door closed. There was no sound as he walked down the carpeted hall.

59

The name that popped up on the screen was "Hunter." It was eight o'clock in the morning, Tuesday, July 5th, and the Admitting Office was just opening its doors for the day's business. Aaron stood there riveted by the name and address on the screen, as if he had been given the Hunters' death sentence. So that was the reason Laura had never called him. She'd solved her problem her own way. There was no way he could have been more shocked or distressed. Laura had said he hadn't helped her carry her own baby to term. Now he had to be the executioner of her motherhood a second time.

Mechanically, he copied the address and phone number, though he had them in his own file. The potential for personal disaster had just gotten a lot bigger, both for the Hunters and for himself.

He left the office quickly, forgetting to thank the secretary who'd opened up the file for him. He didn't register anything around him. Not the people, not the familiar hallways filling up after the long weekend. He was thinking the police would figure all this out very soon. He had to move fast. He ran up the stairs and across the Bridge of Sighs.

How did the fact that it was the Hunters alter the way they would handle the devastating situation? They had been waiting for this piece of news all night—Aaron, Tom, and Bettina, each in their separate places. But now that it was someone he knew, Aaron wondered if it changed anything, other than how bad he felt.

In his office the night before, they had discussed what they would do when they had the name. There was no way to be certain it was the couple who had the baby. On the one hand, they had to be prepared for disappointment. On the other hand, if the couple in the computer had the baby, they had to be very careful.

Theoretically, they had no authority to go charging around demanding the return of a baby two people might think was fairly and legitimately theirs. It was a police matter, not a hospital one. Theoretically, they should let the police investigate. But this was not a theoretical situation. And none of them had wanted to leave it to the authorities. It was too risky.

Once the bureaucracy got involved, the couple with the baby could use any number of delaying tactics that might take months to plow through. They could make any claims. They could refuse to let the baby be fingerprinted. Every day that was lost would make the ultimate adjustment harder for the Dunnes and the baby.

In the end, they had decided to wait for the location of the couple before making a final decision. If the adoptive parents were in the area, they would probably go over and talk to them.

With that decided, they had parted for the night. Aaron,

who had missed the parent/child softball game, took his disgruntled family out to dinner and then to a fireworks display.

Tom had driven home to an empty house and spent much of the night cleaning up the mess the police had left there. He didn't want Bettina to see the bedroom the way she'd left it. He ran the washing machine and dryer for hours, and scrubbed the floors meticulously with lemon-scented ammonia. Bettina was taken back to the eighth floor, where she was given something to make her sleep. From what the nurse on the floor told Aaron early this morning, she'd gotten some rest.

Aaron checked his watch. They were scheduled to meet in just a few minutes. He went into his office. Lorna was at her desk, canceling his appointments for the day as he had instructed her. Tom and Bettina were in his waiting room. They were holding hands. Both were haggard but calm. Bettina had been quietly released a few minutes ago. Even the reporters had left them for the exciting new murder.

Aaron hurried through the waiting room, crooking his finger at them to follow him.

"Who is it?" Bettina asked.

"I wanted you to be here when I made the call," Aaron said. Now he was sorry he had made that decision. He put his hand to his head and rubbed out the creases in his forehead as if that could take the pain away. There was always so much pain. And now more than ever before. He couldn't stand back from this one, he thought, couldn't wait to see what happened and pick up the pieces later. He was deeply involved with all of them.

"I know them," he said. He didn't say the woman was his patient. He still considered her a patient. He felt that about all of them—once a patient, always a patient, even when they didn't need him anymore. Well, this patient was going to need someone now. And now it couldn't be him.

He reached for the phone and dialed Laura's number. It was busy. He looked at the slip in front of him and dialed Wendal's number at the office.

"Is Mr. Hunter there? This is Dr. Simon calling."

He didn't have to wait long. Wendal came on almost immediately.

"Dr. Simon. You're Laura's psychiatrist."

"Yes," Aaron said.

"Well, the most wonderful thing has happened," he said happily, before Aaron had a chance to say anything else. "We're parents."

"That's what I'm calling about," Aaron said. "I need to talk to you right away."

"What is it?" Wendal said. "Is something wrong?"

"Could we meet downstairs at your apartment? I think it would be better if we were all together."

"Is there something wrong with Laura?" Wendal said, anxiously. "Did she call you?"

"No, I'm sure she's fine. How about fifteen minutes?"

Aaron hung up and nodded grimly at the tense faces in front of him. "Let's go."

60

After Wendal left, Laura took the phone off the hook so no one could call her. She knew she would be scared if the phone rang. Better to be unavailable, she decided. Then she checked on the baby, who was still sleeping, and went into the kitchen to clean up. It felt strange with Wendal back at work. She felt very alone.

The silence of early morning made her nervous. A minute later she put the radio on. She began clearing the table, stacking the dishes in the sink. She put the butter away, rinsed the dishes, all the time listening for the baby. One more day, she told herself. I'll keep her one more day. And then I'll give her back. Mom for a day. Now she was willing to settle for that little.

She reached for the bag of garbage in the kitchen and opened the door to the back hall. At that moment, Peter had just finished putting a stocking over his head.

Laura had the door all the way open before she turned and saw him. She froze.

For a second they made an awful tableau, predator and prey caught motionless just before mortal combat. Then Laura found her voice and swung the door closed.

She was an instant too late.

Peter moved quickly and shoved his foot into the doorway. Laura gasped as she tried to pull the door closed. As she held it against his weight, she began to cry, softly at first, and then louder and louder until she was shrieking for help.

Even with the stocking on Peter's head, she knew who he was, and what he was there for. They hadn't paid for the baby, so he was taking it back. Suddenly she was a jungle cat, a wild animal that would do anything. She felt she was stronger than she had ever been. She was not going to let him in. With one shoulder against the door, she looked around for a weapon, didn't see anything within reach.

Peter swore grimly as he shoved against the door, then got it open enough to wedge his body in. They were both panting and sweating with the effort. It was barely nine o'clock and the heat was intense. Laura cried for help, but inside every sealed apartment in the building the central air-conditioning whirred on monotonously. No one came.

Finally Peter wrenched the door open. He tried to knock Laura aside, but she came at him fighting and screaming with all her strength. She managed to kick him and scratch him in several places before he got a grip on her and was able to push the door shut with his foot.

"Shut up," he said sharply.

He twisted one of her arms behind her back and put his hand over her mouth. Laura yelped with pain and sank her teeth into the fleshy part of his thumb.

"Bitch," he gasped, yanking his hand away.

Fury at his violation of her home, her fortress, was greater now than Laura's fear for herself. She did not, in fact, think of herself. She had the baby to protect. Who knew what would happen to it, if Peter took it away. Then two mothers would lose. Laura had planned to give her back to her real mother, but she would never let her go to Peter. Fighting was not a decision. It was a reflex action.

"Shut up," Peter said again.

He smashed her hard in the face. Her body swung away from him, slammed into the wall, and went down on the kitchen floor, where she was finally silenced. He went into the baby's room.

Then he was ready. He took the stocking off his head and put on the fisherman's hat that he had stuffed in his jacket. He planned to take off the surgical gloves in the elevator. Not until then.

He left the baby on the floor in the entrance hall and turned toward the kitchen.

When he returned, Laura was still on the floor, half-propped against the wall. Peter set down a laundry basket full of baby blankets and picked up a rope.

A moan escaped Laura's lips as he pulled her to a sitting position.

"Peter, why are you doing this?" she muttered.

He jerked. "Shut up," he answered.

"Where's the baby?" she whispered. The laundry basket didn't make sense. Her face was swelling and the rope cut into her wrists. Laura was aware only that Peter was taking the baby.

"Shut up," he said again.

Her voice rose to a wail. "Don't take the baby. Please, I'll give you anything."

"Damn you, I said shut up." He reached for a dish towel to stuff in her mouth.

She tried to knock him over with what little strength she had left, and Peter stumbled.

"You won't get away. You won't get away," she cried over and over.

"Yes I will," he cried wildly. By then his fingers were shaking so much he couldn't untie the towel that she had knotted around the handle of the refrigerator door. He moved out of reach, but still her legs kicked out at him.

"You bastard! You're not taking that baby."

Instead of collapsing, she began to revive. She seemed to swell until she was an enormous, howling, thrashing animal. "God damn it, don't you know you'll go to jail for life?"

Peter gave up on the dish towel. She was kicking so hard he couldn't get close enough to tie her feet.

"Shut up," he said, "or I'll kill you."

"No," she said. "No, you won't."

Suddenly she knew that he would kill her, just to get rid of her. He still had the rope in his hand. Before Laura could say anything else, he had a section wrapped once around each hand and was moving toward her.

61

They took Aaron's old white Subaru because he knew the fastest way to get to The Oaks. He had to take a precious second to gather up the piles of books and periodicals that littered the backseat and dump them in the trunk. No one said anything as they waited for him to make space.

The sky was the kind of deep blue they didn't see in New Jersey much anymore. The air was hot and humid. Bettina was wearing real clothes that Tom had brought her, a shirt and skirt that hadn't fit in months. No one took any notice of them as they walked out of the hospital. No one looked their way as they stood in the parking lot.

"Where is everybody?" Bettina asked.

Aaron had warned her they might be surrounded by reporters when they came out, but interest in them had waned now that there was a murder with a real body.

"They'll come back," Aaron said. "They always do."

They fell silent again as they got in the car and buckled their seat belts. After so much discussion the night before about what they would do if they found the baby alive in somebody's home, they could not say anything about it now.

Aaron drove quickly, speeding up through changing lights. He was thinking about what language he should use to tell the Hunters the baby they had longed for could not be theirs. How could he help them understand they must pack it up and give it back? He cranked his window down, set his chin.

At no point had anyone asked if Bettina was sure she could recognize her baby. But Aaron had considered that, too. How many times had she seen it? She'd seen it a number of times, but she'd been beaten up and drugged since then. She was better, but there was no question she wasn't a hundred percent. He wasn't convinced her mind was really clear yet. Could she be sure? Another question that worried him was what if it wasn't the Dunne baby, *clearly* not the Dunne baby. It would put them back at square one.

There were a lot of things they hadn't talked about. They hadn't discussed in depth what they would do if the baby was clearly theirs but the Hunters refused to give it back, threw them out, and phoned the police. They could call a lawyer and start some sort of suit against them. Getting a court order could take months. There was no way to prove the baby was theirs without blood tests and fingerprints. If a battle began, there was always the chance that Laura could freak out and run away. The Hunters had to be willing to accept disaster. They were all relying on that.

Tom's shirt was soaked. He looked over at Bettina, held her hand tightly.

"Somebody murdered that poor girl," she murmured.

"Who would do that?" Tom said.

Aaron shook his head, couldn't imagine.

"Isobel must have helped someone take my baby. She knew everything." Bettina sniffed a little.

"I thought she was just being nice, and all the time she was going to take my baby." She shook her head. "Why would she do that?"

"She's dead," Tom said.

"It's horrible."

Hot air blew in their faces from the open window.

Aaron made a right turn and caught sight of a large, fair-haired man in a business suit standing in the curved driveway that was set back in its own little park.

"Oh," Bettina cried unhappily.

They had come to a large, extravagant building on the edge of a golf course. It had tennis courts no one was using. It was early. Sprinklers were still spraying water on the lush grass.

"Oh, no. What a place," she murmured.

Aaron pulled into the curve of the driveway and turned off the motor. For once he wasn't going to worry about authority— about a ticket, or someone getting mad.

The man in the business suit walked slowly over to the car. His body moved like it was made of brittle sticks. He looked puzzled and confused at the number of people in the car.

Aaron climbed out of the front, and Bettina and Tom got out of the back. For a second they looked at each other.

"You're Wendal Hunter?" Aaron asked.

Wendal nodded.

"I'm Dr. Simon," he said. "And this is Bettina and Tom Dunne."

"Hello." Wendal nodded grimly.

"They're the parents of the baby that's been missing since last Friday," Aaron explained.

"Oh, no!" Wendal said explosively. "No." The color drained from his healthy pink face, leaving him suddenly as faded and worn as the young couple in front of him.

"It can't be our baby; I know it can't." Wendal put his hand out to the car to steady himself. "It can't. You've made a mistake. Why did you come here?"

"The baby that was meant to be yours died yesterday. It had a heart defect." Aaron said it as gently as he could. But the words came out sounding very harsh. It was a fact. He couldn't change it.

"I can't believe—" Wendal started to protest. "Why would you bring these people to my house? This is an outrage. Disturb my wife. How could you? You'll have to leave right—"

"The nurse in Laura's doctor's office has been murdered," Aaron interrupted. They had been standing in the driveway long enough. They had to move somewhere else now.

"Didn't you see it in the paper this morning?" Aaron asked.

"No, I didn't. The paper didn't come this morning, for some reason." Wendal shrugged.

"What does that have to do with it?" he asked.

"Can we go upstairs?" Aaron said. "I think we should talk about it there."

Wendal hunched his shoulders defensively for a moment.

"I don't want to do that." He licked his lips and looked at Tom and Bettina. "It wouldn't be good for my wife."

"Laura won't be able to keep the baby anyway," Aaron said. "Think about her. It will be worse for her if you fight it."

Wendal wavered. Somebody came out of the building and waved to him. Wendal nodded. Then he turned back to Tom and Bettina. The muscles in his jaw relaxed.

"All right," he muttered.

62

They were silent going into the building. Wendal rang 9A and didn't wait for a response. They were silent in the elevator going up. The doors slid open on the ninth floor, revealing a long hallway with burnished silver wallpaper and steel gray carpeting. No sounds came from any of the doorways they passed. Wendal stopped at 9A and turned his key in the lock.

"Laura?" Wendal opened the door.

The radio was on. They could hear the weather report. Sunny and hot through the week.

"Laura?" he called again.

The place had a strange empty feeling about it. Aaron, Bettina, and Tom stood awkwardly in an entry that opened into the living room-dining room area. The kitchen door was closed. There was a new stroller parked in the corner that still had the tags on it.

Wendal opened the kitchen door.

"Oh, God, no."

He plunged through the door, with Aaron and Tom right behind him.

Laura was lying on the floor, facedown on the bisque tiles. There was an empty laundry basket beside her, some broken dishes, and a garbage bag that was torn open and spilling out the remains of breakfast and last night's dinner.

"She's—dead," Wendal cried. "Jesus, she's dead."

Aaron pushed him aside and crouched down beside her,

feeling for a pulse. "She's alive," he said. "Get an ambulance and call the police."

Wendal moved to do as he was told.

Aaron turned Laura over and examined her quickly. Her face and head were bruised in a number of places, but nothing seemed to be broken or bleeding. Her breathing was even and her pulse was steady.

Wendal came back. "They're on their way."

"Good. Get me some water," Aaron said. "Do you have any ammonia?"

Wendal got it for him. Aaron sponged her face with a wet towel and revived her with a sniff of the household ammonia.

Tom and Bettina wandered around looking for the baby. There was nothing in the elegant living room or dining room. They stopped in the room decorated for the baby and held each other tight. It was all yellow and featured a new crib that was similar to the one Bettina had bought. The room had a southern exposure. Sunshine streamed in, and the smell of baby still lingered in the air.

"Oh, God, Tom." Bettina crumbled. "Where is she?"

"Hold on," Tom said. "I'm here."

"Hold on," she muttered to herself.

Laura was coughing and groaning when they came into the kitchen. Wendal hovered over her anxiously.

"Wendal?" Her voice came out scratchy and low.

"Oh, baby, are you all right?" He helped her sit up. The last time he found her unconscious, she was bleeding to death from a miscarriage.

"You saved my life again." She started to cry.

"It's all right. I'm here."

"Peter took the baby," she wept. "He was going to kill me."

She looked uncomprehendingly at Aaron. "What's Dr. Simon doing here?"

"When did he leave?" Tom asked wildly.

She turned her head away from him. "He had a rope around my neck. He was going to kill me."

"When!" Tom demanded.

She wouldn't look at him. She spoke only to Wendal.

"He heard the buzzer and hit me." She broke down sobbing.

It was then that they realized the back door was open. Tom and Bettina ran out into the back hall, empty except for some garbage cans and the back stairs. The light coming from the window opposite was almost blinding. As they stood there for a few seconds, they could hear the faint echo of footsteps.

63

They were the kind of stairs that hugged each other in a tight square. No way to see down. No way to tell if the echo came from above or below. "Oh, God," Bettina cried. "Which way?"

"I'm going down," Tom said.

"I'm coming with you."

"You're not strong enough," he told her. "You stay here."

"I can't stay here," she protested.

"Then be careful," he commanded.

He took off without another word. It was nine stories going down. Bettina followed as quickly as she could. Her feet were very heavy, and she moved slowly.

It kept getting hotter and felt like a descent into hell. Every floor was two sets of stairs. Her whole body hurt. Her head, her healing incision. Her leg muscles screamed with every step. She almost fell into the window at every floor. Some of them were all the way open. She hadn't had any breakfast. She kept going.

In front of her she could hear Tom's footsteps clattering down the stairs. Above her she heard another set of footsteps coming down. It was Dr. Simon. He passed her, telling her to sit down on the stairs and stay where she was. She ignored him. She was holding on. It was her baby.

Down another flight. She told herself she could make it.

Tom got to the ground floor first and charged out the door. For several long seconds Bettina didn't hear anything as she scrambled down the last two flights. She felt like she was crawling, but she was on her feet. Hold on, she told herself.

At last she stumbled out into the full heat of morning. The glare was so intense she couldn't tell what was happening. Dr. Simon and Tom had stopped short just outside the door. They were watching a man in a fishing hat about ten yards ahead of them.

The man was holding a white bundle tightly against his chest and seemed to be using the tree as a shield. It was eerily silent. Tom and Dr. Simon waved her back. What was going on? Bettina ignored their instruction and took a few steps forward.

Now she could see two other men advancing on the one by the tree. They had their hands in their pockets and walked casually toward him. There was something very menacing about them.

"Bettina," Tom said, warning her back fiercely.

"Why don't you put that down and come with us?" the shorter of the two men said.

The man in the fishing hat shook his head. "Where'd you come from?"

"A friend of yours sent us. Come on, Peter, get in the car." The bigger man moved his weight from one foot to the other.

"No way. Don't come near me."

"You're going to come with us one way or another. Why don't you make it easy on yourself?"

The two men stood there, unaware that three people were watching them from behind a screen of forsythia bushes. Bettina moved closer.

"He has the baby," she said softly.

"If you take me, you have to take us both out," Peter was saying. "You don't want to hurt the baby, do you?"

Suddenly the baby began to cry, and Bettina stepped out from behind the bush. At the words "hurt the baby," she could no longer stand there quietly. Her legs trembled so much she could hardly stand, but she moved forward into the three men's view.

"It's my baby; give her to me," Bettina said.

The three men turned to her in surprise. Aaron and Tom rushed out to stop her.

"Get away from me," Peter yelled. "All of you."

Bettina pulled away from Tom's grip on her arm and started walking toward Peter. "Give me the baby," she said again.

"Come near me and I'll pound it on the tree," Peter shouted. He swung the baby toward the tree.

"No!" Bettina screamed. She broke into a run.

For a second all was confusion. The two men who had been

menacing Peter crossed the street and melted away. Peter moved to the other side of the tree to get away from Bettina. Tom and Aaron went around the other way to catch him.

Bettina was closer. In a second she was at Peter's side, reaching for her baby. The baby was screaming. Peter grunted. He had two men coming at him from one direction and a woman pulling at him from the other.

"Give me the baby," Bettina demanded.

Peter held it away from her. As she lunged for it and missed, Tom and Aaron stepped forward. Tom grabbed the baby just as the back of Peter's head exploded into a fan of bloody bits of bone and tissue that sprayed all over and sent Bettina reeling into the bushes.

She screamed and went down like a rock thrown into a pool, her neck and chest a violent red against the grass.

Aaron got to her first. She could hear the baby crying.

He crouched beside her. "Hold on. I'll get an ambulance," he said.

She gasped and tried to sit up. There was blood all over him. "You're hurt," she cried.

"I'm fine. Don't move." He pushed her back to the ground, searching for the entry point of the bullet. It must have hit the tree and ricocheted into her, he thought.

"Where's Tom?" She struggled to sit up.

"Don't move," Aaron commanded, frowning. There didn't seem to be a hole. She was covered with blood, but there was no place where it was pouring out of her. She resisted his attempts to keep her still.

"I'm not hurt," she insisted. "I just fell."

She got up, pulling the pieces of herself back together one more time. Her body was numb. It felt as if she had been hit. But she knew she wasn't.

"Are you sure you're okay?" Aaron said, looking from her to the blood on his hands.

"I'm okay," she said. Her legs were still trembling, and she was sickened by the smell.

The heavy, sweet odor of the first moment's violent death had passed. And now the blood and brains, the body on the grass, were beginning their cycle of decay. Police sirens shattered the silence.

"Tom?" Bettina cried.

The numbness turned to horror as she realized Tom was not standing where he had been. He was lying on the ground, not far from the body. The baby was on his chest, shrieking.

"Tom," she screamed. "Hold on. Hold on, Tom. I'm coming."

Even as she said it, he began to struggle to his feet, soothing the baby at the same time. It was his first moment with his child. Two police cars pulled to a stop near them on the grass.

"We're all right." Tom started walking shakily toward Bettina. "We're going to be all right."

They met halfway and embraced tearfully, the baby between them.

Aaron headed back inside to Wendal and Laura.